DESTROYER OF CARTERVILLE

DESTROYER OF CARTERVILLE

A CARTERVILLE MYSTERY

ROBERT J. MCCARTER

LITTLE HUMMINGBIRD PUBLISHING

CARTERVILLE MYSTERIES

Each Carterville Mystery is stand-alone, but things do change in Carterville. The chronological order of the books are:

- **Out of a Christmas Sky**
- **Destroyer of Carterville**
- **The Blood of Carterville**

Note: The events of this story take place seven months after *Out of a Christmas Sky* and over a year before *The Blood of Carterville*.

PART 1
LEADS: JULY 1

ONE

SUNDAY, JULY 1. THE CARTERVILLE
BREWERY

I hate the Carterville Brewery. It doesn't belong here.

I say that as a descendant of Samuel Carter—the prospector that founded this town—and the chief of police of Carterville, Arizona.

The brewery sat on the Carterville Circle, the retail hub of our small town of 290 residents that was frequented by tens of thousands of tourists.

It was in a historic, two-story-tall red brick building that was originally the Carterville Mercantile back when Carterville was a booming mine town. The inside walls were that historic red brick with high ceilings and big exposed ventilation ducts. Support posts stood every eight feet made of whole pine trees stripped of their bark and polished to a high shine, the bottom four feet clad in stainless steel and clever round bar tables circling the wood at a standing height.

There was a long wooden bar with stainless steel accents at the back with a mirror behind. Dangling from the ceiling were "old tyme" artifacts like an antique toboggan and skis. On the walls were black-and-white photos of Carterville from the mining boom days of the late 1800s.

A wooden counter with stools underneath it lined the tall windows that looked out onto Carterville Circle and the majestic fir tree that marks the center of the town and the epic view of the desert as it reached towards the Grand Canyon and beyond. Tables were scattered throughout wherever there was room.

To one side was a small, cramped stage that promised live music in the small space.

The air smelled of beer and the brewery was crowded with locals and tourists alike. It was opening day, and this was the first time I'd been able to bring myself to even look inside, much less come inside.

While many of the touches were authentic and it was clear that money had been poured into the space, it felt more like Disneyland than Carterville to me. It was forced and the industrial touches in the historic building just felt wrong. This was the kind of place you expect to find in Scottsdale, not in our little mountain town.

Karen Winslow, the mayor of Carterville, smiled at me and strode over, her cowboy boots clicking on the polished cement floor. She had upped her elegant western wardrobe, wearing a black cowboy shirt with twisting silver embroidery. Over that was a deep blue vest with the yellow Carterville Brewery logo on it. Her long turquoise skirt fell in layers with a black belt and large silver buckle around her waist. A big chunk of polished turquoise on her bolo tie brought it all together.

"You came, Henry," she said with a smile so big, it seemed like it was genuine. "I wasn't sure."

Despite myself, my eyes darted over to the far side of the building. That was where Peaks Gift and Coffee had been, where Lila Chang had womaned her gleaming beast of an espresso machine until she had been murdered seven months ago on Christmas Eve.

Lila had been a friend of mine and Karen had been a suspect in the murder because she was trying to force Lila out of the building so she could start this very brewery.

"I wouldn't miss it," I said to Karen with a smile, touching my cowboy hat and tipping my head towards her.

Truth be told, it was my job to be here. My title may be chief of police, but there was only one other officer in our department and then our office manager. We all do everything, and that includes me walking around downtown in uniform on a busy July Sunday right before a big holiday keeping an eye on things.

"Good," she said, her hazel eyes lighting up in her lean face and her expensive perfume becoming overwhelming now that she was close, drowning out the more pleasant smells. She grabbed my arm and pulled me to an empty section of the high counter that ran along the outside wall of the brewery. The bustling Carterville Circle was visible. "Here's the best spot, you can see the Canyon between the branches of our noble fir."

She pointed and I just stared at her, the happiness and energy in her voice was quite compelling. There were dark smudges under her eyes, but opening a new restaurant will do that to you. Karen was a few years older than me, in her mid-fifties, her plaited blonde hair shot with a bit of grey and wrinkles beginning to furrow into the forehead of her well-tanned face. She didn't dye her hair or hide her age which was something I appreciated. She was a horse woman through and through and spent a lot of time outside, so that tan was earned.

"So," she began, leaning against the counter. "First drink is free for you every day. Any beverage you want. And all food is half off. The whole staff knows to treat you right, Henry."

She must have seen the puzzled look on my face. "Seriously," she said. "No strings. We just want you to feel at home at Carterville Brewery. And that goes for Officer Ortega too."

"And Annabelle, I presume," I said. Annabelle Unger was my office manager, dispatcher, accountant, and everything else. She was who really kept the CPD running.

Karen opened her mouth to object. Annabelle was a civilian, but it was only a moment and she smiled and said, "Of course. I know that bad business with Lila got us off on the wrong foot with this, and I want you *all* to feel comfortable here."

Her eyes strayed to the far section of the building like mine had. Karen had taken advantage of a financial issue Lila had had and maneuvered her into a poor lease and kept raising her rent trying to force her out so she could build this place.

Her eyes wandered back and met mine, and I swear I could see regret there. "Lila was the best of us," she said, her voice a bit thick.

Now it was time for my jaw to drop open in surprise.

"Really, Henry," she said. "She was the best of us. I miss her too. She had that smile that could always make you feel better."

I nodded, still shocked to see this side of her.

She put her hand gently on my shoulder and gestured back to the crowded room. "Look. This place is going to be good for our town. It's another destination. We have plans to start bottling our beer soon, and the Carterville name will spread even farther. I know this level of tourism makes you nervous, but the dollars will make this a better town."

I looked at her skeptically. All I could see would be the calls to deal with the drunk and disorderly, trespassing, and the other problems the tourists caused.

"You know it does," she said patiently. "Since the meteor hit and we got our powers, how many fewer overdoses have you dealt with? How many fewer domestic disturbances?"

I gave her a look a parent would give a kid that did their homework without asking.

And, yes, if you've been hiding under a rock and not heard, about six years ago a meteor hit Carterville, burying itself in the mine on the other side of the hill and bestowing powers on everyone that was here at the time. But only when you are in or near Carterville. And the powers are rarely something you would see in the movies.

"I read your reports, Henry," she said. "Every word."

I nodded. She was right. The money had helped the town, but it had also changed the town. I leaned close and lowered my voice. "Have you heard the 'blood of Carterville' rumors?" I asked.

Her brow furrowed and she shook her head.

"Ortega stumbled across this on the internet," I said. "Seems some are theorizing that the blood of someone who was in Carterville when the meteor hit could convey their power... somehow."

She got a sour look on her face and shook her head.

"The more tourists we get," I said, "the higher chance someone will do something truly stupid."

She put her hand on my arm. "At least we have you," she said.

Now it was my turn to have a sour look on my face.

"Don't worry," she said. "That business about defunding your department and contracting all our policing through the Coconino Sheriff's Department is done. I took care of it."

After the whole mess with Lila was over, Karen had told me "someone" on the town council was thinking of defunding the department. My position is an elected one so I can't just be fired, but the town council controls my budget. It was clear that that "someone" was her. I had countered saying that I might just run for mayor if I was out of a job.

I don't like politics, but I can play the game when I have to.

"This makes our need for a new officer even more urgent, Karen," I said.

She nodded and stared out the window. "I'll fight for you, Henry," she said without looking at me. "I will. I'm sure we can bump your budget a bit, but not that much. Not yet. But enough for some more gear, for sure." She turned to me and had a grim smile on her face.

I nodded. I wasn't expecting any concessions from her, but since she was offering, I was happy to get more funds.

"But for now," she said, her smile brightening and reminding me of her when she was much younger, "what can I get you? I do hope we'll be seeing plenty of you."

I smiled and nodded. I would be coming around because it was my job. But it wasn't lost on me that this wasn't a "no strings" offer as she had indicated. My presence would benefit her directly. The locals seeing a Carter in the Carterville Brewery would legitimize it. And me being in here with my badge would help the tourists mind their Ps and Qs.

I opened my mouth to tell her I wanted some coffee when my radio squawked to life. "Carter, this is dispatch. We have a ten-eight-nine up off Fir Street. On the *end* of Fir Street. Over."

"Maybe next time," I said.

Karen nodded, thanked me for coming, and swept off.

I walked out of the bar, the heat of the summer day hitting me. I adjusted my cowboy hat and put on my aviator sunglasses. The aviators were the cheap ones you get at the dollar store since I tend to lose them or sit on them all the time.

The Carterville Circle was busy, lots of tourists milling around, cars slowly making their way around our tight roundabout, people sitting on the low wall that surrounded the seventy-foot fir in the middle of the circle. But my eyes went to the view.

Carterville sits on the northern side of the San Francisco Peaks, draped on Carter Hill with a spectacular view of the desert to the north. It's the kind of view you only get in Desert Southwest. The trees, turning from ponderosa pine to piñon at this elevation, getting smaller as you go downhill until they melt into bushes and then grasses as the desert takes over.

There are shades of brown, taupe, and a bit of red all the way to the horizon. If you know what to look for, you can see the cut of the Grand Canyon from here.

I breathed it in. This was the view I had been seeing all my life, and I still loved it.

"Copy that, Annabelle," I said on the radio. Knowing who lived on the end of Fir Street, I added, "Is Ortega available for this one? Over."

"Sorry, Chief," she said. "He asked for you specifically. Over."

"Roger that," I said. "I'll head up there now. Over and out."

I walked towards our single CPD vehicle, an old SUV, wishing I had had the time for a coffee because I knew this wasn't going to be fun.

TWO
SUNDAY, JULY 1. THE SMITH RESIDENCE

BUILT ON A HILL ON THE NORTHERN SLOPES OF THE TALLEST mountain in Arizona, Carterville has some great views as I have described. The higher up the hill you go, the better the view. Down at the bottom of the hill where the ground is nearly level, the view is just of juniper and piñon trees. On the top of the hill at the Carterville Overlook, ponderosa pines dominate, and the view is spectacular.

The bottom of the hill is a gentle slope and towards the top it gets quite steep, Main Street chugging up it at a steep enough angle that your car better have a working low gear.

As a consequence of the view and the grade, the higher you go up the hill the pricier the real estate gets and the smaller and more precarious the lots.

The only thing above Fir Street is the Carterville Overlook and our one and only church. Fir Street means money. Or history, there are folks that have houses up high because they inherited them from their ancestors. The house that I share with my sister, which was built by Samuel Carter, is one street down on Engelmann.

So, Annabelle sending me to the end of Fir Street meant that the 911 call had been from Winston "Smitty" Smith.

Earlier I said that most of the powers bestowed on Carterville residents weren't the kind you'd see in the movies, but Smitty's was. It was a real live superpower. He could heal people. If they weren't all the way dead, he could bring them back.

Seven months ago, while doing my duty and trying to capture Lila Chang's murderer, I suffered a fall from a spectacularly high place.

I'm not going to go through it all here. I've already written about it. Let's just say it took half the town and everything Smitty had to save my life and I owed him.

And that's just the way Smitty likes it.

Most of the streets in Carterville have houses on both sides of the street. But not Fir. It's too steep up here with houses only on the downhill side, the road itself dug into the hill. Fir wasn't one of the original streets, so when my ancestor built his house on Engelmann that was as high as you could go. Fir was first built in the early 1920s by the Winslows. They had been here a while by then and had more or less taken things over from the Carters. A lot of the money they made during Prohibition ended up here.

Yes, the mayor is a Winslow and I am a Carter. A town like this is rich—stifling rich—in history.

Most of the private property on Fir Street was now owned by Smitty. He was living in one house and in the process of bulldozing three other houses. While these were built in the

1920s not the 1880s, they were still historic. A lot of people weren't happy about it.

When Annabelle had called, she used the code 10-89. After what happened with Lila, I got a bit paranoid and we threw out the standard usage of codes and reassigned the numbers. Too many people with police scanners around here.

For us, a 10-89 is "Threat to life or limb."

Honestly, we don't use the codes that much. With two officers and one dispatcher and our radios almost always in range with good reception we don't need them. It's not the kind of vibe we want. But sometimes we want to deal with an issue before the Carterville rumor mill gets a hold of it.

So Annabelle had told me that someone had threatened Smitty's life, and he had asked for me to handle it. Personally. Because I, quite literally, owed him my life.

Smitty may have a superpower but was no hero. He had bought half of the western part of Fir Street with all the money he charged those he healed. The price tag to pay my debt to him was fifty thousand dollars. As if a cop in a tiny town could come up with that kind of cash.

It took all of a minute and half to drive from where I was parked on the Circle to Smitty's end of Fir Street, but it was long enough for me to be in a foul mood.

Smitty used to be a part-time mechanic and a full-time petty thief before the meteor hit. Now he was trying to take the town over. He had cured Karen Winslow of cancer and helped several others on the town council. He had put me together after my long, hard fall. The people that ran this town all owed him, and I didn't like it. Not one bit.

I pulled up in front of the fourth house from the end… well, it was the end house now as a backhoe picked at the remains of the last three houses Smitty had just flattened to make space for whatever gaudy monument to his own ego he was going to build up here. There was heavy dust in the air from the churning of the earth on the steep hill and the beep-beep of the dump truck backing into place.

The residence still standing was a quaint two-story house that someone had sheathed in off-white vinyl siding in the fifties that ran in horizontal planks. The windows were narrow and tall, a short gravel driveway led to the covered front door.

My boots crunched over the gravel as I looked around. The hill was steep here, the short driveway on solid ground, but most of the house dangling on stilts over the hill. I couldn't see it, but I knew the back of this house because my house was below it and to the west just a bit. It had a modest deck and a small basement at ground level that the former owner had turned into a woodworking shop a couple of decades ago.

Before that it had belonged to the Smiths, no relation to Smitty, another family that has been in Carterville since the beginning. In fact, the house just to the west that was now a shrinking pile of rubble had also belonged to the Smiths. The owner of the Carterville Inn and my former on again, off again girlfriend, Annie Smith had been born there.

It's all a bit confusing because Smitty is a Smith but not closely related to *the* Smiths that had been here since the late 1800s. Smitty was born here, but his parents were not directly related to Annie's family which goes all the way back.

In a small town, history is not just the buildings but the people. After our especially disastrous breakup last Christmas, the day Lila Chang died, Annie and I don't talk anymore.

But I'm sure she was more than a little pissed about what Smitty was doing up here.

The house was fronted with colorful flower beds, the scent fighting with all the dust in the air from the beeping yellow monsters busy chewing up the past. I stood in front of the door and stared at the carnage. It looked like a tornado had hit, the mechanized monsters churning the old homes into broken boards and bent pipes.

Being on the end of the street, Smitty's new house would have a massive 180-degree view of the desert. The only view better is the Carterville Overlook and I'm sure he would have bought that land and built his house up there if he could have.

But I was stalling. I didn't want to see Smitty. While he did heal me and I did owe him, he didn't heal me all the way. It took me two months to start feeling like myself again. He claims that was all he could do, but I had my doubts.

There was nothing to do for it, so I knocked. Smitty opened the door, and I was relieved to see he wasn't in his new-age getup, trading the long flowing layers for shorts, flip-flops, and an Arizona Diamondbacks T-shirt. His blond hair was more scraggly than usual, the premature grey really standing out. He was tall and thin and all sharp angles, his legs looking to be a little too thin to actually hold him up.

He also looked worried, his face pinched into a deep frown, dull green eyes flickering out at the road behind me as he hurriedly waved me in and shut the door.

"Thank you for coming, Chief," he said, his voice a little more nasally than usual.

This had officially become a weird day. Karen Winslow was kind to me and Smitty was glad to see me.

We stood in a small, tiled entryway that opened to a

modest-sized living room. There was an overstuffed leather couch with a broad coffee table in front of it covered in paperwork with a sleek laptop sitting on top. Beyond were sliding glass doors that led to the small deck.

"What can I do for you, Smitty?" I asked.

He bit his lip and nodded, walking me into his living room. He pointed to the top of a pile of papers. On it was a sheet of off-white paper that had been previously folded. It had been ripped along all the edges and said, "Destroyer of Carteville, I AM comming for you."

The letters were bold and blocky with little bites out of the edges. Some fancy faux beat-up font someone had found on the internet. "AM" was oddly capitalized and "Carteville" and "comming" were misspelled which was odd since the latter was the kind of thing a modern word processor would autocorrect, and the former was the name of the town we lived in and everyone should know there are two Rs in it.

The spacing of it was also odd, the phrase in three different lines

Destroyer of Carteville

  I AM

    comming for you

Smitty reached for it, but I held up my hand. "Where did you find it?" I asked. "And how much have you handled it?"

He gave me a puzzled look. "It's evidence, Smitty," I said. "The more you mess with it the less useful it is."

He pursed his lips and rubbed at his chin. His usually shaved face had several days' growth of blond beard. "It was in my mailbox, and I've… I've handled it. I… I won't next time."

"Next time?" I asked.

He nodded and pointed to a rolltop desk on the other side of his living room. It was an antique in good shape, all shiny dark wood. Probably expensive. He pointed at the top drawer. I grabbed a pen from the desk and opened the draw with it. There was a pile of paper in there. I'm not sure how many. The top one said.

Destroy Carteville
   AND I will
      destroy YOU

The same misspelling of Carterville, the same edge-eaten font, the same ripped edges. But I noticed a random black blob of toner on the page and realized that the paper wasn't off-white, the toner cartridge was leaking, leaving it with a grey haze and that blob.

That had happened to us at the department when Annabelle tried some cheap, off-brand toner cartridges for our printer.

I poked the top paper with the pen. I couldn't see enough of the other papers to read them, but they were the same. Torn edges. Bad toner cartridge. Strange heavy font.

I went back to the coffee table and looked at that one. It had a small toner blob and the same grey haze.

I looked up at Smitty who had his hands shoved into his pockets. "How long?" I asked.

He looked away, his gaze going out the sliding glass doors to the view of the desert beyond. "Three weeks," he said.

I bit back a curse and asked, "And what made you call today?"

He met my eyes, and I could see that he was scared. I didn't know if Smitty could heal himself, but I figured he could and that had made him cocky. Since the meteor hit, he's been insufferable, lording his superpower over everyone, trying to remake this town in his own image.

Smitty used to be an annoyance. He saw a lot of me before the meteor. If there was a robbery in town, he was one of the first doors I would come knocking on. Sometimes he was behind it, but I never had enough hard evidence to put him away. Sometimes he wasn't behind it and that just built up the bad blood.

We had history, and even though I owed him, he had been reluctant to call it in. Something else had happened.

He bit his lip, sighed, and his head bobbed up and down a couple of times like a nervous bird. He pointed to the second drawer of that rolltop desk.

I walked over and used the pen to open it.

"Shit," I said. In it was a small straw doll dressed in flowing earth-toned fabric with a bit of corn straw for hair clearly meant to be Smitty. The head had been mostly twisted off and was hanging by a single straw.

THREE
SUNDAY, JULY 1. THE SMITH RESIDENCE

I watched as Annabelle worked. We were both gloved up and I was ostensibly part of the effort, but I mostly just watched. I watched the look of concentration on Annabelle's face as she pulled out one sheet at a time from Smitty's desk. Read the phrasing as I wrote it down on my little notepad, photographed it and slipped it into a plastic evidence bag. Later we would look for prints, but I was pretty sure there would be none but Smitty's.

Annabelle's purple-streaked red hair was pulled back, her wavy hair contained in an unusual ponytail. She was still dressed in her usual tight jeans and high heels with a red blouse, but she somehow looked more in her element. Her face impassive, her brown eyes focused as she worked, all business.

With an office so small, everyone wore a lot of hats, and Annabelle was best with the CSI stuff, so I let her take the lead. She was a few years older than me, her age and her many years smoking showing in the fine wrinkles on her face.

I watched Smitty as he paced and bit his nails and looked more or less like a nervous heron ready to take flight. He was scared instead of his usual post-meteor arrogance, and I have to admit that seeing him like this did engender some empathy.

Later when Officer Isabella Ortega arrived and Annabelle was out dusting the mailbox for prints, I stood and watched as they sat in that small living room, and she took his statement.

Ortega was short, young, strong, and stocky with long black hair pulled into her usual ponytail. She was seven months on the job in Carterville and not much more than that being a cop. I stole her from the Coconino County Sheriff's Office after the business with Lila Chang and she proved to be useful and interested in this weird little town.

She had her police blues on and asked all the right questions. I caught her glancing shyly at me a couple of times. She thought I was testing her. I wasn't. Not really. I just didn't trust Smitty, and by taking a step back I hoped to see things more clearly.

I did trust that he was scared, but that was about it.

"Do you have any enemies?" Ortega asked.

Smitty snorted out a half laugh, and I was relieved to see the old arrogance. "You try having a power like this and see how hard it is to not make enemies."

Ortega's smooth forehead wrinkled in puzzlement. "Can you please explain?" she asked.

Smitty looked to me like he wanted me to explain how the

world worked to the young woman, but I just gave him a small nod, indicating that I wanted him to answer.

He sighed and slouched into his expensive leather couch. "I can't save everybody. It costs me. A lot. I was shitting blood for a week after I saved the chief there," he said, his sharp chin jabbing at me.

"And I strongly believe in equal exchanges," he continued. "That I should receive something back for my efforts and for my suffering." He pointedly looked at me. "I'm not some pro bono softy. If I was, I would have been living in a shack and killed myself from the effort long ago."

"So, you haven't helped some who needed it...?" Ortega asked tentatively, her tone making her sound like she was as naïve as they came. I suppressed a smile because while she was really just a kid, she was smart and driven and playing Smitty as I watched.

He snorted again. "So many," he said. "People fly in from the other side of the world so I can heal them. I turn down most. I give a deal for locals, of course, but even then, I can't do everything. You stub your toe, don't come calling on ole Smitty."

"Let's start with the locals," Ortega said. She had a small notebook out, same brand that I carry, her pen poised. She's got a great memory and used to rely only on it, but I have encouraged this habit. Memory, even a good one, is a lot more squirrely than we like to believe.

"Annie Smith," Smitty said, glancing at me.

I suppressed a groan. The last thing I wanted to do was question Annie about another crime.

"It would be impolite to describe her problem," he continued, "but she couldn't meet my price and she was pissed." He looked at me again. "You know Annie."

I didn't quite suppress a groan this time. "And what about you tearing down her childhood home," I said. "Has she mentioned that?"

Smitty shrugged. "Not a word. She was up here a few weeks ago, right after the heavy equipment got here. Didn't say a word."

Now that was strange. Heritage can be a big deal in a town like this. My name is Carter so it's all out in the open what my relationship to the town is. But Annie's family was here from almost the beginning, and she rarely missed an opportunity to make sure people knew that. The Carterville Inn, which she owned and ran, had plenty of period pictures with the Smiths in them.

"Who else?" Ortega asked.

"Felicia Marin," Smitty said. "I did end up helping her out, but the price did not sit well with them. Her and Harold have been giving me the stink eye ever since. Which is a little funny coming from those two hippy lawyers."

"What happened with Felicia?" I asked.

He shook his head. "Sorry, Chief. Patient-healer confidentiality." He was definitely getting back to his arrogant self now that he wasn't alone and this was all about him.

I shut up and watched. The list also included Lisa Bass, the pastor of the Carterville Church, and Frank Paulson, the owner of the Carterville Diner and my best friend.

I wanted to ask more questions but just watched Ortega do her job. After she left, I just stood there staring at Smitty.

"What?" he asked. "You gotta thing for me now, Henry? You felt the power of Smitty and want some more?"

He was trying to push my buttons, but the tables were turned. He was the one that needed me.

"Do people do that?" I asked.

His brow furrowed and he smiled. It was a predatorial thing that showed off his overly bleached teeth. Another thing about the new Smitty that I just couldn't stand. "Do people do 'what'?" he asked, although from his tone he knew exactly what I was asking.

"Do people hurt themselves on purpose so they can feel your power?" I asked. The beeping of the equipment outside stopped, and the room suddenly felt too quiet, like people were listening. It was hot in there. It was July and above eighty degrees. The windows were open so there was a slight breeze, but these old houses don't usually have air-conditioning. Up at this elevation it's silly—you only need it a few weeks a year.

His smile got bigger and more sharklike. "You're a big boy, Henry. You know how the world works and you know the answer to that question."

I nodded because I did know. I remembered back seven months when my body was broken. I was dying from that fall and Smitty healed me. It was this deliciously warm sensation that felt like the first rays of sunshine on your face after a long cold storm, or how it felt when you first held hands with someone you had a crush on, or the feeling of safety you feel as a kid when your mother picks you up and holds you as you cry. That sensation was everything when he was healing you. Everything you had ever wanted and didn't think you would ever have. I could understand how someone might get hooked on that.

"How many regulars you got, Smitty?" I asked.

He shrugged. It was lazy and sloppy with him slouched there on the couch. "Handful," he said.

"Did you cut off any recently?" I asked.

He leaned forward, his hazel eyes finding me. His eyes are like that, sometimes full green, sometimes with enough gold to make them look hazel. He nodded, the confidence running from his face. "They wanted too much," he said. "It wasn't worth the cash anymore."

I nodded for him to continue. Because I could relate to whomever this was. As much as I hated owing Smitty, as much as I never wanted him to lay his hands on me again, I wanted to feel that feeling again.

But he didn't say anything, and I couldn't stop myself. "I suppose the worse you are hurt the better it feels to be healed," I said.

He licked his dry lips and nodded as he stared at his hands, the instrument of his power. "You got the full monty, Henry."

He usually called me "Chief," and I didn't like this more familiar exchange. We were not friends. Not by a long stretch.

"And I suppose it feels good to you too while you are doing it," I said.

He nodded again, still staring at his hands. "But I take some of it on myself and I feel like shit afterward." He looked up at me and for the first time I really got how hard this must be for him. His patients went from pain to ecstasy. He went from ecstasy to pain, taking on a bit of what he healed the person from.

I wanted to ask him if finding out who was doing this would clear my debt with him, but I didn't. It was my job, and I would do it regardless. Smitty was the one that tried to extract something from everyone with his power. Me, I just do my job.

Don't get me wrong. I almost said something about ten times during our conversation. I wanted out of the debt. I didn't want to feel obliged to him. And the hate that was smoldering in my heart for him burst into flame.

But that's what a job is, when it's a good one. It gives you opportunities to be better than you are if you take advantage of them.

"I need a name, Smitty," I said quietly. "I need to know who you cut off and no bullshit about patient-healer confidentiality. I'll keep it quiet unless it's material to the investigation."

He nodded, his eyes meeting mine again. "But you deal with this person alone," he said. "No telling little miss officer there or Annabelle."

"Agreed," I said. "Unless they become a viable suspect, I will deal with this myself."

He nodded and rubbed at his pointy chin and gave me a name.

My jaw hung open for a moment before I shut it and nodded. "I'm leaving Ortega here for now," I said. "Don't mess with her, Smitty. She's a good kid. You do and I'll take it personal."

He stared at me. I could see the arrogance trying to take a hold of his face, but he nodded and slumped back onto the couch.

I left with a knot in my stomach. Little towns like this are full of secrets. This wasn't one I wanted to know any more about.

FOUR

SUNDAY, JULY 1. THE CARTERVILLE INN

Annie Smith wasn't the name Smitty gave to me, the name of the person that was addicted to his power and kept hurting themselves so they could feel it. But she did have a couple of reasons to hate Smitty. Unfortunately, she was a suspect and she needed to be questioned. Besides, I needed some time to process the name he had given me.

I left Ortega our one CPD vehicle and set out on foot. Nothing is that far away in Carterville and, besides, my sister had been harping on me to get more exercise and lose some weight. I had put on a few pounds recovering from my fall.

As I walked into the Carterville Inn, I knew it wasn't going to go well. I knew I shouldn't even be here, that I should let Ortega take this one. But—and I could be fooling myself here —I didn't want to foist this on Ortega. It was going to be worse for me, but it would be bad for anyone, and I didn't want to subject her to it. And, besides, I had left Ortega with Smitty.

Yeah. I was definitely fooling myself to some degree. I was aware of my growing fondness of the young officer, and I did want to protect her, but I did want to see Annie too, even if it was going to be terrible.

Our breakup had been spectacularly bad. Brutal even. And it happened around the investigation of Lila Chang's murder where she was a suspect. But I still missed Annie.

The inn sits in a three-story red brick building built in 1890 as a saloon. The lobby was dominated by the original bar and Annie was standing behind it talking to a customer. She didn't notice me, and I got a moment to just look at her. Petite, long black hair, high cheekbones, and piercing blue eyes. She had a smile that could light up your world and cut you to shreds depending on her mood and intent.

She was dressed in a white dress shirt with a thin black tie and a black vest. The standard uniform at the inn. It's an upscale historic hotel. The high ceiling was decorated with the original stamped tin tiles and the arched windows let in enough light to show off the antique furniture and the historic photos hanging on the walls.

It was just a moment there when my breath caught at her beauty. She was my age with fifty just in the rearview mirror and looked even more beautiful than when she was younger. The crow's feet and other minor signs of age on her well-tanned face only enhanced the overall effect. She wasn't a child. She was a woman. She knew her mind.

I have been having that reaction to Annie since puberty hit and I started to see her differently. I couldn't help it. But it was just a moment while she talked to some tourists and didn't know I was there. When they left, she turned to me, the smile melting off of her face and a frown taking its place.

"Brooke," she said to a young woman dressed just like her farther down the counter. "I'm going to take a break and talk to the chief here. You okay?"

Brooke was a student at NAU in Flagstaff, one of the interns from their school of hotel and restaurant management and had started working for Annie this summer. She was petite with a round face, long blonde hair braided in the back, and striking grey eyes. But she looked off today, her skin pale, sweat at her hairline.

Brooke nodded carefully, like she might have a migraine or something, and stared at me, her mouth forming an "O." She had probably heard the stories of our breakup and I'm sure they had grown in the telling. Although they didn't need to—the truth would easily warrant that expression.

"Henry," Annie said as she opened the door to her office which was behind the old saloon bar.

"Annie," I said, tipping my cowboy hat to her as I walked behind the bar and into her cramped office.

It was even smaller than mine over at the department with just enough room for a wooden desk with a chair on either side, a low bookshelf that served as a printer stand, and a couple of filing cabinets.

On the wall behind her desk was a picture of our graduating class taken in Flagstaff. It's all awkward youth full of hope and promise ready to take on the world. In the center of that picture is Annie with me on one side and Frank Paulson on the other.

When we were together, I used to love seeing that picture. Now it feels like an indictment and reminds me of how far gone my youth and that kind of confidence is.

"I take it from the fact that you came to see me that this is official business," she said, the frown on her face looking like it had taken up residence and wouldn't be leaving anytime soon. It deepened her frown lines and made her look older.

"I'm afraid so," I said.

She leaned against her desk, piled high with paper that was threatening to bury her computer, and crossed her arms, one eyebrow raised.

"I need our conversation to be confidential," I said, taking out my notepad. "I want to get ahead of this before the rumor mill gets a hold of it."

"Very well," she said.

The stilted nature of our conversation was driving me nuts. We had known each other our entire lives. We had been a couple as teenagers and then we had an on again, off again thing after my divorce that had finally ended for good seven months ago. This was a ridiculous way for us to act. But it was probably better this way. There was too much regret and anger for us to try to be real with each other.

And that hurt. But being real would hurt more.

"No recorder this time," she said, her frown still firmly in place. "Does that mean I am not a suspect?"

She hadn't forgiven me for treating her as a suspect in Lila's murder, and she was a legitimate one.

"It means I'm not dealing with a murder or a serious crime at this time," I said evenly.

I hadn't forgiven her for cheating on me and the way she acted before and after the murder.

We stared at each other for a few breaths, the room silent and hot.

"Well...?" she finally asked.

"This is about Smitty," I said, and her frown deepened.

"He's had some threats against his life, and he told me you two had a recent… ummm… *disagreement* over his services."

Her eyes narrowed and her cheeks flushed a bit even with her deep summer tan. "You should leave now, Henry," she said.

She must have seen the puzzled look on my face because she added, "Or I will not be held responsible for what I do." She wasn't yelling, but I think it would have been better if she had been.

"Annie, I need to know what happened," I said, backing up a small step despite myself.

"No, you do not," she said, standing up, her 5' 4" petite frame looking a lot more imposing than it should. "It is personal. And while I can't say I'll lose any sleep over Smitty finally reaping some of what he's sowed, I know nothing about it."

She continued to stare at me, and the room seemed twice as hot, sweat trickled down my back, and I wanted to do nothing more than escape.

"Then leave the personal part out," I said. "Tell me what happened."

"No," she said. "Arrest me right now or get the hell out of my inn."

Her tone was still low and even and that didn't mean she was mad, it meant she was furious. Now Annie knows me, just about as well as anyone does. If she was behind the threats against Smitty, she would have thought this encounter through and could have come to the conclusion that stonewalling me was the best tact.

And right there was the real reason our breakup stuck. She was a legitimate suspect in Lila's murder and that changed something in how I looked at her. That was playing out now. With her fiery nature and fierce temper, it was believable that she could be messing with Smitty.

I took another step back. I had decided to leave. I couldn't trust myself when it came to Annie. But then I saw the piece of paper sitting on the top of her pile. It was a flyer for a Fourth of July fireworks viewing party up at the Carterville Overlook and hosted by the Carterville Inn. The paper had a few random black blobs and a grey haze to it. Just like the papers Smitty showed me with the threats on them.

I walked around Annie and picked it up. "Good thing we've gotten some rain this year," I said. "It'd be a shame if the fireworks got canceled again."

She looked at me like I was crazy.

"You guys print this up in house?" I asked.

Her brow furrowed and she slowly nodded her head. "Yeah. Why?"

I shrugged. "Just wondering. Mind if I take this?"

She was still looking at me like I was crazy. Which was frankly better than the look she was giving me before, like if she could kill me with her gaze, she happily would. She gave me a confused nod.

"Thank you for your time, Annie," I said. I opened the office door and could feel her eyes on my back.

This wasn't good. Annie was officially a suspect. Again.

FIVE

SUNDAY, JULY 1. THE CARTERVILLE POLICE DEPARTMENT

AFTER LEAVING THE CARTERVILLE INN, I WALKED THE Carterville Circle which the inn sits on. The circle joins Main Street and Cedar Street in a brief flattening of the hill. It's the center of town and prime real estate. I wasn't trying to go anywhere, I just needed to move. It had been so hot in that little office and Annie being a suspect again was just not right.

I mean, it couldn't be, could it? Was Annie Smith even capable of misspelling the name of the town we lived in? But the paper looked like it was printed on the same printer with the same bad toner cartridge.

Town was busy, even for a Sunday. It had to be the upcoming holiday. I walked past the brewery, and it was even more packed than it had been earlier. I looked in through the glass but didn't see Karen Winslow and was glad for that.

My mind tumbled around with what little I knew.

Someone was threatening Smitty—not at all hard to imagine.

They were doing it with bad spelling, odd formatting, and a crappy toner cartridge.

Annie hadn't detailed what her disagreement with Smitty was, but it was clear there was one. Her behavior had confirmed that. And she's got a crappy toner cartridge in use in there.

I needed someone to keep an eye on Annie. It couldn't be me, not with how our first talk in months had just gone. And it couldn't be Ortega. I wouldn't subject the girl to it, and Annie wouldn't take kindly to being staked out.

And then it hit me. I knew who could help. With a nod I finished a loop of the circle and walked to the station.

———

I handed Annabelle Unger the Fourth of July flyer from Annie's desk.

"What?" she asked. "You invitin' me for an evenin' out on the town, Chief?" Her southern lilt was turned all the way up. "Why I do declare, I just might pass out from the thrill of it all."

She placed the back of her hand on her forehead and tipped her head back dramatically, her purple-streaked bright red hair spilling over her silky red blouse. She was close to sixty years old, and I think quite proud of that hair, any hint of grey beat back by a chemical barrage.

I would prefer her to wear a uniform despite her not being an officer. But that would never happen. I gave up asking years ago.

She was at her desk in the big open room of the Carterville Police Department. It's not much. Three desks, filing cabinets, and a big whiteboard. There're two holding cells in the back, a bathroom, and a converted closet that is my office and the armory.

The entrance to the CPD is off Cedar, but we're in a historic building on Main that was the original post office in back of a bakery, the sweet smell making it obvious why my belly kept getting bigger the deeper I get into middle age.

"You wish," I said with a grin. I don't think you would call this flirting, although it has been established that I am not very good at knowing what exactly flirting is. Annabelle and I go way back, and we have a relaxed working relationship. "See the blobs of toner and the grey haze?" I asked.

She nodded as she pulled the paper close and squinted. I could relate. I've never needed glasses, but the years have made it harder to see things like this. I was past the need for a pair of readers but was fighting it still.

"See if it matches what's on those delightful little love notes to Smitty," I said.

Her eyes widened and she whispered, "Shit. It can't be Annie, can it?"

I shrugged. "I've got to make a call," I said and went into my closet of an office and closed the door.

I don't actually close the door much. Especially not during June or July where it can get roasting hot in here since we don't have air-conditioning either.

I pulled my cell phone out and found the number for Martin Lester and hit the call button. Up until the Lila Chang thing, he had worked for me. But things went so sideways with Lila I had to fire him, or, more specifically, force him to retire, and he ended up leaving town.

But he had a power I needed right now.

"Yeah?" he answered.

"How far away are you?" I asked.

"Ummm… about three hours," he said. "I'm on a hike near Sedona right now. Why?"

"I need you to watch someone for me," I said.

He was quiet, but I knew we hadn't lost the signal because I could still hear him breathing. This may sound like an odd conversation, no small talk and few words, but that was Martin Lester. He was a quiet man and he had lost a lot, more than most, when Lila was murdered. The prospect of returning to Carterville could not be a pleasant one.

As I've explained before in these stories, the powers we were granted when the meteor hit often fit the person and their personality. Martin Lester was a quiet man, and his power was not being seen when he doesn't want to be. It's not invisibility or anything like that—he'll show up on photos—people just don't notice him.

"Who?" he finally asked.

"Annie," I said.

He was quiet for a few breaths and then asked, "Why?"

"Someone is threatening Smitty. I have circumstantial evidence that the threatening notes are being produced at the inn," I said.

He was quiet again for more than a few breaths.

"I wouldn't ask if it wasn't important, Martin," I said.

"She knows that she's a suspect?" he asked.

"Unfortunately, yes," I said.

"Well, that ain't good," he said. "See why you need me. But…"

He left that word hanging there and I didn't need any help filling in the blanks. He had left Carterville and with good reason. There was too much pain here, the loss of Lila too real.

"You got other suspects?" he asked.

I thought for a moment. Lester wasn't working for me, but I had known him all my life, and up until the business with Lila he had never given me reason to question my trust of him.

"It turns out Smitty has regulars," I said slowly. "They get addicted to the feeling of him healing them."

"I can see that," he said calmly.

"He had to cut one of them off recently," I said. "I need to go talk to them next. I've got Ortega watching Smitty, and with her heels, Annabelle couldn't tail someone if her life depended on it. But the evidence warrants keeping an eye on Annie."

"You sure this ain't personal?" he asked.

Now it was my time to pause. If you don't use a lot of words, like Lester, you've got to get to the point quickly.

"Anything involving me and Annie Smith is personal," I said. "But there is evidence here. Annabelle has a sample from the inn and she's comparing it to Smitty's letters right now."

"Okay," he said. "I'll be in and out, watch Annie, and I won't talk to no one. Not even you, Henry."

"Yeah," I said. "Sounds good."

"I'll need someone to drive me into town," he said. "Wouldn't be good if anyone recognized my car."

"Sure," I said, getting that by "someone" he meant not me. "Go to Bo Larson's place. I'll tell him to expect you and have Ortega come bring you in."

"That works," he said and then hung up.

I sat there second-guessing my decision. To pursue Annie

as a suspect. To bring Martin Lester back into town. To follow this case where it led.

It's the last one that kept me sitting there. The name Smitty gave me as the repeat customer he cut off was echoing around my head. Almost anyone would be better than her.

With a sigh I pushed myself up and headed out. It was time to talk to Karen Winslow again.

SIX

SUNDAY, JULY 1. THE WINSLOW APARTMENT

An hour later I was sitting on an elegant and uncomfortable couch in the apartment above the Carterville Brewery. The couch was a deep blue with a velvety fabric and cushions that were too hard. With its hardwood accents and elegant lines, it was made more for looking at than sitting on. The true test of a couch, for me, is that you can get a decent night's sleep on it.

The view was good. Half of it was the tall fir tree that is at the center of the Circle, but beyond its branches was the vast desert of Northern Arizona. The dark green needles covered where the Grand Canyon was some forty-five miles away, but east of that I could see the desert that was part of the vast Navajo Indian Reservation.

The room had this stark feel with hardwood floors and exposed brick on the exterior walls. Lots of room and high ceilings. It was filled with more elegantly uncomfortable furniture like the couch, one piece of furniture here costing as much as every piece I owned.

The air was warm and still, the windows closed, and I sat on the edge of the couch like I was a kid waiting to go see the principal.

Karen Winslow and Ken Fischer have a ranch a little ways out of town and spend most of their time there, but this is their "in town" apartment in case they don't want to make the "long" fifteen-minute drive to their ranch.

It's also their offices. They own a lot of real estate here and a few businesses. If you're familiar with Arizona and the Winslow name sounds familiar, it is with good reason. Karen is a descendant of Edward F. Winslow, the founder of Winslow, Arizona. A family disagreement around 1900 saw part of the family splitting off and coming to Carterville to make it their own. Judging from where I was sitting, they largely succeeded.

Karen Winslow has been mayor of Carterville almost as long as I have been chief of police. It's always been a bit tense between us. Because of our names and because of our jobs.

Karen had been a suspect on the Lila Chang murder and now she was a suspect on this Smitty thing. Just like Annie Smith. I know this is a small town, but it was getting a little ridiculous.

I had walked from the department back to the brewery and told her I had an urgent police matter to discuss with her. She had rushed me up here and left me waiting. I suspect there was intent behind it. What better thing to do when the police come to question you than to keep them waiting?

The room had a floral odor that was Karen's overly strong and very expensive perfume. There was a desk on the other side of the room with a bookshelf behind it in dark wood. I recognized a few of the books—they were histories of the local area.

History is important to people around here. Carter. Winslow. Smith. These are some of the names that have been here the longest. History is a matter of pride. And history is full of bloody conflicts. More than once the Carters and the Winslows have pulled guns on each other with only one surviving. The violent history of the Wild West is often glorified. Look no further than the conflict between the Earps and the McLaurys and Clantons in Tombstone, Arizona, in 1881.

Karen was being a kind host to me downstairs just a few hours ago, but that doesn't change the history. Not of our ancestors and not of the two of us. It's the mayor's job to create prosperity for their town and it's the chief of police's job to create safety. The two jobs are often at odds.

I almost left. About half a dozen times. I have better things to do, but that would be playing into her hand. And that's the problem with the mayor. She's always playing chess, looking several moves ahead with her decisions, and it can cause a simple man like me to question his motives.

I was leaning forward to get up, to leave, when she swept into the room, her turquoise skirt flowing around her long legs and her blonde braid wagging behind her.

"What is the urgent business, Henry?" she asked, sitting in an uncomfortable chair across from me, her back erect.

"I'm sorry if I gave you the impression this was a business discussion," I said. "There is a police matter involving Winston Smith that I need to question you about."

Her brow furrowed and her hazel eyes focused on me. "Smitty?" she asked. "What's going on with Smitty?"

I pulled out my little recorder and asked, "Do you mind?"

"What is going on here, Henry?" she asked.

"Someone is threatening Smitty, and I need to ask you about your recent dealings with him," I said.

Her eyes narrowed and she bit her lip and leaned back in that uncomfortable chair. "No recorder," she said. "And no notes. Just a conversation between two friends. Please."

I hadn't planned on the recorder, but knowing Karen I had opened with it. "I need to take notes," I said. "Procedure. But I won't use your name. No one on my team knows about this yet and I hope it stays that way."

She swallowed and nodded, her eyes flicking away from me and staring out the window at the view of the desert. She sat there and didn't speak.

"I'm guessing this started when he healed your breast cancer," I said.

She nodded, still not looking at me. "You know how it feels, Henry. It feels like…"

She fell silent but I did know how it feels. I have used metaphors to describe it, but right then I thought of a word that would probably work better for her. "It feels like heaven, right?"

She nodded and looked at me and I could see pain behind her eyes. Longing. Regret. These are unusual emotions for her to show, at least to me. "Even with Smitty, curing cancer doesn't take just one treatment," she said. "I think I would have been fine if it had just been one treatment. But we did one a week for eight weeks and…"

"And you were hooked," I offered.

She shook her head. "Not quite, but I was most of the way there. I drink, of course, but I've never had a problem with that. A little weed now and then is fun, and I tried a few other drugs in college but…" She ended in a shrug. "What Smitty can do makes all of that seem like nothing, like shadows, like a cheap knockoff of the real thing."

She was right. I remembered what it felt like when Smitty healed me after my fall. The feeling of bright warmth that flowed through his hands into me. The utter peace I felt as I gave into it and my body healed. Gin can never do that. No matter how much of it you have.

"How often were you going back to him?" I asked.

She glanced at me and then looked away. "I didn't go back after he cured my cancer. I wanted to but I could fight it. The first time was a mistake. Katie, our Appaloosa, stepped on my foot. She didn't mean it, but she broke a couple of bones. I was looking at a long recovery, so I went to Smitty."

I nodded. "I remember hearing about that."

"This was almost six months after he healed me of the breast cancer and…" she said, trailing off again.

"And…?" I prompted.

"The cancer hadn't been painful," she said. "But this was something different. Feeling my bones and tendons and muscles heal… It was… Well, you know…"

I nodded. I did. I had empathy for her situation. And that must be why she was telling me so much. She needed to talk to someone who could relate to her experience.

"How often after that?" I asked.

She shrugged. "A month after that I 'accidentally' smashed my thumb while shoeing one of the horses."

"And after that?" I prompted.

"It was a slow progression. It got to the point where I would have a standing appointment every two weeks and I'd just bring the hammer with me and do it there." She was staring at me, her gaze defiant as if she was daring me to say she did something wrong.

"And when he cut you off?" I asked.

"I was going every week," she said. "And I kept needing… more."

"So… smashing your thumb wasn't enough?" I asked.

She shook her head and looked away. I didn't ask her what she had ended up doing, what was enough. I didn't want to know.

"And Smitty was good with this?"

She nodded. "Encouraged it for a long time. And I'm not the only one."

I wrote a few more notes and turned away, looking out the window at the view. This is the problem with being a cop. You have to peer into the dark recesses that most people never discover.

I had known Smitty was using his power to heal to gain power over this town. I had known that Karen was one of the people he had on his side, I just didn't know how.

And it seemed I was one of the ones too. I owed him for healing me and saving my life. He said the bill was 50K, which I hadn't been able to come up with yet. But Karen could easily pay a bill like that, so it finally made sense how she became beholden to him. He got her hooked on his power.

"Are you sure it really took eight treatments to heal your cancer?" I asked.

Her jaw dropped open and she stared at me blinking too much. Clearly the thought had never occurred to her.

"I had eight different broken bones, a punctured lung, a

lacerated liver, and a ton of internal bleeding," I said. "He saved my life in one short session."

She continued to stare at me.

"I'll admit that I hobbled around, and it took me a month or two to be completely better," I said. "I could have benefited from another session, and I've always wondered why he didn't heal me all the way."

She was pale and still staring.

"Maybe he only went that far," I said, "hoping I would come back for more. Maybe he wanted me to be a regular. Maybe he wanted you to be a regular."

The silence was thick in the hot room. While this was a dark recess I didn't want to peer into, Smitty and his growing hold on this town suddenly made a lot more sense.

Karen shook her head like she was trying to wake herself up and stood up. "I need to get back downstairs," she said, starting for the door.

I stood up and followed her. "I need those other names," I said.

She stopped. "Names?"

"You said you weren't the only regular," I said. "I need those other names."

She nodded and walked to her desk, pulled a small pad of paper out of her drawer, and started writing names down. It was an odd choice since I was standing there with my notepad out, but maybe she didn't want to say the names out loud.

She tore the piece of paper off the pad and handed it to me. There were three other names.

"There may be more," she said quietly.

"Thank you for your honesty, Karen," I said. "I understand

this is a big day for the brewery, but I have more questions for you. What time can I come back?"

The sour look on her face made it clear that she wanted to be done with this discussion, that she thought she had given me enough. And we had talked about her addiction to Smitty's power, but not about him cutting her off which is what made her a suspect in this whole business.

She looked at her watch. It was an old-fashioned watch worked into a Hopi silver bracelet with chunks of turquoise. "Eight should be fine."

I nodded and walked out with her, shoving the list of names into my pocket. It turns out there were far too many people who might have reason to mess with Smitty.

SEVEN

SUNDAY, JULY 1. MAIN STREET, CARTERVILLE

After talking to Karen, I needed to clear my head and my stomach was starting to grumble at me. I don't know about you, but sometimes it seems like my stomach runs my life.

I'm thirsty, get me something to drink. I'm hungry, let's eat something, preferably fried. Oh no, you stuffed me too full with all the things I told you to eat, why are you so mean to me?

Which makes the whole "trusting your gut" thing laughable. If you did everything your stomach told you, you'd end up fat and sick and heading towards a heart attack with a side of diabetes. But being in my role with only one other cop on the team, I have learned to trust my gut. Sometimes. Well, it's more a trust but verify kind of a thing. Trusting your gut intuition is often right, but knowing it is sometimes wrong.

As I walked through the brewery, Karen Winslow already talking to customers, a smile lighting up her face like nothing at all had just happened, the smells of the brewery hitting me and my stomach getting loud. Beer. French fries. A whiff of coffee. But I kept walking. While there was comfort food aplenty here, it wasn't the comfort I really wanted.

I walked out and rounded the Carterville Circle and headed down the east side of Main. There was a breeze and it felt good to cool off a bit. The sun was high above me in a clear blue sky and the tourists were everywhere. Shorts. Flip-flops. Taking pictures and selfies. Chattering about things. I heard the word "powers" drift over more than once just getting out of the Circle.

I smiled and nodded at the tourists and said hello to the locals. There are sidewalks on both sides of the street and once you get on Main proper, trees planted on the inside edge of them. Mostly fir and maple, some of them a century old.

Main had started its steep descent down the hill when I saw Crazy Carl.

Well, that's not a nice name, but the name had stuck and with good reason. Carl has a power, one that edged towards "super," but it was a heavy one to bear.

He was a tall man in his early forties with dark skin and was swaying as he walked, his black hair falling into his eyes and unkempt. He had on jeans and a white T-shirt, his feet bare. He was from Lebanon and had been a visiting professor at Northern Arizona University six years ago and had been in Carterville when the meteor hit.

"Hi, Carl," I said with a tip of my cowboy hat. "How are you doing today?" Carl had good days, bad days, and crazy days. Judging by his dirty bare feet, this was one of the latter.

It used to be that he could be in Carterville for a while before the crazy would hit. For the last few months it seemed to hit him almost right away. He hadn't been here that often, but every time he was, he ended up like this.

"Smitty," he gasped, grasping my arm, his hand shaking but his grip strong and painful. His halitosis was potent and he was way past the need for a shower. He swayed and twitched as he talked to me. "Danger for bad man. Danger for good man. Be wary of promises made. Be strong, for you will be tested."

His accent was intense, his Rs rolled, verbs dropped, using "z" instead of "th," but understandable. I looked around, there was no one too close to us, but I pulled him to the side, down the short sidewalk that led to an old house that was an accounting office now.

Carl's power was seeing the future. Sometimes it seems like he had already lived in the future or was living in the future, his sense of time and timing badly disjointed. It almost seemed like he was possessed by it.

He didn't live in Carterville, well, not most of the time. After the meteor hit, he left not knowing he had a power. Two years ago, after the story of Carterville powers got out, he came back and discovered it. He lived forty minutes away in Flagstaff but came here pretty often. He was a psychologist and visiting was kind of his own experiment in experiencing powers and studying those with powers.

"What about Smitty?" I asked, keeping my voice low.

"He rreaps what he sowed," he said, the rolled "r" lending weight as he leaned close to me, gesturing with his hands, his breath making my eyes water. "We all rreap what we sowed. Even you, Henry. Especially you, Henry."

Well, that was foreboding but not very helpful. Someone Smitty abused with his power was abusing him back. I got that. And the fact that my mistakes were going to come around and bite me in the ass didn't surprise me at all. It was the nature of reality.

"Who?" I asked. "Who is threatening Smitty?"

He stopped his swaying and twitching and looked me straight in the eye. "This town not big enough for the both of you," he said and then giggled, recognizing the bad cliché even in his state. And then his face got serious. "You, Henry. You threaten him. I know you want to hurt him, but you must fight ze impulse. Do not kill him."

I was always fighting that impulse. While my stomach rattled on a lot about what it wanted to eat, my fist wanted to connect with Smitty's pointy jaw every time I saw him.

"Is Smitty okay?" I asked, going with the fact that all time is often the same for Carl when he's like this. "Did someone hurt him?"

He looked away, the swaying and twitching starting again. "Agents here," he said. "Zey study us, you know. Zey want to extend our powers outside mountain." He looked at me and his eyes were all the way crazy. "Sacred Kachina of mountain have granted powers. Zat makes us more zen human and our powers will never leave zis mountain."

The Kachina are spiritual beings that the Hopi say inhabit the San Francisco Peaks. The mountains are sacred to them and the Navajo—the Carter Mine was something they never liked on their sacred mountain.

Carl was deep into conspiracy now. It seemed to be something about his mind in this state. He saw the future as the same as the present and conspiracy theories all made sense.

Are we being studied? Of course. Many scientists have been here studying our powers. Carl George was one of them.

It took a few years before much of anyone believed the rumors, but then the scientists came.

Were there secret government agents? Doubtful. There were certainly some non-secret agents a few years back. Like most of us, they theorized that the meteor was the source of our powers. They went into the mine. They searched for the meteor but failed to find it and concluded it had disintegrated on impact.

When they became convinced that our powers only worked within about five miles of the center of town, they lost interest. You can't fight wars with Carterville powers.

"And that's a good thing, that our powers can't leave," I said, taking his arm and guiding him back up Main Street. Carl had been here too long. While I had other important business to attend to, Carl was liable to hurt himself like this. He would certainly freak some tourists out. "Let's go take a ride, Carl. I want to hear more about those agents."

"Yes!" he said, his eyes way too wide. "Zey have tunnel to ze east. Zey long to get back in mine. Zey want to find meteor Kachina called down on mountain. Zey believe zat zere must be piece of it buried. Source of unbelievable power. Zey want to take it away."

I chuckled but it didn't sound that far-fetched. I could see several different parties wanting to make Carterville powers mobile or figure out how to give others the same kinds of powers we have. And, yes, I know that correlation does not equal causation, but the meteor struck and powers showed up. In this case, there is no other explanation.

EIGHT

SUNDAY, JULY 1. OUTSIDE THE CARTERVILLE ZONE OF INFLUENCE

CARL WAS MORE CRAZY THAN ANYTHING ELSE AS I WALKED HIM back to the department. I radioed Ortega, asking her to move our old Ford SUV, our one and only official CPD vehicle, back to the department and walk back to Smitty's. The SUV was there when I got Carl there—not easy, the guy's as focused as a butterfly when he's like this—and drove him out of town and past the zone of influence.

Sure enough, his little red Prius was sitting parked on the side of the road. Carl and I have done this dance dozens of times. He parks right outside of the zone of influence and walks into town.

I have no idea where his shoes went and he usually doesn't run around in an undershirt, but this was the way of it. He kept his wallet locked in the car and hid a key in one of those magnetic boxes stuck to the bottom of his car.

"How are you feeling?" I asked him.

His eyes were too wide, but the twitching had stopped. "Little better, Henry. Gratitude."

I nodded.

He patted his pockets and then looked at me. "You got any paper? A pen?"

I pulled an extra notepad out of the glovebox. One of the small ones that I keep in my back pocket all the time. I gave him a pen and he scribbled for a few pages.

His power was gone, and the memory of his visions fade pretty quickly. While he wrote, I got out and went around the back and grabbed a water bottle and a granola bar out of my emergency supplies. I got back in and put them next to him and just watched.

His brow was furrowed in concentration as he wrote.

Everyone that was in Carterville when the meteor hit ended up with a power. It's different for all of us. I've been claiming for years that I don't have a power. And since it's not relevant to this story, I'm not going to tell you what it is. But watching Carl and feeling that sense of relief I feel every time I leave the zone of influence, I was once again struck by the weight of our powers.

Smitty and his superpower is a case in point. Not only is there a cost for using it, but it has changed him. With his premature grey hair and his inability to gain weight, it's quite apparent. The same is true for all of us even if it is not so obvious. The more potent the power the greater the change.

After a few more pages, Carl looked up at me, his brown eyes wide. "Change coming," he said. "Big change. I..." He trailed off and looked away.

"I can take it, Carl," I said. "I need to know what's going on with Smitty."

He nodded. "The futures... I... I see... so many. No knowing what will happen, only knowing what might happen."

I nodded for him to keep going. Even without his power in effect, Carl can be fairly obtuse.

He opened the water bottle and took a few gulps. "Zere is a change coming, Henry. It is already in motion, and it will take time but..."

"Please, Carl," I said.

"All a jumble. One with great power will die. One with a kindred power will leave," he said.

I nodded. "I suppose I'm in that equation," I said.

He nodded.

"Does this have anything to do with who is threatening Smitty?" I asked.

He shrugged his shoulders. "Many have dark thoughts towards the healer. Many regret the price he has extracted. Some with dark intent. Fading now to my sorrow. But I see a woman. Does that help?"

I nodded. "Narrows down a long list, thank you, Carl."

He nodded back. "Walk with care, Henry."

He took the water bottle and got out. I watched as he retrieved his key and got into his car and drove off.

There wasn't a view here, we were in a dip in the forest and all I could see were juniper trees and a few piñons. I sat there after he had driven off remembering his words, "All a jumble. One with great power will die. One with a kindred power will leave."

Was that Smitty and me? No, it couldn't be. Our powers are not at all similar.

My stomach grumbled and I shook my head. I didn't have

time to deal with possible futures, I had the present to deal with. I started up the old SUV and headed back to town.

NINE
SUNDAY, JULY 1. THE CARTERVILLE DINER

I WENT WHERE MY STOMACH SENT ME, TO A PLACE OF substance and comfort, to the Carterville Diner. It was set back from the street farther than most buildings, giving it some room for parking. It was a little early for lunch, so I was able to snag one of the parking spots. I stopped and stared at the squat brick building. It's old but not historic, with a fifties-style sign done in neon that said "The Carterville Diner."

I got out of the SUV and smiled. My best friend, Frank Paulson, owned the place and did the cooking. But the smile didn't last because he was one of the names Smitty gave me. An incident he didn't tell me about. And despite what Carl said about it being a woman, I had to check the leads.

The bell on the door dinged as I walked in. Despite it being before noon, the place was busy, tourists and a few locals filling the high backed dark green booths and most of the high stools in front of the long counter. This made me happy. I would hate to see Karen Winslow's new brewery make this place any less vibrant.

The walls were outfitted for tourists with old, rusted signs, vintage posters, and bits of old, worn memorabilia from Carterville's history. One of my favorites was a beat-up old metal sign that hung above some of the booths and said, "Last Gas Before the Grand Canyon." It didn't bother to tell the hapless tourist low on gas that Carterville was five miles off of 89A and that the gas in the middle of nowhere Carterville is more expensive than just about anywhere else.

Eyes lifted up from burgers and shakes or late breakfasts as I stepped in. The locals didn't give me a second look, the eyes of the tourists lingered. If experience was any indicator, plenty of them had questions for me. About Carterville powers and where they might witness one in action.

"He's in back, Chief," Patty Walsh said as I strolled through. There was concern in Patty's green eyes, her curly red hair pulled back into a voluminous ponytail. Patty was beautiful, not in a Hollywood way, but more in a girl next door kind of way. She had an amazing smile with a splash of freckles on her cheeks, generous curves, and a decidedly Irish look.

She also had a power. She knew what people wanted before they even asked. It made her a hell of a waitress and it's how she knew I needed to talk to Frank.

When Annie and I were breaking up, she said Patty was part of my "Carterville harem." She hadn't been completely wrong. Patty and I were friends, but the thought of more was intriguing. The thought of being with a woman who knew exactly what you wanted was… well, intimidating comes to mind, but so do a whole lot of other words.

"Thanks," I said with a tip of my hat, wondering how much of that she got as I walked behind the counter and into the kitchen.

The air was hot, the sound of sizzling meat and the smell of hamburgers making my stomach take notice as it started making strident demands.

Big Frank Paulson was manning the grill with a pimple-faced teenager at the fry station. Frank was a large man, about 250 pounds, but only average height. His kind blue eyes were embedded in his round face and his head was shaved clean and shined with sweat in the harsh fluorescent light of the kitchen. He was dressed in his ever-present white apron over jeans and a green T-shirt, the apron stained and dingy.

"Well, if it ain't Henry Carter himself," Frank said with a nod as he flipped a few burgers and pressed the spatula to them causing fat to drip out and sizzle on the grill. "Come down from on high, having decided to slum at the old diner after being offered all the free food he can eat at the sparkling new brewery."

I smiled. This is a small town, nothing done in public is ever private, and stories grow in the telling. "And if it isn't Big Frank Paulson," I said, "master of the grill and savior of hungry bellies throughout Northern Arizona."

Frank flashed me a smile and focused on plating a few orders. A cheeseburger and fries, a cobb salad, and a tuna melt. He was meticulous, and sure this was diner food, but it was precise and neat and vibrant.

Frank Paulson's food was the best in town. There was no way the brewery could beat it. His power was one of the good ones, one of the ones that didn't come with a heavy burden.

Which was just as well, Frank was a good man, and he deserved a good power.

His was the power of growing plants. Saying he had a green thumb was like saying that the Grand Canyon is deep. Most of the produce he served he had grown, and you could taste it. His lettuce was always crisp, his carrots bursting in flavor, and his tomatoes were to die for, a dessert all unto themselves.

Frank could get a meat and potatoes kind of guy like me to eat vegetables they were so good.

After the meals were plated and on the passthrough and he had rung the bell, he looked up at me. "I suppose you are here for more than a burger."

I nodded. It wasn't normal for me to walk back into the kitchen. I usually situated myself on a stool at the front counter where Patty worked, letting her keep me fully supplied with coffee.

"Sure," he said, "I can give you three minutes." He nodded at the teenager, a local, one of the Larson kids, and handed him the spatula. I followed him past the long stainless-steel table that dominated the middle of the kitchen and had a bun toaster and lots of half-prepped plates, past the big walk-in cooler, and out the back door.

The air outside seemed cool after the kitchen. It wasn't much back there, just a dumpster and a place to park when unloading supplies.

"What's up, Henry?" Frank asked, a curious look on his face.

"Smitty," I said and watched the curiosity melt into a sour look. "Keep this to yourself, please, but he's getting threats." Frank's blue eyes widened but he didn't say anything. It felt unnatural, but I had left my notebook in my back pocket. Frank has been my best friend since we were toddlers and I had to keep this casual. "He said you two had a professional disagreement and I'm just following up."

Frank was a man who was way more comfortable with plants than he was with people, probably one of the reasons he's always back in the kitchen. That could be the downside of his power—it has made the introvert more introverted. We've had our difficulties over the years, the worst when Annie Smith stopped dating him and started dating me when we were in high school, but I felt lucky to be one of the humans he regularly interacts with.

We didn't have much time and there was a lot I didn't say. I didn't say he was a suspect. I didn't ask him why he didn't tell me about his medical problem. And I didn't need to spell all that out for Frank.

He pursed his lips and nodded, his blue eyes darkening and slipping away from mine. "Yeah," he said. "You could say that. I've got a little problem and he wanted way too much money." He shrugged his big shoulders.

I didn't say anything. I knew Frank. Words could take time for him to find, especially if the emotions underneath them were uncomfortable. "I yelled at him," he said, looking at his shoes. "I was loud. Mighta punched his wall. He really pissed me off."

He clenched one of his fists which had fresh scabs on a couple of the knuckles.

Frank seemed like a cuddly bear most of the time, but "bear" is the operative word. His belly may have been bulging and he may have been middle aged, but he was a strong man.

He was an all-state wrestling champion in high school and was not the kind of guy you wanted mad at you.

I faced that bear in high school when I told him that Annie and I were dating. When I told him that we were in love.

His blue eyes found mine again. "But I didn't touch him, and if I was going to hurt him, I would have done it right then. You know that."

And I did. When I told him about Annie and me, he had me on the dirty linoleum of Flagstaff High School so quick, I hardly knew it had happened. He punched me once in the face before leaving me there bleeding with a broken nose, half the senior class gawking at me.

I nodded. "Know anyone else as pissed at him as you were?"

He snorted. "Half the town. Lord Smitty makes it hard not to be pissed at him. But I don't know of anyone that would do anything about it."

He didn't ask me what kind of threats Smitty was getting, he knew I couldn't tell him. And I didn't ask him why he went to Smitty because I knew he would tell me in his own time. Nearly fifty years of friendship will give you a kind of shorthand.

"I need to get back in there," he said, nodding at the screen door. "Before Bryant burns something." He took a step forward and then turned back to me. "I'll think about Smitty's problem. Come by the house tonight and we'll talk more."

I nodded.

"And go sit down," he said. "Patty already put your order in."

TEN

SUNDAY, JULY 1. THE CARTERVILLE CHURCH

CARTERVILLE HAS ONE CHURCH, WHICH IS SOMETHING OF A miracle. Congregations form, something goes south, and some of them leave to create the kind of church they really want. Happens all the time.

I think there's a couple of reasons this kind of thing hasn't stuck in Carterville. First is where our church is. It sits on top of Carter Hill and has the best view in town. Second is the church itself. It's over a hundred years old and made out of local volcanic rock, the peak of its roof thirty-five feet up and the stained glass that lets light in at the front utterly spectacular. And the third factor is Flagstaff. Churches on the east side of town are a little over thirty minutes away. You don't want to worship here, you can do a little driving and go to the grocery store while you're in Flag.

That makes the Carterville Church nondenominational by necessity.

Nestled behind the church was a cement block structure

that was built in the sixties. It was painted a light brown and was as plain as the church was grand, the utilitarian nature of it a sharp contrast to the church. Inside it was mostly one big room that was a kitchen, community center, and Sunday school. It had that kind of look that all rooms like this had with calendars, posters with bible verses, and lots of kids' drawings covering the walls. On one end of the room were bathrooms and an office.

After lunch I drove up to talk to Lisa Bass, our pastor. I found her in the big room cleaning up from Sunday School.

As humans in their late thirties go, she was entirely average. Not that tall, not that thin, not remarkable except for her lovely brown eyes. They were comforting and compassionate which befit her calling. She also had the dark skin and the tight black curls of her South African heritage, which was unusual around here. Not that many Black people in rural Arizona.

She was sweeping when I came in, dressed in jeans and a white blouse, which was unusual. I was used to seeing her in smart pantsuits or a skirt and jacket.

"Henry," she said with a bright smile. "To what do I owe this pleasure? I haven't seen you around here much."

She didn't add, "since Lila Chang was murdered," and I appreciated that. I don't know if it's a sign of middle age or my line of work, but I can't tell you in any certain way what I think about God. I want to believe there is some order to this madness, but I don't know that I can anymore.

"Sorry, Pastor Lisa," I said, taking my cowboy hat off. "I've been seeking solace in different ways."

She nodded, her eyes going to my notebook and pen

which I hadn't realized I'd pulled out. "I take it this is not a social call."

I shook my head. "I'm afraid not, but it shouldn't take long."

She smiled and leaned her broom against the wall and walked over to her office. She was limping a bit, placing her right foot down carefully.

Her office was a nice size with a desk facing the door and a large wooden cross on the wall behind it. There were filing cabinets and a couple of bookshelves along the walls, but one corner of it had two small sofas and she sat on one and gestured for me to sit on the other.

This was where she counseled her parishioners. It was a comfortable space, a place for conversation, but I was wishing we were still in the big room. I had sat here before and talked to Pastor Lisa and other pastors before her. Not confession but counseling. It was a place for intimacy, and the questions I brought felt uncomfortable here.

"How can I help you?" she asked, a gentle smile on her face.

I nodded. "I am investigating some threats that Winston Smith has received."

She licked her lips, her eyebrows darting together and then her face relaxing. "What kind of threats?"

"I have to ask that you keep our discussion private," I said.

She nodded. "Of course."

I flipped back in my notes. "The threats are a bit vague, but they promise to destroy him."

She pursed her lips. "And why have you come to me?"

This was the hard part. While I wasn't at church much these days, I respected Pastor Lisa. In my experience, she was a good person, and I didn't think she was part of this, but I have learned that we don't really know each other as well as we think we do. Hell, I don't even know myself sometimes. We humans are complicated.

There was no avoiding it, so I dived in. "Smitty told me that you two had a recent disagreement regarding his services."

She nodded, her eyes locked with mine.

"And another source," I continued, "identified you as a… a repeat customer." Smitty hadn't told me she was one of the "regulars", her name was on the list Karen Winslow wrote for me.

She just stared at me, and I decided that if I was ever in a poker game with Pastor Lisa, I had best be careful. I let the statement hang there, and after a couple of breaths she asked. "Do you have a question?"

This wasn't what I expected. Maybe because of her hearing people pouring their hearts out so much, I figured she'd take those statements and give me something. Confirmation. Denial. Something.

"Were you one of Smitty's repeat customers?" I asked.

She paused, her eyes finally drifting away. "You asked me for privacy on this matter," she said. "Can you provide me with the same?"

I nodded. "This is between us as long as you tell me the truth and what you tell me does not become material to the case."

She pursed her lips and sighed. "Henry, I need you to promise me this stays between us." Her eyes met mine and I saw a side of her I had never seen. Doubt, regret, fear.

"I promise that I will keep our conversation between us unless it becomes essential to the case."

She nodded slowly, took a deep breath, and sighed.

"I believe Winston's power is a gift from God," she said, the words coming out slowly but crackling with energy like she was winding up for the crescendo of a powerful sermon. "I believe he has a great calling to fulfill. I believe it is of paramount importance that you protect him from this threat, whatever it may be."

She proceeded to tell me the details like I was a priest receiving her confession. It was a story that sounded familiar after what Karen Winslow told me but colored heavily with her faith. She was full of energy, her spine rigid, her voice strong, her breath coming quick. It was like she wasn't quite human anymore, the energy of it transforming her into something else.

"His healing is like feeling the direct touch of our Lord," she said at the end. "How am I to turn away from something like that?"

"But Smitty turned you away," I said.

She blinked and nodded, her shoulders slumped, and she seemed mortal again. "He did. But God chose him as the instrument of His power so I must have faith."

"Do you know why he stopped working with you?" I asked. This was delicate territory. It wouldn't be kind to spell it out, to ask why she could no longer take a hammer to herself and then go see Smitty so she could feel the touch of God through his hands.

With Pastor Lisa it felt different than it had with Karen Winslow. For Karen it felt like addiction, for Lisa it seemed like she was trying to reach something spiritual. But that doesn't mean it wasn't an addiction.

She looked down at her hands which were gripping the couch cushion. "Sunday was my day," she said. "I would see him early before church. I would go from feeling the Lord work through him to heal me right to the church, take that holy feeling to the pulpit. I…"

"He practically raised me from the dead," I said gently. "I know what it feels like. It must be hard to not have that anymore."

She shook her head and looked up, her brown eyes filling with tears. "It has been devastating. A test like none other God has put in front of me. I thought coming to this town and being the only Black person here was a test, but I was wrong. That was nothing compared to this."

I nodded, trying to make my eyes as compassionate as hers. It seemed like the least I could do. I knew enough of Smitty's power and enough about faith to glimpse how hard this must be for her.

The trouble was this made her a serious suspect.

"So what happened?" I asked, my voice quiet. "Why won't Smitty work with you anymore?"

She took a deep breath and rubbed at the tears just escaping her eyes. "I don't blame him," she said. "It was selfish of me to keep going back for more. To use his energy and not let him share God's gift with others."

"What happened?" I asked again, keeping my tone gentle and even.

She shook her head, like she was trying to shake something loose, took a deep breath, and looked at me, her face steady and clear. "He just told me he didn't have the energy anymore. That he was busy helping people that really needed it."

I knew Smitty and I knew he would not have been that kind. That he would have sneered, and his words would have been sharp and biting.

"That must have been hard," I said.

She nodded. "I was angry. I didn't take it well. I had a broken toe that day and it is still healing."

I wrote a few notes and was about to ask another question when she continued. "You have to understand, Henry. While there is much about Smitty that I find... questionable, I would never hurt him. His power is God's, of that I am sure, and I wouldn't think of taking his gift from the world."

I nodded and did my best to smile. While I wanted to believe her, I still had to consider her a suspect. And while the notes Smitty received with their misspelling and focus on how Smitty is destroying "Carteville," didn't fit her, I had to seriously consider her as a suspect.

Addictions can make you do crazy things. Add a heavy dose of faith onto that... well, that could be a combustive combination.

"I appreciate your time, Pastor Lisa," I said.

She looked surprised that we were done and then smiled and nodded. "Of course, Henry. You are welcome here any time."

"One more thing," I said, nodding over to the laptop on her desk and the small laser printer on a stand next to it. "Can you print something out for me on your printer?"

Her forehead furrowed. "Why?"

"Sorry, I can't tell you that, but it's for the case."

She shrugged and went over to her laptop and poked a bit

and the printer whirred to life and spit out a piece of paper. It was still slightly warm when she handed it to me. It was the July calendar for the church and the paper was crisp white with no random blobs of toner.

I smiled, relieved to have a reason to suspect her less. "Do you know of anyone else that was going to Smitty regularly?"

She stared at me. "You think that…" she began but then her face opened up in comprehension. "I know of one other person that has recently had an experience like mine with Smitty."

"Who is it?" I asked.

"Our mayor," she said.

ELEVEN
SUNDAY, JULY 1. THE CARTERVILLE OVERLOOK

After talking to Lisa Bass, I walked to the overlook and let the view wash over me. The mountain rushing down to the desert and the desert cruising to the horizon, the cut of the Grand Canyon visible on this sunny Arizona day. From forest to desert, the color going from a dark green to the taupes, creams, reds, and browns of the desert.

It was hot but a nice breeze licked at the sweat on my forehead and cooled me down some. I took a deep breath and leaned against one of the hulking metal coin-operated binoculars, the metal warmed by the sun.

I needed a moment. I'm a cop in a small town, I deal with addictions all the time. Drunks mostly, but we've had our share of meth, and recently we had few people hooked on heroin. It's ugly and not pleasant but part of the job. But what were we dealing with now? People addicted to the healing power of Winston "Smitty" Smith? It deserved a moment. A lot of moments. And a stiff drink or two.

Smitty had encouraged these addictions, I was sure of that. Especially with people like Karen Winslow and Lisa Bass. People of power and influence. And when he had healed me after all the craziness surrounding Lila Chang's death, he had set me up for the same addiction. By not healing me all the way. By leaving me hobbling around for a month thinking I would come back to him and go further into his debt.

But I was just too damn stubborn for that. I toughed it out and my body eventually healed. Sure, I feel older, my knees creak more than they did, but it was not in my nature to carry debt if I didn't absolutely have to.

"You okay there, Chief?" a voice near me asked. "You don't look so good."

I jumped and turned, my heart thumping hard. Martin Lester was standing next to me. The quiet man had arrived, his power making so I didn't notice him approaching.

"Christ, Martin," I said. "You just about scared the crap out of me."

He shrugged, his thin shoulders not coming up very far. He was still tall and slim with a slight bulge at the middle and a full head of grey hair, dull blue eyes, and a bushy grey mustache. "Sorry 'bout that."

"What are you doing up here?" I asked.

He shrugged again. "Annie ain't at the inn. So, I decided to take a walk. See if I could find her. See what's new."

I nodded and smiled, but the overlook was a weird place to look for Annie. And then I really looked at him. He looked older, the lines on his face deeper, more fully reflecting his sixty years than I remembered. He was thinner too, his cheeks hollowed out, his jeans baggy and the tan polo shirt he was wearing just hanging off his frame.

"You okay?" I asked. There was a lot in that question, and by the pained look on his face he knew it. After the mess with Lila Chang and what he did, I had forced him to retire from his decades long position as a CPD officer and he had decided to leave town. The only town he had ever lived in. He called it retirement, but the pain in his eyes made it clear it was hard being back.

He did another weak shrug. "Ain't easy. But I like exploring. Didn't do enough of that."

How many places had Marin Lester visited where no one noticed him. Not because of his power, which didn't work outside of Carterville, but because of his nature. Just an older man keeping to himself poking around the Southwest's many interesting places.

His dull blue eyes met mine and he asked, "What about you, Chief. You okay?"

I shrugged. "This stuff with Smitty and the regulars... Some of them he addicted himself, with intent. Others he encouraged. He tried to do it to me. It's not right."

Lester crossed his thin arms and stared at me, his mustache wagging a little like he was chewing on his lip. "Lots of folks wouldn't agree, but this town would be better off without Smitty."

I knew Lester and he wasn't hinting that I shouldn't do my job, that I let something bad happen to Smitty, he was just stating an opinion. And that opinion sounded like fact to me.

"I have to do my job, Martin," I said.

He was staring at me, hard. "What exactly do you *have* to do, Chief? Sounds like no real crime has been committed."

"Yet," I said. "There is clear intent."

He shrugged again and this time it was chilling. Lester was

right, I could slow down, deal with the pile of paperwork waiting for me back at the office, or patrol downtown as it fills up with tourists for the Fourth of July holiday. But that wasn't me. And it didn't used to be him. What happened with Lila had damaged him.

"Sorry to scare you," he said as he turned away. "Wasn't going to say anything, but you didn't look okay."

"Thanks for doing this, Martin," I said.

He looked back, nodded, and ambled off.

My gaze went back to the desert, and when I looked for him again a few seconds later, I couldn't see him.

My mind went back to Annie and why she wasn't at the inn. It was Monday and that was a kind of day off for her, as much of a day off that a small business owner is likely to get. I had been lucky to catch her earlier, she must have been short staffed. Annie got a massage on Mondays and was religious about it.

"Check Carol Wick's place," I said. I couldn't see Lester, but he couldn't be that far away yet. "She gets massages from her on Monday."

Lester didn't answer and I turned back to the view letting the calm of the desert wash over me, but it wasn't helping like it usually did.

TWELVE
SUNDAY, JULY 1. THE CARTERVILLE POLICE DEPARTMENT

Annabelle's brown eyes were wide when I walked into the station. She had the letters Smitty had received laid out on the empty desk in the middle of the room, each in a plastic sleeve. She had been chewing on her nails and looked pale.

She was pacing in front of the desk and was the only person in the fluorescent-lit room. The cells in back were empty and Ortega was still at Smitty's.

"What's wrong?" I asked.

"Look at this one," she said, handing me one I hadn't seen up at Smitty's place.

Destroyer
Retrobution will be
>*mine*

I shrugged. It fit with the others with "retribution" spelled wrong.

"And this one," she said, handing me another one.

Destroyer of Carteville
  I know your sekret
    I AM your end

"AM" was capitalized like in the first one I saw and another odd spelling mistake. "Secret" is an easy word to spell.

"Wait," I said. "Do they all have a silly spelling mistake?"

Annabelle nodded. "Yes, they do. Every damn one. An' they never spell Carterville correctly."

I went over to the table and scanned them. They were all similar. Three lines. "AM" always capitalized. The paper streaked grey with a few black toner blobs. That weird moth-eaten font. The ripped edges.

Another one said

Destroyer be warned
  I AM equalizer
    firewerks will ensue

I did a quick count. There where thirteen of them, which added to the creep factor.

"The misspellings are on purpose," Annabelle said. "The three lines. The capitalizations. It's all on purpose. There is a message here."

"What? Besides Smitty having finally pissed someone off enough to do something about it?" I asked, my tone light, but the levity failed with Annabelle's eyes still wide and her biting her red fingernail.

"There is a message here, Chief," she said, her words coming slow. "Whoever did this knew they'd end up here. Knew that we'd be lookin' at them. Knew that…"

"That what?" I asked.

"What if these here messages ain't for Smitty," she said, her southern accent thickening. "What if all this here was meant for us." She gestured at the thirteen messages laid out on the desk, almost covering it completely.

She started pacing, her heels clicking on the linoleum.

"That seems like a stretch, Annabelle," I said.

She paused, her eyes wide. "Is it? Is it really?" she asked and then started pacing again.

"Are you suggesting that the threats are for us and not for Smitty?" I asked.

She snorted. "No. That boy deserves every one of these threats. Someone is more than a little bit mad at him. I am suggestin' that the games are for us. That whoever did this is playing a game *with* us."

I nodded. That made sense. "What about the printout I brought in from the inn. Does it match."

She shrugged and went over and pulled the Fourth of July flyer from her desk and put it with the batch of threats. "No real way to tell for sure," she said. "Some color laser printers print out a machine identification code in yellow dots. You'd never see it if you didn't know what to look for. But her printer is just black. Same as the one used to print these letters.

"That said," she continued, "how many laser printers are in Carterville that have a crappy aftermarket toner cartridge that is leakin'?"

I nodded. Annabelle was more herself now that we were

talking about technical details, but I could tell she hadn't told me everything. "But…?"

She shrugged and then folded her arms. "But, someone is messin' with us, Henry. Maybe these were printed out at the inn. The printer is in Annie's office, right?"

Annabelle calling me Henry was unusual—it really caught my attention. I don't know if it was her upbringing in Georgia or not, but she almost always called me "Chief." I nodded in answer.

"Well, if I were goin' to send bizarre messages," she said, "I'd use an easily identifiable printer that wasn't mine."

"Annie doesn't leave her office locked during the day," I said.

"And how hard would it be to distract whoever is on the desk," Annabelle said, "sneak in, and print this stuff out? All you would need was a thumb drive and a couple a minutes to print 'em all."

"So that I would investigate her and not the real perp," I said.

She bit her lip and nodded. That's the trouble with conspiracy theories—and make no mistake, this was becoming one—once you start seeing them, you see them everywhere.

THIRTEEN

SUNDAY, JULY 1. THE PAULSON RESIDENCE

Showing up at Frank and Lisa Paulson's house at dinnertime was a good way to get fed something amazing. After Annabelle and I had some coffee and I went rounds with the letters, I had headed out for a walk and ended up down at Frank's place. It wasn't entirely planned. I needed to think. I needed some exercise. I had drunk too much coffee and needed to chill out a bit. I should have gone and talked to more people on the list of people mad at Smitty, but I just couldn't stand the thought. Especially with another discussion with Karen Winslow planned for later.

Dinner at the Paulson house is usually early, around 4:00 p.m., when things are slow at the diner. Frank's wife Lisa cooks and she's no slouch in the kitchen. While Frank is a master of the grill, Lisa is an amazing baker.

I was standing in the kitchen. It wasn't big, but newly remodeled with a large gas stove, stainless-steel appliances, and granite countertops. My belly was full and I was basking in a moment of happiness after this day, about to thank Lisa for the meal. Frank had already headed out to the greenhouse to get some vegetables for the diner and I had lingered.

Lisa was taller than Frank and willowy compared to his bulk with short dishwater blonde hair that had hard-to-see strands of grey. She was nothing like Annie Smith, being gentle and soft spoken, which makes Frank a much smarter man than me.

Frank ended up marrying a woman who was the opposite of Annie Smith, and I ended up marrying a woman quite similar. He's the one still happily married.

"I'm sorry he didn't tell you," she said, nodding toward the kitchen door to the backyard which was dominated by three greenhouses.

It took my brain a moment to catch up. I shrugged. "It's his business."

"Which he should be talking to his best friend about," she said.

"Is it serious?" I asked.

Her lips pursed. "Depends on how you look at it," she said. "If he does the right thing, it probably won't kill him, but…" She paused, her soft green eyes finding mine. "This is his to tell. If it had been up to me, he would have told you a month ago."

A month? That hit me like a slap. How many conversations had Frank and I had in the last month where he had kept this to himself? I felt weak in the knees. Frank and I had grown up together, and except for our issues around Annie, we had always been close.

"Best go out there, Henry," she said. "I think he's finally ready to talk."

I nodded and wandered out. I had lost a lot in this life, but losing Frank wasn't something I could even conceive of.

———

FRANK WAS PICKING CHERRY TOMATOES, THE BUSHY GREEN plants heavy with fruit.

We were in one of his newer greenhouses, with plexiglass sides and roof, pavers for a floor, and long tables of happy plants, their leaves emerald green and their branches bent from the weight of the fruit. It was hot and humid, the air smelling like the depths of a forest, pungent and loamy. Even for this simple task, Frank's concentration seemed complete. I stood there watching the big man, not sure if he knew I was here.

"It's prostate cancer," he said, the words unadorned, without emphasis or emotion, his big fingers gently pulling off the little tomatoes. "We caught it pretty early thanks to Doctor Lion. She likes my vegetables and Lisa was worrying about me, so we did a deal."

Jenny Lion has a power. She can see into your body better than any MRI machine and spot issues. It takes a toll on her, so she limits how many times she'll do it in a day. And unlike Smitty, she charges a reasonable price for her services, and the same price to everyone.

"I'm sorry, Frank," I said.

He nodded without turning toward me. "The treatments suck. Either chemicals that would suppress my testosterone, which is pretty awful, or yanking the prostate out and risking incontinence and impotency."

His voice was still steady, but it had gotten quieter. I stepped closer. "That's bad," I said. "So that's why you went to Smitty."

He nodded. "He asked for thirty thousand dollars," he said. "It wouldn't be easy, we wouldn't have any cushion anymore, we could scrape it together, but…"

"It's too much," I said. "He told me it was 50k for saving my life like he did last Christmas. And I was barely savable. It's too much, Frank."

He shrugged his big shoulders. "I told him that. He said prices had gone up. He laughed at me. Asked me how much being a man was worth to me."

I knew Smitty well enough to know that his language would have been much harsher than that.

I started pacing on the cement pavers. I had helped Frank lay them in last year. When we talked, it was often in here or in one of the other greenhouses, our words muffled by the moist air and the dense foliage. We talked about the easy things and the hard things, but he hadn't told me about this until now.

"When did you go to Smitty about this?" I asked.

"Two weeks ago," he said, still plucking cherry tomatoes and facing away from me.

Two weeks. Smitty's thirteen threats had started three weeks ago. Something clicked in my brain and my hands formed fists seemingly of their own volition.

"Shit!" I said, stopping my pacing.

"What?" Frank asked, finally looking at me, his blue eyes wide.

"I'm so sorry," I said, turning to go.

"What, Henry? What did you figure out?" he asked.

I turned back and sighed. "That amount Smitty gave you. It's about me," I said. "Smitty is using you as leverage to get to me."

FOURTEEN
SUNDAY, JULY 1. THE CARTERVILLE POLICE DEPARTMENT

I didn't go right to Smitty. I wanted to, but I needed to wait until my hands could be anything but fists and my desire to pummel him with them faded. Smitty was playing chess and I couldn't barge in all Neanderthal-like and expect to get anywhere. But Smitty deserved it—he was playing games with my best friend's health.

So I went back to the department, which was empty, Annabelle's shift having ended. I went into my closet of an office and slammed the door, hard. I slumped into my squeaky old chair behind my banged-up metal desk, and I went through my notes.

The many suspects.

The copious threats.

Annie's printer.

Frank's prostate cancer.

Smitty addicting the powerful and influential to his healing power.

Pastor Lisa's view of Smitty's power as a gift from God.

I got on my radio. "Ortega, this is Carter, come in. Over."

Her reply was immediate. "Ortega here. What's up, Boss? Over."

"Sorry to make you walk, but I need you down at the department. Tell Mr. Smith I'll be up shortly to see him. Over."

"Roger that. See you in five. Out."

I went back out into the main room and looked at the threats one at a time. Reading them, my eyes got caught by the silly misspellings and the odd capitalizations. Was Annabelle right? Was there a message here intended for us?

"For me," I said aloud, my voice hushed. This was Carterville and my last name was Carter. I was the Chief of Police. It didn't seem too egotistical to think that if there was a message here, it was meant for me.

My eyes landed on "Carteville." The second "r" was missing. Consistently. Carte-ville. I pulled out my phone and searched for "carte." A French word for menu. A playing card. An archaic word for a map or chart.

Carteville. Maybe the message was for me. Taking the "Carter" out of "Carterville." Remove one letter from the word and it's not the same anymore. Remove one person from this town and it's not the same town anymore.

My sister is the only other Carter that lives in town, and she's only here about half the time. She works long shifts as a nurse in Flagstaff and stays with her daughter several nights a week.

I looked through the letters again and pulled out the other misspelled words: retrobution, firewerks, comming, sufer, sekret.

I walked over to Annabelle's desk and grabbed the straw doll. She had bagged it and it looked even more pitiful encased in plastic. It was crudely made with twists of straw tied off at the limbs and neck with simple twine. It was dressed in a light brown shift, the kind that Smitty wears when he's in his Zen savior mode. The fabric was roughly cut and not hemmed, threads unwinding. The little straw head had been nearly twisted off—it was attached by a single straw.

The last straw.

It was hard to deny Annabelle's assertion that there were messages here for us. That this thing with Smitty had a bigger purpose than just messing with him. But I am not a fan of conspiracy theories. Something about our brains make us suckers for them, but there is usually a rational explanation.

Like we really did land men on the moon.

But this wasn't some world-spanning conspiracy that involved multiple governments and thousands of people. The kind of conspiracy theory that plenty ate up but never made sense to me since humans are not very good at keeping secrets, much less thousands of them.

This was an effort by one or maybe a few individuals. This was the kind of conspiracy that could be real. And it really didn't seem like Smitty was the only one they were messing with.

———

It took Officer Ortega more than five minutes to get back to the department. It was more like fifteen, and by that time I was pacing and staring at the evidence.

"He's freaked, Boss," she said as she came in. "He didn't make it easy to get away."

I nodded but didn't say anything, just kept pacing, my eyes on the threats and the straw doll.

"He's afraid," she said. "Eager for you to get back up there."

I nodded again.

Ortega leaned against a desk and just watched me pace the worn linoleum of our small office. I wished it was bigger—my legs needed to stretch. There was something I was missing. Something important.

"I can sleep in the car tonight out in front of his place," she said. "Might make him feel better."

"No," I said without thinking about it. What was I missing?

"Did you find anything useful?" she asked, poking at the letters. "Boy, does this person have a spelling problem."

"No. They don't," I said and kept pacing, her brown eyes widening as she looked closer at the letters. She was smart and I should be taking some time to explain it to her, but I could feel that thing just out of reach and didn't want to lose it.

She started sorting through them. Each plastic sleeve had a small sticker with the date the threat was received. I glanced as I walked close, and she was putting them in order. I stopped and watched, her hands moving quickly.

After she got them in order, I scanned through them again and didn't notice anything in particular.

"They all begin with 'Destroy' or 'Destroyer,'" Ortega said. "Three lines. No punctuation. A spelling mistake in each besides not being able to spell Carterville."

None of this was new or that interesting. I started pacing some more.

She ran to her desk and rummaged around and came up with a small magnifying glass and went back to the letters, leaning close.

"The grey crap on the page is leaked toner," she said slowly, "but the blobs are not."

"What?" I asked.

She looked up, a smile lighting up her face. "I can see the pixels. The blobs are on purpose." She held out the magnifying glass.

I took it and stooped down.

"You can make them out along the edge," she said. "And look at the inside of the blobs. They are flat black, no variance."

I leaned close and squinted, but I couldn't quite make it out. "I don't see it," I said.

She went over to Annabelle's desk, pulled the digital SLR camera we use for CSI work, and came back and took a picture of one of the blobs and blew it up on the LCD on the back.

"Okay…" I said. "That doesn't look right. But why?"

She shrugged and looked away, maybe remembering that she was shy. "No idea," she said, "but they are on purpose."

I went back to the pieces of paper. Each one had a couple of blobs on them, some bigger than others, all of them seemingly at random positions. It made no sense, but maybe that was the point.

I sighed. "Well, it's something," I said. "Good eyes there, Ortega. Can you text Annabelle and let her know? Tell her I want her to look into it tomorrow?"

She nodded. "Sure, Boss. Should I go camp out at Smitty's place tonight?"

I shook my head. "No. If Smitty needs 24/7 babysitting, he can hire himself some private security. I'm going to go tell him that right now. Go get some rest. I'll need you tomorrow."

She smiled but didn't leave, leaning down and looking at the letters again.

I still couldn't see it, but I was convinced we were missing something important. And it wasn't just the blobs.

FIFTEEN
SUNDAY, JULY 1. THE SMITH RESIDENCE

"Took you long enough," Smitty said as greeting when he opened the door to his house. He sauntered into the living room and slumped on his couch. He had a black Glock 9mm sitting on the coffee table.

It took a force of will to not form my hands into fists and do something about it. That game he had played with Frank was beyond unacceptable. "The CPD can't provide you with round-the-clock security," I said instead. "We don't have the personnel."

Smitty's dull green eyes found mine and there was disdain written on his face, a sour expression like he had something awful in his mouth and knew he had to swallow it. "I must say," he said. "I am disappointed in you, Henry. You owe me your life, after all."

I smiled, or at least came up with my best approximation of a smile, and said, "I do. And I'm grateful to still be breathing. But two officers can't investigate this and provide security for you, not to mention dealing with the day-to-day needs of Carterville."

He leaned back, his eyes narrowing and a smile playing on his lips. "What do you want?" he asked.

Smitty was always playing games, so he figured I must be. And I was, but not on this topic. "We have a limitation here, Smitty. Ortega can't be here 24/7. And I can't be here if I'm going to investigate all these *sensitive* matters of yours."

I pulled out my notepad, wrote a name and a number on it, ripped off the page, and handed it to Smitty. "He's reliable but not cheap. I checked with him on my way up and he's already on the road. He'll be here in thirty minutes. I'm sure you can afford it."

I turned to go and Smitty said, "What do you want, Henry?"

I stopped at the edge of his living room but didn't turn around. "I want you to tell me everything, Smitty. I know you've left some things out."

He snorted. "Is that all?"

I turned back to face him and folded my arms in front of myself. "No. Not even close."

His brow furrowed and he brushed at his blond going to grey hair. He kicked at the coffee table. Besides the Glock, it had a laptop and a bunch of paperwork strewn on it. In an odd and unexpected moment of empathy, I realized I had no idea what it was like to be Smitty. How complicated it must all be getting as he spun his webs and sought control. And all of this on top of it.

He sat up straight and really looked at me. He must have seen something in my face because he looked away and nodded. "I'm listening."

"One," I said. "I get to the bottom of this, and our debt is cleared."

"Are you saying that you won't do your job if I don't agree to that, Chief?" he asked.

"No," I said. "I will do my job if you don't agree to that. My *entire* job. Like working on the stupid report I have to give to the town council next week, issuing parking tickets because we badly need the revenue, and walking downtown during this busy holiday to make sure things are in order."

What Martin Lester had told me up at the overlook had rumbled around my mind, and because of the games Smitty was playing it made more sense than it did when he said it.

Smitty opened his mouth to speak, but I held up my hand. "Oh, I'll investigate this matter too. But no real crime has been committed so it will get shuffled down the pile a bit. Mary and William Reilly have been having some break-ins. Someone's messing with one of their Airstreams. It's costing them money and disturbing their business. Now that's an actual crime I should be focusing on."

He looked like he was going to say something, but I forged on. "And you know how the Fourth is around here. Dummies coming to town with fireworks not realizing how dry the forest is. Seems pretty important that I make sure someone doesn't burn the town down."

"Are you done?" he asked.

I shook my head. "One. I figure this out and we are even."

He flapped his hand in a lazy gesture to say I should continue. "You're counting, so there must be more. Get to it."

"Two. You tell me everything," I said.

"You are repeating yourself," he said with a sigh. "Is that it?"

I shook my head. "No. Three. You heal Frank Paulson for free. You do it first thing in the morning and you pay Doc Lion to confirm and to check again in six months, a year, and then two years. It comes back, you heal him again. You apologize to him and act like a decent human being. You find out what Lisa's favorite charity is and you throw a bunch of money at them."

He leaned forward, a real smile on his face. "Tough thing Frank is going through," he said. "Sounds like it's important to you, so I'll tell you what. I'll do two and three, but not one. I saved your life, Henry. At great cost to myself, I might add. This hardly seems like enough. I—"

I turned and walked to the door, opened it, and went outside. With part of the mountain to the west, the sun goes down early here and the air had already started to cool. My hands were fists, my nails digging into my palms. I took a deep breath and relaxed them.

Smitty had found the right lever for me. Not my own health—I battled back from his partial healing without asking for more from him—but Frank. I just couldn't bear to see him suffer. He was a good man and deserved better than this.

"Wait," Smitty said. He had actually gotten off the couch and come after me, his flip-flops slapping against his hardwood floor.

I turned around. "What do you want, Smitty? Really. You waited weeks to tell me about this. Why now? What the hell do you want?"

And then it hit me, the little thing that had been bothering me that my pacing in the office with Ortega didn't dislodge. It was fueled by Annabelle's belief there was a message in the notes for us and Ortega's faux toner blob theory.

The thought really did hit me. It was like a blow. And the thought was, what if Smitty was behind all of this? The notes, the straw doll, everything. What if he was playing a long game that I couldn't see?

My face flushed but he didn't see it, his head down and his shoulders slumped. He sighed and nodded. "I agree to your terms," he said, slinking back inside.

I stood there staring at him. He seemed defeated and genuinely scared about what was happening. If this was part of a long game, then I was in trouble. I didn't have a clue what it might be.

I knew I couldn't trust him, but I had a job to do and I had to help Frank.

SIXTEEN
SUNDAY, JULY 1. THE SMITH RESIDENCE

Smitty was never going to tell me everything. I knew that. I'm not a fool. By getting him to agree to tell me everything, I was just ensuring that he told me more. Telling someone "everything" is quite literally impossible.

In writing these stories, I can't tell you everything. Most of it has passed on, evaporated into the past, and was not captured by my frail human memory. Much of it is below the threshold of me noticing, our brains constantly editing out information so we can actually function. And you sure as hell wouldn't want to suffer me sharing every thought in my head, even if it was possible to capture them.

But even that wasn't the "everything" I was asking Smitty for. I was asking him to tell me the things that he had intentionally left out. The things he knew to be important that he hadn't shared.

That was the meaning of "everything" in this context and

we both knew it. And still I knew he wouldn't even go that far. But the more information I had, the better. The closer I might come to finding out what he was really doing.

It was silent when we got back into his living room. The view out the sliding glass doors past his deck was quickly approaching spectacular. While the sun had set in Carterville, the golden light of a summer evening was bathing the desert, enriching the colors and edging them more towards yellow. This time of day at this time of year, I would prefer to be on my own deck, a drink in hand, sunk into an Adirondack chair and letting the view and a little gin wash away the trials of the day.

Smitty was standing there, his foot scraping at the area rug that covered the hardwood in most of the living room, his head down and his hands in his short's pockets.

We weren't friends. In fact, much of his pre-power days had included me showing up and asking him about robberies in town, including a number of arrests but nothing that ever ended up with him doing jail time.

Smitty was smart but lazy. He had, arguably, a gift, the best power of all of us, but he used it to manipulate and control. I wanted nothing more than to see Smitty out of this town permanently. And I suspected that the feeling was mutual.

But I gave him a moment. I sat on his couch, ignored the gun sitting there, folded my arms, and stared at him.

He started pacing and my gut reaction was to think that this would be bad, that he had something terrible to tell me. But paranoia had been introduced into the equation and I had to wonder if this was an act, if he was moving chess pieces that I couldn't even imagine.

"You remember where I was when the meteor hit?" he asked. He was pacing and wasn't looking at me.

"Sure," I said. "Your mom was still alive and you were laid up at her house. You had fallen off a roof, a house up here on Fir you were fixing to break in to. You broke a leg, a few ribs, and bruised the hell out of your spinal cord. The doctors didn't know if you would ever walk again."

He glanced at me, that sour look on his face again. Maybe he didn't like my characterization of the event or maybe the truth was bitter. "Right," he said. "I was almost thirty and living with my mother because I couldn't take care of myself." His tone had lowered, making him sound more nasally than usual.

I kept quiet as he started pacing again. Quiet seemed much more likely to get him to talk than poking him with words.

"The next day, after the meteor, I could walk, barely," he said. "A week later I was pretty much back to normal. A week after that, Mom had her heart attack and I hadn't figured out I had a power yet, that it had helped me heal, that I could heal others. I watched her die."

He glanced at me, his eyes haunted, and I nodded. I knew the story and it was a tragic one, but I didn't know what he was getting at.

He chuckled but it was an awful thing, stilted and haunted, raspy and dry. "My powers of healing are limited, Henry," he said.

I opened my mouth to ask about it, but he forged on. "I can directly heal others to a very limited degree in real time. My real power is that I can take on their damage or disease and heal it in myself. And I can heal it faster, but it takes time and takes a toll." He brushed at his head where the grey was particularly dense.

My mind spun. How had I not put this together—the signs were all there. How the thirty-five-year-old Smitty looked to be over fifty. How he had told Ortega, "I was shitting blood for a week after I saved the chief there." How frail and weak he always seemed. Sure, I knew his power had a cost. That's just a given. All exercise of power has a cost whether it's meteor-granted powers or plain old human power. But I hadn't thought that he was taking things on from others.

"It's an awful burden," he said. "As more people have come from all over the world to have me heal them, I have had to start prioritizing. Using the tools I have to keep myself well amidst the onslaught of damage and disease I've been taking on."

Empathy wasn't what I wanted. Empathy didn't feel safe. But here I was, someone who claimed to not have a power to keep people from always wanting me to use it to help them or using it against me. I understood the cost a Carterville power can extract.

It also explained Zen Smitty. How his demeanor was often that of a Sedona guru with loose, flowing clothing, lots of meditation, and an obsession with healthy food. These were the tools he was talking about, the ones he used to try to stay well.

Because he was always taking on the disease and damage of others. Because his power was most potent when healing himself, not healing others.

I have stated multiple times in these writings that our powers often seem to make us more of who we are. Patty Walsh being more empathetic. Frank Paulson being even better with plants. But Smitty's power never seemed to fit. He used to be a petty thief and he now robs people blind and they happily pay him or do him favors. And I guess it did make him more of what he was but in a sideways kind of way.

But the thought that was new as I watched Smitty pace and watched the distant desert turn golden behind him was that who he was now was about his power.

I mean, he had started out with taking advantage of others being as natural as breathing and now he was even better at it. But the burden of the power, the cost it has extracted, pushed him down this road. Made him fall back to capitalism to decide who gets healed and who doesn't.

"So, I had to cut back on my regular clients," he continued as his feet took him back and forth across the small living room. He stopped, his eyes now looking hazel and particularly haunted. "I had to, Henry. I had to start prioritizing. I know it has been hard on some of them, that they miss the feeling. I get that, I do. But I had to."

He started pacing again, and I kept watching, kept silent. I didn't tell him that he didn't have to do what he did. That he could have turned down some outsiders, took some time to wean back the people he addicted to his power, that there is always a choice and the choice you make says a lot more about you than about the circumstances forcing them.

I wasn't Smitty's father. He didn't want to hear that kind of stuff from me, and I doubted that he was capable of hearing it at all.

"I got myself in trouble," he said, his voice low and nasally again. "I said yes too many times and I could barely get out of bed. I couldn't hold food down. I was dizzy all the time. I was afraid my powers weren't enough, that I was going to die."

He paced some more and then stopped in front of the sliding glass doors and stared at the desert. "I had to cut them off," he said. "All of them. If I didn't help myself then I couldn't help anyone else. You gotta put on your own oxygen mask first, right?"

He was rationalizing, but I just kept silent. I get getting in over your head, but he did a poor job of the transition. But at least that transition made sense now.

"None of them took it well," he said. "I don't think I understood how much they needed my power."

As silence settled in, he just kept staring out at the desert. "Can you explain one thing to me?" I asked.

He nodded but didn't turn around.

"After that fall I took, after you healed me, you walked away," I said. "But Doc Lion had said I had eight broken bones, a lacerated liver, punctured lung, and more. If you took all that on, how could you walk away?"

He took a deep breath and sighed, slowly turning around. He was biting his lip. "The part of my power that can take on things from others… it's not a direct translation. The disease and damage are distributed, a little taken in by every cell. So I didn't have your actual broken bones and lacerated liver, but I had an equivalent amount of damage."

I nodded and had to look away. It made sense. If he took on all the damage I took or a heart attack directly, he wouldn't survive. His body distributed the disturbance differently, but he ended up with what he took from others.

"I need you to give me all the names," I said. "Every one of your regulars."

He told me. Karen Winslow and Lisa Bass were on that list

but a couple of others too. Smitty had too many people who had motive to do this. I had no idea who could be behind it.

But one thing had changed. The thought that Smitty was somehow behind all of this, somehow playing this large and complicated game, faded. Well, that he was behind the threats did. I knew he was playing a large and complicated game, and that game was for the control of Carterville itself.

SEVENTEEN

SUNDAY, JULY 1. THE WINSLOW APARTMENT

JUST AFTER 8:00 P.M., I WAS BACK IN THE WINSLOW APARTMENT above the Carterville Brewery. There was muffled music filtering up from the bar, a band playing for opening night.

Karen looked tired. She still had on her turquoise skirt and embroidered black cowboy shirt, but the blue Carterville Brewery vest had come off. She was sitting on one of the uncomfortable chairs in her living room and I was sitting across from her on the uncomfortable couch.

Blonde hairs had escaped her braid and were gently waving around her face, the open window bringing in a cool breeze and the sound of tourists on the Circle outside.

"So, what were your other questions?" she asked.

I nodded and took out my notebook and flipped back to our previous conversation and then to a new page. "Once again," I began, "I appreciate the candid nature of our previous conversation."

She nodded as if rushed, like she had somewhere else to

be. I knew this was opening day for her, but she had set the time.

"But I need to know more details," I said. "Particularly when Smitty stopped working with you. What the conversation was like. How you have coped with the absence of his power."

One eyebrow arched and her hazel eyes became intense. Her eyes were the same color as Smitty's but a bit brighter. I don't think I had ever put that together before.

She sighed and leaned back. "He first told me six weeks ago. But I talked him into healing me then. Four weeks ago was when I broke my toe and he cut me off." The words were flat and lifeless. I didn't know if that was fatigue from her very busy day or something else. "I pleaded. I cried. I yelled. It was ugly and he was a smug, sanctimonious ass."

She leaned forward, her jaw set. "As to how I dealt with it, I threw myself into my work and hobbled along as best I could."

"Have you seen Smitty since?" I asked.

"So, I'm a suspect?" she asked, more energy in her voice now.

"Officially, no," I said. "This is all off the books right now. But I would be remiss if I didn't question all of Smitty's regulars. They have motive, to be sure."

"You talked to Lisa Bass?" she asked. "Asked her questions like this? Did you talk to Gary?"

I paused, searching for the right words. "I have or will be talking to all of his regulars. I am sorry, but I cannot discuss an ongoing investigation with you."

She sighed, leaned back, and nodded.

"What have your interactions been like with Smitty since?" I asked.

She rolled her eyes briefly. "Civil and as brief as possible."

"No more arguments? No altercations?" I asked.

"No," she said. "I saw him at the gas station once and then at the diner. I think that's it."

It felt like something was missing, like there was something she was leaving out. I looked back over my notes and there was one name she hadn't mentioned. Her husband.

"I'm sure Ken has been supportive through all this," I said.

She blinked a couple of times and looked down at her hands. "He is always supportive," she said.

"He doesn't know," I said.

She looked back up at me and her eyes were fierce. "And it's important that he not find out."

Ken Fischer was a gentle man, at least these days. He has spent the last couple of decades in AA and was a driving force of the local AA community here and in Flagstaff. He could actually be helpful to her. I could almost see a group of locals in a circle. "Hello, my name is Karen and I'm a Smitty-a-holic."

But she had chosen to hide it. Which made this delicate territory. Ken may be gentle these days, but that wasn't always the case. What would his reaction be if he found out that Smitty addicted his wife to his power with intent? Would he think that meant Smitty was trying to "destroy" Carterville?

The suspect list just got longer, and a new name was on the top of that list.

"I'm serious, Henry," she said. "Do not bring Ken into this." There was plenty of energy in her voice now, this thought being like a double espresso to her demeanor.

"I don't know if I can do that, Karen," I said evenly.

"Why?" she asked, her arms crossing and her spine straightening.

"Because an angry spouse fits with the evidence we have," I said.

"But he doesn't know," she shot back.

"Are you sure?" I asked.

She blinked and looked away. I was married and it ended badly. I knew there are times when couples don't talk about the things they should when they should. I also knew Ken. He was a smart guy, an engineer working in Flagstaff for a company that creates implantable medical devices. He was the quiet type but very observant. He had to notice that his wife was seeing Smitty regularly. And being an addict himself, there was a good chance he had noticed the addiction in her.

She rose and stared down at me. "Leave Ken out of this, Henry, or I swear to God…" She swept out of the apartment leaving me alone, the thumping bass of the band below vibrating through the couch.

EIGHTEEN
SUNDAY, JULY 1. THE CARTER RESIDENCE

Arizona. Views during the day and stars at night. July often brings monsoons, but the evening was clear, and the moon was just past full, casting the desert in a ghostly glow.

My uniform was off and sweats were on, my equipment belt and gun locked up, and I was sprawled in an Adirondack chair on my deck, my favorite drink in hand. And that would be gin and soda with lime and a dash of bitters.

I heard footsteps on the deck coming around from the side. Loud, exaggerated footsteps. "Hello, Martin," I said without turning. "Can I get you a beer?" Martin hated my drink of choice.

"If it ain't too much trouble," he said, easing his long frame into the chair next to mine with a sigh.

The only light I had on was the stove light in the kitchen, so Lester's long face and mustache were only dimly outlined in the dark. Still, he looked tired.

I got up and walked through the open sliding glass door

into the kitchen, opened the fridge, which seemed bright to my night-adjusted eyes, and got his beer.

When I walked back out, my eyes just wanted to keep sliding over the Adirondack chair he was sitting in. His power was still engaged. It would be hard for any of my neighbors to notice him, especially if they didn't hear him.

I handed him the beer, sat back down, and took a sip of my drink, the cold glass and tinkle of ice cubes welcome. The day had cooled but the memory of the heat still lingered.

"I pulled out the sofa bed," I said. "It's all ready for you and comfortable. Wendy is in Flag tonight, but she's fussy about other people sleeping in her bed."

He nodded in the darkness. "Much appreciated. I didn't know that about your sister."

"How would you," I said. "You've never needed to stay here before."

The silence that descended was awkward. He hadn't ever needed to stay here because he used to have his own house. Carterville used to be his home. It wasn't logical, but I felt bad about forcing him out. His actions around Lila Chang's murder were more than enough to justify firing him, but I understood his actions and can't say that I would have done too much different in the same circumstances.

It got quiet enough with just the gentle glug of his pulls on the beer and the tinkle of ice cubes from my drink that we could hear the noise from the Circle floating up. A random voice or two and distant music that was annoyingly familiar but undefinable.

"Don't like the brewery," he said, clearly hearing the same thing I was. "Too fancy."

"Me neither," I said. "Don't like the name either."

He chuckled. It was a quiet thing. "I bet you don't."

More silence and quiet drinking. I wanted to know what he found out tailing Annie, but I wasn't in a hurry. Anyway, it was best not to hurry Martin Lester, especially since I dragged him back here.

It almost seemed like old times. The two of us had done this more times than I could count. While my house may be small and historic, the deck was big and not so old. I helped my father build it when I was eight and rebuilt it two years ago. It was one of my favorite places.

I got up and walked over to the telescope and trained it on the moon, centering it towards the bottom of the glowing orb on Tyco Crater. It's not an unusually big crater, but it's a relatively new one which makes it more distinct and easy to find. It was my father, much on a night like tonight, that showed me the moon through a telescope when I was a boy.

And the moon seems important around here. Back in the sixties, astronauts trained around Flagstaff in the cinder fields not too far from Carterville.

"You want to see the moon?" I asked, stepping back. "I've got Tyco right in the center.

Lester ambled over and stared for a while.

"Annie's not your perp," he said when he stood up. He still had his beer and took a swig.

"Yeah?" I asked.

He nodded. "She got her massage and then went and cleaned her house and then went back to the inn."

"Okay," I said. This was a Martin Lester conversation, so the words were kind of shorthand. "Okay" here meant something like, "Okay, but why does that make you think Annie didn't do it?"

"But later, I saw someone come in when Brooke was out on the counter," he said. "I was outside but saw it clear enough. He handed her a twenty and slipped into the office. Came out with a manila folder in his hand."

"Shit," I said. Because Annabelle had been right. The messed-up paper was a misdirect. And this meant I would need to get Annabelle some time on Annie's computer because it might have evidence. I didn't ask Lester who it was. I knew he was getting there.

"I followed this person," he said. "I didn't get a good look at the paper, but they addressed the envelope and put it in a mailbox. Wearing gloves the whole time. Got it in right before the mailman came."

"Get any pictures?" I asked.

He nodded. "I'll share them with you."

He was drawing out revealing the name of the person which just made my stomach sink. It meant it wasn't going to be good, and "good" in this context meant "bad," very bad.

"You know the suspense is killing me," I said.

He nodded. "Figured." But he didn't tell me. Not yet. "I don't want to do this again," he added.

I sighed. "I'm sorry, Martin. I'm used to relying on you."

He nodded again. "But it ends here. Right? I don't want to ever come back."

"Yes," I said. "This is it. I won't call asking for your help again." I don't like making statements like this. It's not like I know the future, but he wanted my word and was friend enough to deserve it.

"Ken Fischer," he said. "The mayor's husband," as if I didn't already know.

I swore. Like I was a teenager. It lasted a while. After my

conversation with Karen Winslow, I can't say I was surprised, but this sure made things a lot more complicated.

PART 2
PERP: JULY 2

NINETEEN
MONDAY, JULY 2. THE CARTER RESIDENCE

I woke up hungover and tired. Martin and I stayed up late and drank. It took us a few drinks and quite a while to get back to being friends, which felt important.

And then after I went to bed, I didn't sleep much, my mind roiling around two words: Ken Fischer.

How the hell was I going to investigate the mayor's husband quietly in a town this small? As soon as Karen got wind of it, she would make it very uncomfortable for me. She was a lawyer, as well as mayor and a businesswoman. She would tie me up with paperwork and legal hurdles.

And I didn't have much to go on. Everything I had was circumstantial and quite thin.

All of this was still on my mind as I rolled out of bed. The old Carter home is small. It was originally a cabin built by Samuel Carter and then added on by my ancestors. First a second floor and then a new kitchen on the back, and then a master bedroom addition. It left the house with some odd corners and little steps up and down.

Wendy had the master bedroom even though she wasn't here all the time. She was the elder of the two of us, after all, something I didn't often let her forget. She offered to let me have it, but I insisted because that's the way I was raised.

I was in the upstairs bedroom with creaky hardwood floors and drafty windows. I tried to get up quietly, but the floor creaked under my bulk, telling me quite clearly that I needed to lose a few pounds.

I brushed my teeth, shaved, and combed my hair, not entirely recognizing the man in the mirror looking back at me. It wasn't last night. I mean, I had a soft throbbing headache from the quantity of gin consumed, but it wasn't anything special. It was the bags under my eyes and my double chin. It was the lines turning into trenches running across my forehead. It was how my eyes seemed further sunk into my face.

It was just my age, fifty feeling like a big number. I still related more to my thirty-something face than my fifty-something face. Maybe when I'm seventy-something, I'll relate to this face, but I doubt it'll happen before then.

I snuck downstairs as quietly as the creaky old stairs would let me, not wanting to wake Lester, but he was already gone. The sofa bed was back to being a couch and it looked like no one had been here last night.

I sighed. I had wanted to at least drive him out to Bo Larson's place to get his truck. I wanted to make sure it felt like we were friends in the sober light of a new day. That we could be friends without our work. I couldn't talk to him about the case, although I really wanted to.

My phone chimed. I pulled it out, it was one of those many google alerts as the phone slowly subsumed more of my life. The alert told me that Martin Lester had shared an album with me, the name of the album was "Be Careful."

I just stared at the alert.

For Lester this was a dire warning. It should have been bolded, underlined, italicized, and blinking.

If he was urging care at all then he thought it was dire.

I tapped on the alert, put in my code, and looked at the pictures. Ken Fischer in front of the Carterville Inn looking nervous. Ken Fischer through the front window of the inn talking to the blonde-haired Brooke, a twenty being passed. Ken Fischer walking into the office behind the counter. Ken Fischer coming out with a manila envelope in his hand. Ken Fischer dropping it off in a blue mailbox on Main Street.

Lester may have left, but he did good by me. This wasn't enough to get a warrant or arrest him, but it was something. It was a start.

And now that I had a suspect, it was time to bring the team in. To make a plan. To stop these threats and get on with a life that has a whole lot less Winston "Smitty" Smith in it.

TWENTY

MONDAY, JULY 2. THE CARTERVILLE DINER

I watched Patty Walsh walk away as Annabelle and Ortega stared at me. We were in a corner booth of the Carterville Diner, the smell of bacon and coffee waking up my tired brain.

Patty worked the long counter with those round cushioned stools kids liked to spin on, but she saw me when I came in and knew what I wanted. And that was food, comfort, privacy, and a good view of people coming and going.

"You really should go and—" Annabelle began, following my gaze.

"Not now, Annabelle," I said.

Well, the food, comfort, privacy, and view were what I wanted that she could supply right now. I'm sure she knew I wanted more. Or at least I thought I wanted more. But it was complicated. How can a man be enough for a woman with a power, a power so she knows everything you want? Wouldn't that make intimacy hard? Or would it make it easy? Or would it be unbalanced with her knowing me so well and me fumbling around trying to know her? And is that any different than the normal male/female dynamic?

As those thoughts percolated through my aching head, Patty turned and flashed me a smile, her curly red hair sliding over her green Carterville Diner polo shirt that couldn't hide her generous curves. I grinned back—how could I not? Since Annie and I split, I kept thinking about Patty and kept not being able to do anything about it. Every time I looked at her, she seemed more beautiful and the prospect more tantalizing and more intimidating.

There was a truckload of buts. Including a divorce and the epically horrible breakup with Annie Smith last Christmas.

"Seriously, Boss," Ortega said, pouring too much sugar into her coffee. "She's gonna say yes."

Annabelle fanned herself with her hand in a most exaggerated way. "I do swear," she said, leaning into her southern accent, "I just might pass out from the heat of that look."

I felt my cheeks redden and Patty's smile broadened and then she turned away and I could breathe again.

"Go do it now, Boss," Ortega said. "Go ask her out. It'll do us all some good."

I looked at the round face of Isabella Ortega and she was wearing a huge smile that made her look like a little kid in a candy store. The girl was usually shy. Unaccountably shy given her generally high level of competence and clear intelligence. But this was a different kind of interaction. More personal.

"Is there something on your mind?" I asked. "Something you need to say?"

Ortega's smile melted and she looked down at her coffee, stirring it quickly, the metal spoon clanking against the ceramic mug.

Annabelle leaned close and whispered, "She's sayin' that you need some lovin'. You've been a bit tense lately."

They were on either side of me and I looked at each of them a couple of times, my head snapping back and forth, my cheeks hot again.

Annie and I had been on again, off again for years, but our last breakup had stuck. If truth be told, I didn't know how to date and I sure as hell didn't know how to date a woman who knew everything you wanted before you even asked for it.

I cleared my throat and took a sip of coffee to buy some time and burned my tongue. I knew these two women were trying to look out for me despite the teasing nature of it, but this wasn't the time.

"We have a suspect," I said, just ignoring the whole Patty thing. "And we need to act fast and quiet. But this is going to get complicated, so this is a strictly volunteer operation."

Ortega's smile was gone and there was an intensity in her brown eyes. Annabelle tucked a curl of red and purple hair behind her ear, her furrowed forehead emphasizing the network of fine wrinkles from all her years as a smoker.

I leaned forward and lowered my voice. "Ken Fischer."

Ortega looked puzzled and Annabelle swore fluently under her breath. "The mayor's husband," Annabelle whispered to the puzzled Ortega.

"Oh…" Ortega said. "That's…."

I smiled. It was the kind of reaction I was hoping for. This was serious. They got it.

"What's the motive?" Ortega asked.

I looked around. The booths on either side of us were empty and no one was close. "This is confidential," I said. "I do not know how much of this will end up in the file."

Ortega looked worried and nodded. Annabelle rolled her eyes and flapped her hand for me to continue, more or less saying that if you don't trust me by now you never will.

"Smitty has been addicting people to his power," I said, "producing a roster of regulars. Recently he cut them all off. Karen Winslow was one of them. He left her with a broken toe and no way to get her fix."

Annabelle leaned back, a faraway look on her face. She got it. She knew all the people and all the dynamics. Ortega looked puzzled, but then her young face hardened. "Seriously? Isn't Fischer the AA guy?" she asked.

I nodded, wondering what a girl in her mid-twenties knew about addictions. But I discarded it, that was a silly thought. Youth does not mean innocence. Addictions can hit early and hit hard or be something that has scarred your family.

"If you are in, we need to move quick," I said, pulling out my phone, unlocking it, and giving them each the phone to look through the album Lester had shared.

When Annabelle had it, she asked, "Mind if I share this with both of us?"

"Please," I said, grateful to not admit that I didn't know how to do it and didn't want to know how to do it.

Both of their phones dinged and Annabelle handed my phone back. "I'm in," she said, a grim smile on her face. "You know that. I ain't afraid of the mayor."

I looked at Ortega and she grinned and nodded. The girl actually looked eager. "What's the plan, Boss?"

I smiled. Because of some strange circumstance, I had been on my own for a bit with Lila Chang's murder. It felt good to have my team with me. "Annabelle and I are going to go to the inn to look for evidence on that computer," I said, looking at Ortega. "And you are going to go wait for the mailman."

"Mail-*person*," she said. "It's Monday so there's a good chance it's Ivy driving in."

I heard Anabelle quietly chuckle but kept looking at Ortega. So, the kid wasn't shy about my lack of a love life or about her middle-aged boss using gender neutral pronouns. "I stand corrected," I said. "You will go wait for the mail*person*. All our mail is shuttled down to Phoenix before coming back up north. Sorting is done in Flagstaff, and they send the one carrier out around midmorning."

Carterville has a post office and our own zip code, but that hole in the wall office on Main Street was mostly about PO boxes and accepting packages. Most everything else happened in bigger cities.

"Why am I going to wait for the mailperson?" Ortega asked.

"I want to get that envelope before Smitty sees it," I said. "Provided that it was really addressed to him. We don't see it well enough in the photos."

"Do we need a warrant for that?" Ortega asked. "Don't federal laws govern the mail?"

I shrugged. "Ivy won't mind handing it off to us," I said. "Or Cole if it's him today. I don't trust Smitty and want to see it before he does."

She bit her lip and nodded. She was very "by the book" and this was a stretch for her.

"And watch for Fisher or Winslow," I said. "I want to know their comings and goings."

The door to the diner rang and I looked up. It was Frank walking in, a spring in his step, and I smiled at him. His blue eyes caught mine and he gave me a nod and smiled back. It was a pursed-lip smile and his blue eyes welled up with tears. It was good news. Smitty had kept his promise. Frank's cancer was gone.

He started toward the booth, but his eyes found Annabelle and Ortega, and with a nod he veered off.

Ortega was asking me another question, but I just watched Frank walk back to the kitchen, his shoulders back and his head held high.

At least now I knew something good would come of all of this. I got back to planning with Annabelle and Ortega.

TWENTY-ONE
MONDAY, JULY 2. THE CARTERVILLE INN

I was back in Annie's cramped office behind the counter of the Carterville Inn. Annie was standing in front of her messy desk, her arms crossed. Annabelle and I were standing in front of the door. The young Brooke was outside still on duty, and I worried about our voices getting loud enough for her to hear.

That I was here twice in two days would soon be circulating via the Carterville rumor mill. I didn't want it to be any more than that.

"I am not going to give you any details of my disagreement with Smitty," Annie said, her voice low and controlled. "You should know that bringing Annabelle made that even less likely."

I did my best to smile. "This is not about that," I said, my tongue feeling thick and foreign. It was earlier in the day, so it wasn't as hot in here, but it was stuffy, the air too still.

"What?" she asked. "You got another crime to accuse me of?"

I shook my head. "No, Annie. Annabelle just needs access to your computer."

Her eyes narrowed and she stood up straight. "Do you have a search warrant?"

"I would hope I didn't need one," I said.

She snorted. "Oh, you need one, Henry, believe me, you need one."

"That's it, Annie?" I asked, feeling my cheeks flush. "You refuse when you don't even know what this is about? When you have no idea what the stakes are? Because Lila died and you were a suspect and I was just doing my job?"

She rolled her eyes, and it was suddenly like we were sixteen and back in high school. "You weren't just doing your job, Henry. You were defending your territory. Lila was one of *your* girls and someone killed her in *your* town. So, our history be damned, you thought I could actually do something like that."

Her voice was low again, like yesterday, but her words were sharp, designed to injure. And they hit home. Because there was some truth to it. I had taken what happened to Lila very personally.

But I wasn't going to make the same mistake with Annie and argue with her about why she was a viable suspect, how it was our history and my firsthand knowledge of her volatile temper that led me to believe she could do it.

"We'll get a warrant then," I said with a nod. Not that we had enough for a warrant, but Annie didn't need to know that. "We'll have it by this afternoon and then we'll be coming in and taking your computer and printer away for analysis. God knows how long it will take."

I turned to Annabelle and she shrugged and said, "I don't know. A week, maybe two." She turned and looked at Annie. "Or you can just give me fifteen minutes right now and we'll be out of your hair."

Annie's breathing sped up and her nostrils flared briefly. When we were together, this was a "duck and cover" kind of sign, and it was an act of will not to back up.

Sure, we were pushing this and counteracting her stonewalling with some tactical abuse of power. And this was a very small town, and you definitely have to live with the consequences of such actions, but the situation seemed to warrant it.

"Fine!" she said, her voice finally raising. "You've got fifteen minutes."

She slammed the door behind her, and the old wall shook.

———

AFTER ANNIE WAS GONE, ANNABELLE GAVE ME A WIDE-EYED look that said either "we're in for it now" or "I can't believe you were actually with that woman" or, probably, both.

She walked back around the desk, her steps slow like the office was a minefield, and tapped at the keyboard. Annie's computer was an old tower, the computer itself stashed under the desk, the fan loud in the now quiet room.

Annabelle gave me a sour look and said, "We're going to need her to log in."

I sighed and turned around when Annie came storming back in, the blonde-haired Brooke in tow. The young, round-faced woman was short, and up close I could see her brown roots growing out. She had this look on her face that was half fear and half resignation. It wasn't a charitable thought, but it seemed to me that was the look Annie's employees often had on their faces.

"Stop," Annie said.

Annabelle straightened up and stared at Annie, her eyes hard. There was no love lost between those two. Annabelle watched me break up with Annie on a regular basis, and when we were together Annie's jealousy could often be kindled by the amount of time I spent with Annabelle.

"I will unlock the computer," Annie said, turning and staring at me. "I will give you your fifteen minutes. But Brooke here will witness everything you do. This is not negotiable. You don't like it, get your damn search warrant."

Brooke swallowed hard and didn't seem to be the least bit comfortable, standing there chewing on her fingernail, looking more like a teenager than an adult.

"Of course," I said. "We cannot share details of the case, but it is reasonable to have a witness."

Annie brushed by me, her familiar scent filling my nose and making me wish for something that would never be again. She went to the computer and tapped in her password, the noise loud in the quiet room.

With four people, it was getting hot in here and I just wanted out.

Annie waved Brooke over, looked at her watch and then at me. "Can we have a word, Henry?"

Well, this wasn't how I wanted to get out of this room. I glanced at Annabelle and she nodded to me as she pulled a thumb drive out of her jeans pocket and sat down.

"Of course," I said.

Annie nodded sharply and marched out of the room.

———

WE WERE IN ONE OF THE INN'S ROOMS. THE QUEEN BED SEEMED large, the two antique wooden bed stands pressed against the wall with an antique dresser next to the door. This was a first-floor room, the bed made perfectly, not a wrinkle in the crisp white comforter.

"Can you tell me what's going on?" Annie asked after she closed the door. Her face showed more worry than anger, her frown lines deeper than usual and a touch of fear in her furrowed brow.

I wanted to touch her, to hold her. And I really didn't expect that feeling to go away. She was my first love in high school and then we had our on again, off again time after my divorce. In all, our romantic relationship spanned nearly thirty-five years.

"Off the record," she said. "Please. Trust me enough to give me a clue here. Is this something I need to be worried about?"

"Tell me what happened with Smitty," I said.

She opened her mouth to speak, and it was clear that the words were not going to be kind, so I forged on. "Please. Are you okay?"

She blinked, her mouth moving around the words that didn't come out and then she sighed and looked down, her shoulders slumping. "It's painful, but I'll survive," she said, not looking at me. She sat on the end of the bed. "I know you, Henry, and you really don't want to know the details here. It's female stuff."

I nodded because she was right. I really didn't want to know. And I will admit it was an oddly old-fashioned thing and not something I was proud of.

"It's been happening for a while," she continued, "but got worse early this year."

She looked up and her piercing blue eyes showed pain, maybe grief. Her hands were pressed to her belly. This was something she had hidden from me and now I wasn't there to help her through it.

"And you asked for Smitty's help?" I asked.

She nodded. "The little shit said it wasn't the kind of problem he was willing to take on anymore."

"It got heated," I said. It wasn't a question.

She nodded. "You know how he is. His arrogance is going to be his undoing one of these days."

"Have you talked to him since?" I asked. I kept my voice low and just stood there. Annie was cooperating and I didn't want to do anything that might pop that bubble.

"Nope," she said. "I see him, I turn around."

I got my notebook out and wrote a few notes. When I looked back up she was staring at me.

"Your turn, Henry," she said.

I nodded and licked my lips. I wanted to tell her everything. Her sharing, while it was minimal, almost felt like intimacy and I missed her still.

"Like I told you earlier, Smitty has been receiving threats," I said. "I'm pretty certain the threats were printed out on your printer."

She opened her mouth and her eyes flashed. I held up my hand and continued. "I don't think it was you. I have evidence that Brooke has been accepting cash to let someone use your printer."

Her eyes looked positively dangerous, she took a deep breath, her spine straightening and her shoulders pulling back.

"I have to ask you not to fire her or mention this," I said.

"Why?" she asked.

"I think her actions are as simple as that, her accepting cash for access to your office," I said. "But I'd like to be sure."

She pursed her lips and crossed her arms. "You want me to pretend I don't know someone has been screwing me over for a few bucks?" she asked.

I nodded. "Yes, Annie. You asked me to trust you on this. Can I trust you?"

She sighed and nodded. "Yes, you can trust me. But I'll be watching the girl like a hawk."

I smiled. "I'm counting on it."

TWENTY-TWO
MONDAY, JULY 2. THE WINSLOW RANCH

We were outside the zone of influence in the juniper/piñon forest that dominates the land north of Carterville. These shorter, hardy trees mostly take over from the ponderosa pines as the mountain slumps into the desert and are dominant until about 6,000 feet in elevation. The Winslow Ranch was on the edge of this zone with the house nestled in the low trees, the barn and the corral in the open.

Because of the lack of trees on the north end of the acreage, there were views here of the desert rolling away to the horizon, but we weren't high enough to see the cut of the Grand Canyon.

We were on the edge of an area called the 40s because the land had been split into roughly forty-acre parcels out of square mile chunks of land. The private land was checkerboarded with public land causing an unpredictable patchwork of houses and winding dirt roads.

There are no county roads out here, no services, everything off the grid. Lots of folks had solar power and most everyone hauled their water, and this is where Karen Winslow and Ken Fischer had built their ranch.

They didn't have a forty-acre parcel, though—they had bought every chunk of land and owned 640 acres, a full square mile.

"You okay there, Boss?" Ortega asked as we drove down their long driveway. To get to their ranch you have to drive down Carterville Road to highway 89A, go north a bit and twist around on some dirt roads until you get to their well-maintained gravel driveway.

My stomach was tight and my mouth was dry. I wasn't feeling the normal relief when I leave the zone of influence and I no longer have a power. When that background buzz disappears.

"This is going to get ugly," I said, glancing at the young woman. Sure, she had volunteered for this, but after seven months here, I didn't think she truly understood the dynamics of the town.

"With Mr. Fischer?" she asked.

I shrugged. "Maybe. With Karen Winslow, undoubtedly."

She shrugged back. "The law's the law."

I bit back a laugh. Sure, the law's the law, but enforcing the law has consequences. In this case it could be seismic for our little town.

On her lap was a manila envelope in a plastic evidence bag. It was addressed to Winston Smith. It was the same envelope that Lester had photographed Ken Fischer coming out of the Carterville Inn with and putting in the mailbox. It had creases in it like it had been folded up and shoved into his pocket when he went into the inn. The address was printed with a laser printer, but a color one. Annabelle had already scanned it and found the yellow tracking dots. She was back at the office working on a search warrant. We already had enough evidence to arrest him if the circumstances were right.

And, yes, I told Smitty that there hadn't been a crime committed. I was stretching the truth a bit, trying to get him to agree to my terms. The pattern of harassment against Smitty was on the border of being criminal according to Arizona law. It was most certainly something he could be sued for.

But my goal today wasn't an arrest. Karen would have him out on bail in no time. It was to get in, get more proof in the form of tracking dots from his color printer, and get out. It was to end the threats against Smitty.

We rolled up to their house. It was relatively modest, a single-story structure made of rough pine logs and maybe twelve hundred square feet of living space with a detached two-car garage. You couldn't say the same for the barn. It was a towering red barn with extensive fencing around it. I could see two horses running to the fence, curious about us, undoubtedly. One of them was an Appaloosa with a chocolate brown coat and the distinctive white with dark spots along its back end, looking almost like someone had thrown a blanket on her.

That horse was named Katie and was Karen's pride and joy. I swear she cared more for that horse than her husband or Carterville.

Ken Fisher came striding out the front door and paused on the broad covered desk. He was short, shorter than Karen, about five-foot-six and bald, dressed in tan slacks and a blue polo shirt. He was quite a bit younger than Karen, in his mid-forties, and powerfully built, although I'd lay odds on Ortega if they were to arm wrestle.

He just stood there staring at us. At least he didn't have his cell phone out to contact his wife. That was good.

"Afternoon, Ken," I said as I got out.

Ortega got out on the other side holding the envelope behind her back as instructed.

"Afternoon, Henry," he said, nodding at me. "Isabella," he added to Ortega. "What are you two doing way out here?"

"It's a sensitive matter," I said. "Can we come inside?"

He nodded, a curious look on his face, and opened the screen door. Inside was a wide living room with a high ceiling covered in tongue and groove knotty pine. I could see the kitchen and the hallway that led to the bedrooms, one of which was an office.

The artwork on the walls were horse oriented and the decor was rough, wooden, western-style furnishings. Ken looked decidedly out of place.

"So, what's this all about?" he asked, his hands shoved into the pockets of his slacks.

I nodded at Ortega and she pulled out the envelope. "We know you mailed this to Winston Smith," she said. "We haven't opened it yet, but we suspect we know what the contents are."

He looked confused. "I didn't mail that," he said.

I pulled my phone out and showed him the picture I had.

Ken had thick eyebrows and they danced on his forehead as he looked at the phone and then the envelope, at Ortega and then at me.

"We haven't opened it yet," I said. "But we know what's

inside. We know you printed it at the Carterville Inn on their printer with the bad toner cartridge."

His brown eyes widened and he rubbed at his thinning black hair. He bent his knees and tensed like he was thinking of running, but it was only a moment. He nodded and relaxed. "What now?"

"Now we all sit down," I said, "and you tell us why you've been doing this."

TWENTY-THREE
MONDAY, JULY 2. THE WINSLOW RANCH

Ken Fischer's office fit him much better than the house. The walls were Sheetrock, painted a bland off-white and he had a black standing desk in front of a window looking out onto the ranch. The walls had a framed *Matrix* movie poster as well as a map of France with the route of the Tour de France. There was an exercise cycle, bookshelves full of what looked like math and engineering textbooks, and no place to sit.

"Mind if I record our conversation?" I asked.

He pursed his lips and shook his head. The answer surprised me. Why wasn't he calling his wife? Why wasn't he putting up a fight?

The story that was running in my head—a vengeful husband—didn't quite fit his behavior. But the stories we tell ourselves are often wrong, sometimes a little and sometimes a lot. Strike that. They are usually a little wrong, at least. This one looked to be a lot wrong.

"July 2, 2018, 2:06 p.m.," I said after I clicked on the recorder. "Interview with Ken Fischer by Henry Carter and Isabella Ortega regarding the threats received by Winston 'Smitty' Smith. Please state your name for the record."

I put the recorder down on a shelf next to a cycling trophy and got out my notepad. I was glad to see Ortega had hers out and wasn't just relying on her, admittedly excellent, memory.

"Ken Fischer," he said.

"Can you tell me about the envelope you put in the mail yesterday?" I asked.

The beginning is usually the best place to start a story, but Ken was nervous, alternatingly leaning against the desk and pacing a short path back and forth, and I needed an easy way in.

"I was just following instructions," he said.

The Winslow home had air-conditioning, not at all common around here, but still I felt hot as the story I had been telling myself about this case crumbled around me.

"Can you elaborate, please?" I asked.

He stopped his pacing and looked at me, his arms crossed as he bit his lower lip. "I want your word, Henry," he said. "I want your word that this stays between us."

I cocked my head and stared at him. He was serious and nervous, sweat beading on his forehead.

"Ken, I don't know that I can do that," I said. "Even if we don't file charges, Smitty could sue you for harassment."

He nodded. It was a short, quick thing. "Just for now then," he said. "I… I need to tell Karen in my own way. I've been protecting her, that's all I've been doing, protecting her. I swear."

"Very well," I said. "I will keep this quiet as long as I can. This won't leave my office for a few days at least."

He bit his lip again and nodded, shoving his hands in his slacks pockets and pacing again. It wasn't a big room, so he felt like a caged animal.

"I'm being blackmailed," he said as he paced. "And I have no idea who is doing it."

I struggled to find a question. There was a lot to unpack there.

"What are they using as leverage?" Ortega asked, and I was grateful. That was a useful question.

"Karen's addiction," he said, and this started to make a little more sense. Ken was, as Ortega had called him, "the AA guy."

"What addiction?" I asked.

He stopped and looked at me, his brown eyes wide. Sure, I thought I knew what addiction this was about, but saying it wouldn't be helpful here. I could be wrong.

"To Smitty's damn power," he said as he resumed pacing.

I scribbled in my notepad, not that I needed to. I didn't want him to know that I knew.

"I think we need to back up," I said. "How did this start? How is the blackmailer communicating with you? What do they have on Karen?"

He stopped and opened a cabinet at the bottom of one of the bookshelves. He pulled out a bottle of vodka and three glasses. I saw Ortega's eyes widen and tried not to do the same myself.

He slammed the bottle and the glasses on his desk and opened the bottle and poured three drinks. He handed one to Ortega, one to me, and took one himself.

"Don't shit yourself, Henry," he said. "It's just water. It's just… sometimes…" He shot the contents of the glass back and poured himself another.

I sniffed mine and it was really water. I was thirsty so I drank it.

I had my own relationship with alcohol. I wouldn't call it healthy, but I wouldn't call it an addiction. I did drink to excess, but I didn't drink every day. Now caffeine, that I was addicted to. I could not function in this world without coffee and plenty of it.

Given that alcohol is an addictive substance, I will admit that I could be fooling myself about it. That said, I had never seen someone fake drink. Maybe there was something about the ritual that calmed him. Maybe. I think it would just make it worse for me.

"Okay," he said with a sigh. "It started five weeks ago. That's when I got the first message. It just popped up on my computer." He pointed at the large screen on the standup desk.

"Popped up?" Ortega asked.

He shrugged. "It looked like a web page, HTML, but it wasn't in a normal browser. I work from home some and I was going through email. Just regular stuff. I didn't click on any weird links. It popped up. It had text and pictures. It had a couple of videos. All of it of Karen hurting herself right outside Smitty's place. Her going in. Her coming out with a look on her face. A look that…"

He poured himself another "drink" and shot it back. I don't know all that much about AA, but this faux drinking seemed like a bad idea.

He took a deep breath and let out a heavy sigh. "I know

that look," he said. "I've seen it so many times. I've seen it in the mirror. It was the look of an addict that had just gotten their fix."

I nodded. "And the text, did it threaten to release this information?" I asked.

He nodded.

There are lots of things that go on unsaid that would never be tolerated in the light of day. The mayor of Carterville hurting herself so Smitty could heal her and being addicted to it was certainly one of those. Especially if there are photos and videos of it. And especially in a tiny little town like Carterville. Everyone would know in less than a day. It would change everything for her. She would probably have to resign as mayor. Maybe even leave the town she and her ancestors had put so much effort into.

That thought settled into my stomach like too much spicy food. It wasn't about me, but I felt it like it was. What if I was forced to leave Carterville, the town my ancestor had founded, and generations of Carters had put their blood, sweat, and tears into?

"And then what?" Ortega asked. Gone was the shy young woman. She was not like that when she was working. She was focused but not too pushy.

"There were two buttons at the bottom of the page," he said. "One said, 'I will do what it takes to save my wife' and the other said, 'I am a coward.'" He shrugged. "I clicked the first button."

"Did the page go away?" she asked.

He shook his head. "Not right away. It came up with a set of rules. The title said, 'The Rules of the Game.'"

"What were they?" Ortega asked.

Ken went over to the bookshelf, above where he had pulled the faux vodka out, and grabbed a large hardback book. It looked like some kind of ancient textbook. He opened it and pulled out a handwritten piece of paper. It said:

1. *Do not tell anyone or I will know.*
2. *Do not change anything including misspelings.*
3. *Do exactly as you are instructed.*
4. *Do your assignment in the time limit provided.*
5. *Do not copy any of your instructions in any way for any reason.*
6. *Do save your wife. Do you think she would survive loosing everything?*

"What is with the misspellings?" Ortega asked. "There are two here."

Fischer shook his head. "I don't know. There are always misspellings. In the instructions. In what I am told to write."

"Did the instructions tell you to use the printer at the Carterville Inn?" I asked.

He nodded. "And to bribe Brooke with a twenty each time. And to create the documents as images and add fake toner blobs."

"What's with the fake blobs?" I asked.

He shrugged. "No idea. The instructions were particular too, telling me where to put them, the measurements in centimeters."

On one hand, I was relieved that Annabelle's analysis was good and now confirmed. But on the other hand, it made no sense. Why do that?

"Did you make copies of all the instructions?" Ortega asked.

He bit his lip, his eyes darting between us. He was deciding whether to trust us or not, I could see it in his face. I could also see the desperation. He had kept this to himself for far too long and he was paying a heavy price for that. His eyes locked with mine and he quietly said, "Yes."

I held his gaze. He knew of the friction between me and his wife. He probably suspected that I thought this town would be better off without her. She certainly thought that of me. But my job was more important than my own biases. And my job was to protect the town and enforce the laws.

Ortega read the room and stopped asking questions. I held his gaze for a few breaths and said, "We will do our best to get to the bottom of this without any of it getting out."

"Your best?" he asked, a condescending undertone leaking in.

"It's all I have, Ken," I said. "Whoever is doing this has had a long time to plan and we are just getting fed tiny crumbs, just enough to follow along. I don't know what game they are playing, but I will do everything I can to protect Carterville, all of Carterville, including Karen and Smitty."

He held my gaze for another couple breaths and then his shoulders sagged, and he let out a hissing sigh. "Okay. I copied everything by hand. I'll give them to you."

TWENTY-FOUR
MONDAY, JULY 2. THE CARTERVILLE POLICE DEPARTMENT

I DON'T KNOW IF IT'S HER SOUTHERN HERITAGE OR HER upbringing, but Annabelle Unger sure knows how to swear. It's not casual, like the intersprinkling of f-bombs into everything she says. It's much more varied and creative than that, and it's used properly as a spice at the right time. When we got back to the station with Ken Fischer's notes and updated her, she let loose, and it was amazing.

I am an amateur compared to her. Everyone I know is an amateur compared to her. The shower of swearing was accompanied by her pacing around the room and robust gesticulations.

"I told ya, Chief," she said in the middle of it. "I told ya. This is about us. They are stringin' us along. I told ya."

Ortega's eyes were wide, like a child watching an adult do a novel thing. I could see the wheels turning, she was observing the complexity and nuance of Annabelle's tirade wondering if she could do something like it herself. Or maybe she was just worried about what we had gotten ourselves into.

I just watched, letting the harsh words unwind some of the tension in my shoulders. I sat down in front of the empty desk, the one still covered in the threats Smitty had received, and watched.

Annabelle had some bracelets on today and they jangled as she gestured, her long legs taking her back and forth across the small room quickly. She ended up back by the cells, and a couple of times she had slapped the metal bars as she turned around before she came back, her heels clacking against the linoleum floor as she strode across the room.

The amazing swearing tirade didn't take that long, and I was sorry when it was over. I know Annabelle and this was just her letting off steam. This was just that kind of case. And watching her hands as they went to her red lips, her pockets, her purple-streaked red hair, I could tell she wanted a cigarette. That she was a little like Ken Fischer and his faux vodka. Maybe this energetic cursing was what she did instead of smoking.

"What's next?" she asked standing in front of me, her hands on her hips.

It was almost 4:00 p.m. We had been with Ken for a while but there was still a lot to do. "We go over everything Ken Fischer gave us," I said. "We create a time line. We take the description of the video and photos of Karen Winslow that Ken gave us and try to figure out where that camera was placed. Find out if it's still there, hopefully in a way that doesn't let the owner know we are on to them."

"Is that all?" she asked.

I shook my head. "And we go over your spreadsheet of powers and see if we can find any relevant one."

"Relevant?" Ortega asked.

I nodded. "Yeah. Like how did Ken's computer get infected?"

Ortega narrowed her eyes. "The old-fashioned way," she said. "He's outside the zone of influence and he just clicked on a bad link. Downloaded the thing."

"But how did they target Ken so effectively with the virus?" I asked. "He's an engineer. It couldn't have been easy."

I looked at Annabelle, she was still standing over me with her hands on her hips.

"It's a database of powers," she said. "Not a spreadsheet."

I shrugged. "Okay. It sure looks like a spreadsheet, but fine."

Her eyes narrowed. I knew she was still letting off steam. That spreadsheet versus database didn't matter one little bit in the scheme of things, but in her freaked-out mind it did. And while I needed to let off steam, having a silly fight with Annabelle wasn't the right way to do it.

The spreadsheet in question was something I had Annabelle put together after the murder of Lila Chang. Many of the powers in Carterville were known. When something weird happened, we needed a way to cross check it with known powers.

And this spreadsheet was admittedly way beyond my limited skill of summing columns and doing basic math. It had powers categorized and multiple sheets that summarized and dissected the data.

"Can you bring up the database, Annabelle?" I asked.

"Please. I know it doesn't really look like it yet, but there must be powers involved."

She nodded and went to her desk and logged into her computer. "This is about us, Henry," she said. "We are part of this."

I nodded. "I agree. The threats are one thing, but this game they are playing is with us."

When I looked at Ortega, she was staring at me, her eyes wide. She looked down but I didn't miss the fear in those brown eyes of hers. "Let's get that timeline going," I said to her. She nodded but didn't look at me.

This was a lot. It was too damn much. But we did our jobs and got to work.

TWENTY-FIVE

MONDAY, JULY 2. THE CARTERVILLE BREWERY

Coffee is the most reliable thing in my world. It wakes me up. It keeps me going. And it doesn't extract too high of a price if I don't drink too much.

That latter was currently out. It was past 8:00 p.m. and we were still working. We had coffee we could brew at the station, but I needed to walk, so I offered to "buy" Annabelle and Ortega a fancy coffee at the newly opened Carterville Brewery.

They both like the fancy stuff with foam and sugar and syrups and all kinds of things that disguise the bitter bite of good, strong coffee. I like the bite. I like the harshness of it to be undisguised. I find fancy coffees to be dishonest and far too expensive, but I think I'm in the minority there.

The air outside was cooler than inside as I walked out of the station, and I took a deep breath. Truth is I needed to move, too much sitting and close-up work. A timeline was up on one of the big whiteboards and the notes Ken Fischer gave us were arrayed with what Smitty received. We had spent time with Annabelle's "database," but I had jumped the gun there. We had no idea what powers might have been used unless someone had some computer mind control power and sent out the communications from their brain directly across the internet to Ken's computer. But that sounds far-fetched, even for Carterville.

Out of the station, I went around to Main Street and walked over to the Carterville Circle. There were plenty of people out tonight, shops open late, the sounds of people talking and laughing a pleasant background noise.

I think better when I'm walking, but for some reason pacing doesn't really count. The station wasn't big enough to get any momentum and all that back and forth just kept interrupting my train of thought.

The brewery was packed—Karen Winslow was nothing if not a good businesswoman. She knew this town and she knew what people would open up their wallets for.

I walked in and gave my order to the hostess, a young blonde woman that reminded me of Brooke over at the inn. I know. Kind of presumptuous, but Karen had laid out the red carpet so might as well take advantage of it.

I looked around the crowded restaurant but didn't see Karen or Ken and I felt a pang in my gut imagining the conversation they were having. About her addiction to Smitty's power and how she had hidden it from her husband. About his covert activities threatening Smitty for reasons he didn't know.

Smitty. This all revolved around Smitty. "Destroyer of Carteville" as the threatening notes said. He had his hooks in all over the place in this town with his "regulars," his addicts.

But then he withdrew them. So he could heal out of towners with more serious issues? Smitty?

With more money it makes sense, but letting the mayor go absolutely does not make sense. He addicted her. He tried to addict me. Why? So he can control this town which is the source of his power.

The pieces didn't fit together which meant we were missing something. Something important.

As I waited, as my mind worked, I scanned the restaurant. It was mostly tourists with a few tables of locals. It was loud, the many voices in the small space bouncing off the brick walls making a harsh kind of white noise. Some of the voices rising loud, laughter ringing out, the smell of beer thick.

A few people were eyeing me, as they do anyone in a law enforcement uniform. Their eyes went to the weapons on my belt. But mine wasn't the only weapon in the place. There was a middle-aged man at a table with a pistol on his belt despite the prominent sign on the door that indicated no firearms were allowed.

This is Arizona. I wouldn't call this the "Wild West" anymore, but the spirit of it remains. And while Arizona's carry laws are generous, it is illegal to consume alcohol while carrying. This is the problem with my job—there is always something to do.

Now, I could let it be, but a deadly weapon and impaired judgment are not a good combination. Not in a restaurant packed full of people. And given that the place had just opened, it seemed important to set the proper precedence.

And, yes, having something in my job that was at least simple and clear cut with all this Smitty madness was welcome.

I didn't recognize the man in question. He had brown/grey hair and was in shorts and flip-flops with a T-shirt that was having trouble holding in his protruding belly. He was laughing loudly and drinking a beer. At the table with him was a woman, his wife presumably, and another couple.

I walked over. "Excuse me, sir," I said with a smile.

He looked up at me, his eyes widening. My heartbeat had sped up and I was no longer in desperate need of coffee.

"What can I do you for, Officer?" he asked and then chuckled, his friends joining in.

"I am guessing you missed the sign on the door," I said, gesturing back to the entrance. "No firearms are allowed in this establishment. And even if they were, it is illegal to carry and consume alcohol in Arizona."

He blinked, like the words were having trouble forming in his brain. His companions had gone quiet. He smiled back and it was a nasty thing, more sneer than anything else. His brown eyes were having a bit of trouble focusing and this was not looking like it was going to be easy. "Thank you for letting me know," he said, turning back to his companions with a grin and a chuckle.

A situation like this is all about escalation. I already did this by walking over and confronting him. And I am well aware that most anything I did now could escalate things further. While his companions didn't have any guns visible, it doesn't mean that they weren't carrying.

"And thank you for leaving," I said. "After you stow your firearm in your vehicle you are welcome to come back. Or you can surrender your weapon to me now and pick it up at the police station later. Whatever works best for you."

My tone was even and there was a smile on my face, but

this was no friendly conversation. The restaurant was quieting, and I saw someone scrambling up the stairs to the Winslow apartment out of the corner of my eye.

"And if I don't?" he asked, looking me up and down. I know that look. He was trying to figure out if he could take me like this was some schoolyard conflict and he was the school bully. Problem is, I was never very good at doing what bullies wanted.

"Then I call for backup and I ask you again," I said. My hands were clasped loosely in front of me, but I could have my taser or my gun out a lot faster than he could with all the beer sloshing around his gut.

His eyes narrowed as he looked up at me. "Is that so? How long does it take the cavalry to arrive this far out in the middle of nowhere?"

I shrugged. "Our station is about a minute's walk away. But knowing my people, it will be less than that. And if I have to call for backup, we'll be beyond the stage of small-town courtesy and giving you the benefit of the doubt. We'll be at the point where you end up arrested and spending the night in one of my cells."

"Cliff," the woman next to him hissed. "Just go put that damn thing away. I told you not to bring it."

The comforting noises of the restaurant were gone, replaced by a few whispers and the sounds of clanging and sizzling coming from the kitchen.

I heard heavy footsteps on the stairs and a gasp that sounded like Karen Winslow, but I ignored it, still staring at the man who was still staring back. Maybe he had had too much to drink to be smart about this. I slowly reached up to the mic clipped to my shoulder and squeezed it. "Dispatch, this is Carter. I've got a—"

"Okay, okay," the man said, cutting me off as he stood up, his hands held up at the level of his shoulders. "I'm going. I'm going. What a backwards little Podunk town you all got here."

"Carter, this is Dispatch," Annabelle said on my radio. "Please repeat, we did not copy. Over."

His eyes were daggers as he shuffled by, and he went on with mumbled insults, but he walked out of the restaurant.

"The situation has been handled," I radioed. "Out." I followed him to the door and watched him as he walked around the circle and down Main Street toward the parking lot.

When I came back in, Karen Winslow was standing there, her hands on her hips and a rather complicated look on her face. She was mad with her jaw set and her eyes narrowed, but it looked like she had been crying. She had on a dark skirt and another embroidered cowboy shirt, this one light blue, but the Carterville Brewery vest was missing and even though her hair was in its usual braid she looked a bit disheveled.

"What the hell was that?" she asked, her voice rather loud. There was more noise in the restaurant but not enough to drown her out.

"Law enforcement," I said. "But perhaps you'd like to discuss this somewhere more private."

She blinked and looked around, a rare flash of shame darkening her face before she nodded and marched to the steps.

TWENTY-SIX
MONDAY, JULY 2. THE WINSLOW APARTMENT

COUPLES FIGHT. I AM SURE THERE ARE SOME EXCEPTIONS TO that rule, but my wife and I always fought, and Annie and I did too. And when a couple fights, it's an intimate thing. Each side knows their opponent well enough to do real damage real quick if they are not careful, if they don't pull their verbal punches.

Some relationships seem to be fueled by it, others are destroyed by it. Doing the job that I do for as long as I have, I have walked into the middle of many couples fighting, often when those fights went beyond verbal.

And I hate it.

I don't say that casually, like I hate sweetened coffee, or I hate the unrelenting spring winds around here. I mean that I have a visceral, full-bodied reaction to it, not just some mental resistance.

I followed Karen Winslow up the stairs from the brewery to her and Ken's apartment knowing what I was walking into. My heart sped up and sweat formed at the back of my neck. I wasn't expecting any violence, but after seeing Karen's state, I had no desire to walk into the middle of what must be a very difficult evening for the two of them.

But it's the job.

I've mentioned this before, I think in other stories, but my belief, which I got from my father, is that our jobs are important. They invite us to be more than we are, more than we think we can be. They give us opportunities to grow, to be better, and to collect the scars we all get living these lives of ours.

And while this was part of my job, I sure didn't want to be there.

The living room with its desk and uncomfortable furniture looked the same. Neat and everything in place except for a small stack of papers on the coffee table lying face down, numerous papers sticking out at odd angles as if they had been hastily gathered together.

Ken Fischer was not to be seen, but he had just been here. There were two wine glasses on that coffee table, with a bit of red wine in each and a bottle next to it. The room practically smelled of the difficult intimacy that had been uncorked.

"Explain yourself," Karen said, standing just in the room staring at me, her tone loud and demanding.

I smiled as best I could and ignored my desire to meet her tone. "I came in for coffee, figured I'd take you up on your generous offer," I began. "I saw that you had a customer carrying a gun on his belt that was being served alcohol. Your establishment has a no firearm policy which your employees didn't enforce, and even if you allowed them, serving alcohol to this individual was a violation of the law. I was doing my job, Karen."

Her lips puckered and it looked like she bit back much of what she wanted to say. She was, undoubtedly, working through what I hadn't said. That I could have arrested the man and made a bigger scene. That I could investigate her new establishment for a violation of the law their second night open.

She nodded and sighed, her hazel eyes going to the stack of papers and the wine, and they hardened as she looked back at me. "I told you to leave Ken out of your investigation regarding Smitty," she said. Her voice was quiet, but her tone could not hide the danger in her words.

"I was following the evidence," I said. "He has played a significant role in all of this." Again, there was a lot I didn't say.

Her lips pursed. "Are you planning on charging him?" she asked.

"I cannot discuss an ongoing investigation with you," I said.

"I am his lawyer," she said, and then I realized why Ken was not here. They were playing defense and he must be in the bedroom. I was guessing that Karen was furious he told us all that he did without her being present. "You will run any requests for him through me."

"Very well," I said, feeling my blood pressure rise. Karen kept treating me like a subordinate, like I worked for her, and it was getting on my nerves. "Consider this notice that I expect Mr. Fischer to come down to the station at 8:00 a.m. tomorrow for further questioning."

Her eyes widened. I didn't have further questions for him,

but if this was the game she wanted to play, then we were going to play it.

"He is not available at 8:00 a.m.," she said.

I smiled. "Then I ask you to urge your client to change his schedule. You know what my next move will be if I don't get the cooperation I need in this investigation."

Her eyes narrowed. "I will talk to him," she said. "But I cannot guarantee his presence."

I nodded. "Very well, then I cannot guarantee my ongoing leniency in this matter."

Yes, this had turned into a pissing match between the mayor and the chief of police. Yes, it was all a bit childish. And yes, it was what I had to do. I knew Karen and I knew her well. If I gave an inch on this thing, she would take a mile. She liked to pretend that my position wasn't elected just like hers and that I worked for her. But I was elected and I did not work for her.

"I will talk with my client," she said.

I nodded and tipped my hat. "Well, then our conversation is concluded. Thank you for your time, Ms. Winslow."

TWENTY-SEVEN
MONDAY, JULY 2. THE CARTERVILLE POLICE DEPARTMENT

THE BLONDE HOSTESS HANDED ME MY COFFEES IN ONE OF those cardboard carriers. I had barely noticed her and almost spilled it as I rushed out of the brewery.

I wasn't quite seeing red, but almost. My vision was tunneled in, and I was a good notch or two beyond furious. That hadn't gone well, but I'm not sure how it could have gone any better. Karen was protecting herself and her husband. I was doing my job, what had to be done.

I don't really remember the short walk back to the station, but my coffee was in my hand when I arrived and nearly empty. I put the coffee carrier down on Ortega's desk and stood there staring at the whiteboard that had the timeline of this mess written on it, feeling the buzz of too much caffeine drank to quickly invade my body.

"What's going on there, Chief?" Annabelle asked. "That took a little long for coffee."

"Karen Winslow," I said, spitting the words out. "Enjoy

those coffees because I suspect that is the last of our freebees from the Carterville Brewery."

Ortega took her coffee, they were marked on the side, and handed Annabelle's hers. "What happened, Boss?" she asked. When I glanced at her she was staring at her coffee.

So I told them. In short sentences with all the energy that I had held back when talking to Karen. I didn't curse, like Annabelle did at several points, but they got the picture.

"So we need to come up with some questions for Ken Fischer," Ortega said.

I nodded. "Oh, I have a lot of questions," I said. I hadn't when I first made the demand, but it hadn't taken long.

"What questions?" Annabelle asked.

I stepped back so I could see them both clearly. "What if he's lying?" I asked. "What if all of these notes were just his way of producing some cover for his actions? He has motive, his wife's addiction to Smitty's power. We have a confession of sorts. He has no evidence of his computer being hacked. He didn't even bother taking a picture of any of it."

They were both staring at me, Ortega nodding slowly and Annabelle looking dubious.

"He was worried that his phone was hacked," Ortega said. "Or, at least, that's what he said."

I nodded. "But he's an engineer," I said. "He must know how hard it would be to hack every one of his internet connected devices. And don't they have a camera that's not a phone? Something isn't right there."

Annabelle was leaning back, looking less dubious.

"And what if Smitty is lying?" I continued. "We know that Ken has been mailing the threats, but what if there is something he's not telling us. Something that changes how this whole situation looks. This is Smitty—there is probably quite a bit that he's not telling us."

"Why would he do that?" Ortega asked, her brow furrowed.

"Because he's Smitty," Annabelle offered. "That boy just wants to rule the world and don't give a damn about what games he has to play or who he has to tromp over to do it."

"And because our powers only work here," I said. "Carterville is the world he wants to rule."

Annabelle eyed me. I had said "our powers," an unusual slip for me. I chalk it up to the caffeine and in the moment didn't think much about it. I started pacing, my mind churning through it all, trying to pull things together and find the next logical step. Annabelle and Ortega were quiet, sipping their coffees, watching me or looking at the timeline on the whiteboard.

I stopped when the picture became clear. "Go home," I said. "Get some rest. We have an early appointment."

"And what about you?" Annabelle asked.

I went to the empty desk with all the threats laid out on it and fished out the envelope that Ortega had intercepted today. We had never opened it. "I'm going to deliver Smitty's mail," I said.

TWENTY-EIGHT
MONDAY, JULY 2. THE SMITH RESIDENCE

Going to see Smitty all caffeined up was not smart. But, then again, I was all caffeined up and not thinking as clearly as I thought I was.

We hadn't opened Smitty's mail for a reason. We were quite sure what was in it, and we try our best to steer clear of committing crimes like tampering with the mail. A quick call to Smitty to get permission would have taken care of that tampering part, but he could have said no and that wouldn't have worked.

When I knocked on the door, Smitty answered, in his shorts and flip-flops like last time, but a different T-Shirt. This one was white with large black letters that said, "I Don't Care." It was hard to say whether it was a statement or just what had been clean in his closet.

"Isn't this after normal working hours?" Smitty asked with a little sneer I would have loved to slap off his angular face.

"Long hours come with the job," I said, eying the door behind him. There was one of those fancy deadbolts with a keypad on the door and next to the door was a doorbell camera. I took a step back and saw a camera mounted up under the porch pointing out to the street.

"I guess you hired Steve," I said. He was the security guy I had recommended.

"Yeah," he said with a lazy nod. "Not cheap, but he gets things done."

I nodded. "Where is he?"

"He had to run back to Flag to get more stuff," he said as he turned and walked in the house. "Close the door behind you."

I closed the door and looked carefully around. There was a camera up in the corner of the living room and a motion sensor in another corner. There was some sawdust on the hardwood floor below these and things looked a little off, like everything had been moved and not put back in quite the same place.

"So, to what do I owe the pleasure?" Smitty asked from his slumped position on the couch. The same gun was still sitting on the coffee table in front of it.

"More questions," I said, his eyes going to the envelope in my hand.

He grunted noncommittally.

"I'd really like to understand why you cut Karen Winslow off," I said. He opened his mouth to speak but I kept going. "The others I get—you needed the capacity for other clients. But Karen? I don't get it. It seemed like her influence would be worth keeping her."

He licked his lips and blinked and then sat up straight. "You're not as dumb as you look, Henry."

"I sure hope not with you needing me to actually find out who's behind this," I said. Even with the caffeine running through me, that kind of insult was an easy one to dodge.

He smiled his distinctly predatorial smile and nodded at the envelope. "I'll trade with you. Tell me what that's all about and I'll answer your question."

I shrugged and walked over and handed him the envelope. "Just some mail we came across. It's another threat but we didn't open it."

He took it gingerly, holding it at the edges and turning it slowly over.

"We already dusted it for prints," I said. "But we need the contents. If you don't want to open it, I can just take it back."

He eyed me, his forehead furrowing, and asked, "And... how did you come across my mail?"

"Officer Ortega managed that," I said, being intentionally vague.

"Enterprising young woman," he said. "I'm kind of surprised, though. Tampering with the mail. Isn't that a federal offense or something?"

Now he was just messing with me. "Not when it relates directly to an ongoing investigation," I said, less sure of that fact than I sounded. "And, as you can see, we didn't 'tamper' with it. Delivery was just slightly delayed. If you would like us to no longer use all the means at our disposal on this case, just say the word. I'd be happy to—"

He held up his hand, cutting me off. "No, no, no. It's fine. I'm glad you did." All of that poking was probably because he was stuck here and bored. Or just because he was Smitty.

He was still holding the envelope gingerly like it might hurt him.

"You going to open it?" I asked. I was feeling the need to get the hell out of here. The caffeine was in full force and my heart was pounding and I was starting to sweat.

He ignored me and flipped the envelope over in his hands. Was this an act or was he really this bothered by the threats?

"Did something else happen?" I asked.

He looked at me and his eyes were doing that trick where they looked green. And they looked really tired. He shook his head, his scraggly blond and grey hair falling into his eyes. He brushed it away with a sigh. "No, Henry. This is all a little… overwhelming. I thought I had another day without one of these. I had hoped that…" He trailed off with a shrug.

If this was an act, it was a good one. A damn good one. I wanted to believe him, but I also knew that it wasn't safe.

He fished around in the drawer of a little wooden table next to the couch and came up with a letter opener, a blunt steel blade. He slipped it in and opened it and then paused, glancing up at me.

I gave him a nod, the lingering heat from the day combining with too much coffee catching up with me. The room felt small and I wanted to bolt. I had seen Ken Fischer's notes on this one so I knew what it would say, but still I felt the need to be anywhere but here.

He grimaced and gingerly pulled the sheet of paper out. It was upside down and he set the envelope down and the piece of paper on top of it. He looked at me again and I gave him another nod.

He bit his lip and turned the paper over.

He gasped.

I gasped as my heart thumped in my chest, loud and insistent. This didn't match Ken's notes. It said:

Destroyer of Carteville
I AM here to kil you
while I look in you eye

He paused, staring at the paper—it had the same grey tinge and the blobs. The edges were ripped just like all the others.

I stopped looking at it and watched him, my heart a rushing sound in my head, the walls of the room seeming to close in on me, sweat beading on my forehead.

I didn't think of it then, but in retrospect I couldn't have looked normal, all that coffee coming home to roost combined with the stress of the day and the stress of this betrayal.

Given how I looked and the contents of the new note, it's really not a surprise that Smitty went for the gun on the coffee table, my heart beating even faster.

And I went for my taser.

I fired.

He fired.

————

THIS WASN'T A SLOW-MOTION KIND OF THING, LIKE IN THE movies. Smitty slowly lunging for his gun while my hand reached around for my taser. Me slowly getting the taser out first and aiming at Smitty's chest. Carefully waiting to see if he was really going to do anything with that gun. Smitty raising it up. Me firing. Him firing.

No. This was a blur of a reaction. This was instinct and training and experience taking over and the higher brain functioning mostly staying out of the way.

Smitty went for a gun, a deadly weapon, and I went for my taser, opting for nondeadly force. This was also instinct. But then again, deadly force was what was available to Smitty.

And I can understand his reaction. I was a sweating, over-caffeinated mess at 10:00 p.m. which he probably thought was my nervousness as I built up the courage to kill him in cold blood.

That damn coffee from the Carterville Brewery and my fury with Karen Winslow that had caused me to down it without really thinking.

The taser fired first and hit home, the darts punching through Smitty's "I Don't Care" T-shirt and electricity coursing through his body, causing him to jerk as he squeezed the trigger of the gun. It barked, the sound shatteringly loud in the small space. He missed me completely but only because of the taser. It was close quarters in there and that probably saved my life.

Smitty fell, pushing the coffee table aside as he flopped to the floor.

I felt strange. So hot. My chest getting tight and pain radiating down my left arm. I reached for the mic on my left shoulder.

"Carter to dispatch. I'm..." The pain intensified and I started gasping for air. It was so hot in here. I couldn't breathe. "Send... backup. Send... ambulance."

The pain became even worse like someone had plunged a knife into my arm. And I felt pressure, like an elephant was sitting on my chest. I couldn't breathe. I fell to my knees.

Smitty's eyes found me as he flopped on the floor, and I swear he smiled seeing me suffer.

"Help," I gasped as my hand slipped from the mic and I fell to the floor.

TWENTY-NINE
MONDAY, JULY 2. THE SMITH RESIDENCE

Smitty recovered before I did. The pain in my chest was unbearable, each breath like running a marathon—not that I would know what that is like, but you get the idea. But my heart was still beating and I could still breathe.

Smitty recovered a lot faster than I expected. He was on the floor flopping like a fish as the taser dumped electricity into him, but then he was up before I knew it, the gun in his hand aimed at me. It was probably his power, his body rapidly overcoming the effects of the taser.

I was on the floor, smelling the musty, dusty smell of his throw rug.

"Get up, Henry," he said, breathing hard and stooped over. At least the taser had cost him something.

"Can't," I gasped.

"Looks like you are having a heart attack," he said. "Too bad the hospital is so far away."

I grunted. It sure as hell felt like a heart attack, or at least how I imagined one would feel. But it was starting to ease. Just a little. It wasn't such torture to breathe. And it wasn't lost on me that he wasn't using his power to help me, or even offering to use his power for a price I wouldn't be able to bear.

He straightened up and held the gun steady. There would be no missing me this time.

My radio squawked to life. "Carter, this is Ortega. I am on route. 911 has been called. Are you there? Over."

Smitty blinked. Maybe he hadn't heard me radioing. Maybe he thought he could do anything he wanted. Point to the envelope he just opened. Say that I had tasered him and then promised to kill him. He was weighing whether he could sell that.

"Framed," I said. "We know who has been mailing you. He did this."

Ken Fischer had set me up. I wanted nothing more than to drive out to the Winslow Ranch, arrest him, and throw him in a cell. The pain was easing and I thought I might be able to get up, but I didn't let on.

"Who has been mailing these?" Smitty asked, pointing the gun at the new threat letter and then back at me. "If it wasn't you, then who?"

I gritted my teeth and shook my head. "Put the gun down, Smitty. This is what he wants."

Ken Fischer wants Smitty to kill me? But why? Was this some bizarre plot to get Smitty to murder the chief of police? Was Karen behind it, a one-two punch to punish Smitty and to get rid of me? Were they somehow that diabolical? I mean, Karen Winslow was a shrewd businesswoman and Ken Fischer was a seriously smart guy, but would they do this?

The evidence said yes. Ken printed this out, put it in the envelope, and made his hand-copied instructions that had a different message. He set me up. There could be no doubt about that.

"Carter, this is Ortega," she said over the radio, the stress in her voice clear. "Almost to your location. Come in. Over."

"Put the gun down," I said, trying to put energy I didn't feel into my voice. "Now. Or this gets even uglier."

I sucked in a breath, and it hurt like hell, but I could breathe. I pushed up to my hands and knees as the elephant on my chest decided he had somewhere better to be.

Smitty blinked, looking around like he was hoping to see an ally or a way out. Outside through the open windows I could hear the growl of Ortega's Mustang as it approached. The girl loved her car and she loved to drive fast, too damn fast.

"Now!" I shouted.

I heard screeching tires and a door slamming through the windows. Smitty's eyes went to the door and then to me.

"I didn't do it," I said. "Put the gun down."

His mouth was moving, like he was talking to himself, trying to sort through the possibilities, deciding what the best way out of this was.

A heavy hand banged on the door. "Boss? Smitty?" Ortega said, and then thinking better of that and resorting to her by-the-book nature, she added, "Open up. This is the Carterville Police Department."

Ortega didn't wait. She tried the door which happened to be unlocked. It swung open but she was not visible. Smart girl.

"Stay there, Ortega," I said. I didn't have much volume in

my voice yet, but it was a small house. "Smitty has a gun on me but he's about to put it down. Right, Smitty?"

"Copy that, Boss," Ortega called.

I slowly levered myself up to a standing position using the askew coffee table to get on my feet, my heart whooshing in my ears again, the room slowly spinning.

"Put the gun down, Smitty," I said. "I'll give you to the count of three. Let's get through the day without anyone getting shot, eh?"

In the distance I could hear the warble of a siren, which was surprising. Carterville is off the beaten path—it's not like they are waiting around for a 911 call from a community of 290.

I still felt flattened. It was an epic effort to breathe, but at least I was standing.

Smitty was looking scared and confused. His eyes going to me, the new letter, the door, and then his gun.

"One," I said, my hand drifting towards my gun. He definitely had the edge here. I wasn't in the best of shape and his gun was already out.

His eyes darted around again.

"Is this your plan?" he said. "All along? Killing me in my own home because I drew a gun on you? Even though I had every reason in the world to?"

"No, Smitty. This is not my plan," I said. "I've been set up. Put the gun down and let's sort this out."

"The note," Smitty said, raising his voice so Ortega could hear him. "It says 'Destroyer of Carteville. I AM here to kil you while I look in you eye.' You hear that, Ortega? Henry is behind this. He came to kill me. In my own home. Of course I have a gun on him."

"I hear you, Smitty," she said. "I do. But what are you going to do? Are you going to shoot him now with me as a witness? And then what? Are you going to shoot me too? How will wiping out the entire CPD look? My mic is open and Annabelle is recording all of this. I'm sure the sheriff is on the way by now. The only way out of this is to put the gun down."

I was impressed. She didn't push against his beliefs about what was going on, just laid out where he was clearly and effectively. I had to wonder about the open mic and the sheriff being involved already, but it was plausible.

"Two," I said, to drive her point home.

Smitty pursed his lips and nodded. It was a small thing, two quick bounces of his head and then he slowly placed the gun on the coffee table. I reached over and took it.

"Clear," I said as my legs gave out and I sank to the floor.

Ortega came rushing in, her gun leveled at Smitty.

"Look," Smitty said, pointing at the threatening note lying on the coffee table on top of the envelope I had brought it in.

Ortega's forehead furrowed. "That's… that's not what we were told it was going to be."

Smitty blinked and looked surprised.

"I was set up," I said, as the elephant decided to sit on my chest again. I groaned and lay down on the floor and waited for the ambulance to get here.

THIRTY
MONDAY, JULY 2. THE SMITH RESIDENCE

THIS WAS A MESS. ONE OF THE TWO COPS IN CARTERVILLE down and lots to do. As they wheeled me out of Smitty's place on a stretcher, I talked to Ortega.

The stars were out and the breeze was a cool relief. It gave me hope that I might feel human again someday.

"Tell Smitty he's under house arrest," I said. "He's got private security, a guy named Steve Lancaster. Talk to him when he gets back. He's a good guy, but remember who is paying him."

She nodded, her round face drawn into a worried expression.

"Keep that appointment with Ken Fischer in the morning," I said. "Arrest him if he shows. If not, work with Annabelle on a warrant."

She nodded again, her mouth moving but no words coming out. The three paramedics had me at the ambulance, impatient looks on their faces.

"Get back in there and keep Smitty from messing with any evidence. Have Annabelle come and take pictures. Take his statement. I think he'll be eager to give it."

"I got this, Boss," she said. "You take care of yourself."

I nodded as they loaded me in. The elephant wasn't sitting on my chest anymore, but I was exhausted and wrung out. I was worried about what had happened to me and that it might happen again. Smitty hadn't offered to heal me, which was telling. I'm honestly not sure if I would have refused or not. On one hand, being further in debt to him was not acceptable. On the other hand, whatever was going on with me was scary as hell.

"You got this, Ortega," I said as they closed the doors.

"So do you, Boss," she said, her voice muffled as the ambulance started to pull away.

But the problem was it wasn't at all sure that either of us had anything. While we had Fischer dead to rights, there were too many loose ends, too many things that didn't quite make sense. And being taken away in an ambulance doesn't really bode well, does it?

PART 3
COMPLICATIONS: JULY 3

THIRTY-ONE
TUESDAY JULY 3. FLAGSTAFF MEDICAL CENTER

Hospitals are a terrible place to get better. My father used to say that. With all the noise and the poking and prodding, it made sense. And with my sister Wendy there, boy did it make sense.

"You had a coronary artery spasm," she said, her arms crossed and a disapproving look on her face. Like I had stopped at the drive-through at a burger joint and asked for one coronary artery spasm to go.

It was after midnight and the coffee and all the drama had me wide awake. "At least it wasn't just a panic attack," I said, trying to put some punch into it that I didn't feel.

I was in a narrow, curtained area in the emergency room of Flagstaff Medical Center, one of those thin gowns on and the blanket pulled up. The air was the complicated scent of sharp cleaner trying to hold back the dark scents of various human bodily fluids.

My sister pursed her lips and shook her head. "Are you going to take this seriously, Henry?"

Wendy was a Carter through and through and I sometimes felt bad for her. We all have a splash of freckles and mousey brown hair, which is fine, but the big nose and the weak chin didn't make her the best-looking woman. She was dressed in faded blue scrubs and a few pounds overweight just like me.

Not that any of that mattered to me. She looked a lot like my mom which made her beautiful. But the world seems to care a lot more about how women look than men.

Wendy's hair was shoulder length and browner than mine. She's two years older than me but has fought back the grey with chemicals.

"It would be embarrassing if it was just a panic attack," I said. "It would take two seconds for the whole of Carterville to know, and that wouldn't be a good look in my job."

She shook her head and sighed, a big dramatic expulsion of air.

"Okay," I said. "Okay. At least those words kind of make sense. Why did it happen and how bad is it?"

"The doctor will be in to tell you all of this," she said, "but since… you know…" All that amounted to was that since she was my big sister and a nurse in the hospital whose ER I was stuck in, she was going to tell me all about what had happened to me and give me a good long lecture on how to better take care of myself.

And, frankly, after the last couple of days, I welcomed it.

"Stress is a factor and I think that coffee played a big role," she said. "It usually takes illegal stimulants to trigger a CAS, but I think you managed it with coffee. There are a lot more tests to do, but there probably isn't any long-term damage. You've got to take better care of yourself, Henry. A lot less coffee, less alcohol, and a whole lot more exercise."

"That is almost as bad as a panic attack," I said, pulling the sheet up, but I couldn't get it up far enough to cover my face. I guess there is something about your big sister that makes you feel like a kid even when you are in the grip of middle age.

"It's good news, Henry," she said, her voice softening. "There shouldn't be any permanent damage. But it's a warning sign. We need to get your heart checked out. Thoroughly. And you need to cut back on the coffee. Way back."

I groaned.

"They're about done with you for tonight," she said with a nod. "My shift has ended so I'll drive you home, but let's try to get you in to see Jenny tomorrow."

Doctor Jenny Lion with her power, which made her something of a human MRI machine, would be able to confirm the diagnosis and possibly find other issues.

Doctor Lion had checked me out after my fall, after Smitty healed me. She had counted the bones that had been broken and the organs that had been punctured that Smitty had managed to take care of.

And that brought my mind back to Smitty. If there was a real issue with my heart, he could take care of it. Not that he would be willing to do it at this point and not that I would be willing to ask.

Wendy stepped closer and put her hand on my shoulder. "How much longer can you carry that whole town on your shoulders, Henry? And at what cost?"

I smiled at her and nodded. It felt like a lot, but it also was who I was at a very fundamental level. "But I'm a Carter," I said.

She gave me a pursed-lipped smile and nodded. At least she understood that part.

THIRTY-TWO

TUESDAY JULY 3. THE CARTERVILLE POLICE DEPARTMENT

With five hours of sleep, what I wanted the most was to be swimming in coffee. But the stuff that I loved so much had betrayed me, so I sat in my closet of an office in the Carterville Police Department and gingerly sipped my meager allotment out of an insulated stainless-steel tumbler.

Wendy had gotten up when I did. She had made the coffee and apportioned me my eight ounces and ordered me to take at least an hour to drink it. The tumbler was to keep it hot. Nothing worse than lukewarm coffee.

It was just shy of 8:00 a.m. I was waiting for Ken Fischer to show up and doing paperwork. There was always paperwork that needed doing. And mail that needed to be read. And emails that needed to be answered. And social media outreach that needed to be avoided.

I swear if I let it, the desk part of the job would just take over and I'd sit in this tiny office every day and never get out there and do anything.

I shook my wrist, still not used to the mostly plastic band there. Wendy, somehow, had it at the ready when I got up. "Here," she had said, putting it on me, her hands warm and gentle, betraying her decades as a nurse. "It will track your steps. It will remind you to get up and move."

We had been in the small kitchen of our historic home, one of the first built in Carterville. She was brewing the coffee and the smell was glorious, but my reaction to it was a lot more complicated than usual. The kitchen had been remodeled a few years ago with tile on the floor the color of the desert and granite countertops a darker brown.

Wendy was dressed in a fuzzy blue robe, her hair a jumbled mess like when we had been kids.

"I don't like watches," I said.

She smiled. "Then good thing it's not a watch."

"You know what I mean," I said. It was about the feel of something hanging on my wrist. I just don't like it.

She looked down, her face going slack. When she looked back up, I could see moisture in her brown eyes. Like many men of a certain age, I am not that good with women crying— I just don't know what to do. But when my big sister cries, I can hardly think.

And this was telling. Normally we would have had a rational discussion that evolved into a less rational argument before the tears were threatened and I caved. This spoke to the serious nature of the matter for her.

And, yes, my big sister was likely manipulating me consciously and intentfully. But her intent was good, like it almost always was.

"I can't lose you, too," she said.

Wendy had lost her husband, Jeff, about six years ago. A

brain aneurysm. She had been living with him and their daughter in Colorado. And our parents were both gone and had been for a while.

She came back to Carterville after things were wrapped up in Colorado. She moved into the old Carter house with me since I had divorced a few years earlier and my son was in Phoenix with his mother.

There were a few distant cousins, but she was the only other Carter around. She was my sister. I couldn't say no.

"I'll get used to it," I said with a smile, the best I could manage on scant sleep and no coffee. Because I knew I would. That's one thing us evolved apes are good at, getting used to things.

Back in my tiny office sitting at my beat-up metal desk, I shook off the memory and looked at the silly thing, because it really was a watch. It read 8:03 a.m. I sighed. There had been little doubt that they wouldn't show up. And Karen Winslow had had time to get her defenses in place, and now it was time to see what those were.

———

THE "WATCH" WAS REALLY BUGGING ME. I COULDN'T GET THE fit right. If it was too loose it slid around and kept bugging me. If it was too tight, it felt like it was strangling my wrist and cutting off blood flow.

How long had the world been strapping things on their wrists? Didn't we have a more precise way besides the spaced holes and a buckle? Of course we did—high-end watches had more refined ways of clasping your wrist, but not little plastic fitness trackers.

All of this ran through my mind as I marched to the Carterville Brewery, found that Karen and Ken were not in their apartment, and marched back to the CPD.

When I got back, I tapped on the rectangular face of my "watch" until it showed me how many steps I had gained. Like 250. Oh boy. Only thousands and thousands to go.

And this would be a thing with Wendy. She would want to know how many steps I got every day. Strike that. When she was home, she would want me to show her how many steps I got. She would want to go for long walks with me on the steep streets of Carterville after a long day when all I would want is to sit on the deck with a drink in my hand. She would dedicate herself with the laser focus of her will on me to walk more until I didn't even think about it.

And it's funny. We work so hard to preserve our health, especially as we get older, but it's just bailing out a sinking ship. Our bodies all have an expiration date.

Yup, that's the kind of mood I was in that morning.

"Not there, I take it," Annabelle asked when I walked into the CPD, a sour look on my face.

I shook my head. "Karen Winslow knew what was coming yesterday when I talked to her."

"And that makes her an accessory," Ortega said from her desk.

"Yes, it does," I said with a grim smile. "Get on the phone, Annabelle. Find us a judge in Flagstaff, one that will let us fax in the information. We need some warrants. Ortega, get to work on the affidavits. One for each of them. They need to be perfect."

Ortega smiled and Annabelle clicked away on her

computer. I turned to go. "And what are you up to?" Annabelle asked.

"Loose ends," I said. "Now that Ken is hiding there is no reason not to talk to Brooke at the inn."

Annabelle's eyebrows shot up and she said, "Well, you enjoy that, darlin'."

THIRTY-THREE
TUESDAY JULY 3. THE CARTERVILLE INN

ANNIE SMITH WAS AT THE FRONT DESK WHEN I WALKED INTO the Carterville Inn. It's strange for me to walk in now. Since our last breakup, our final breakup, it's different. I have a lot of good memories in this historic building. I also have a lot of memories of our fights when we went from on again to off again.

There was a question on Annie's face as her blue eyes found me. Actually, there were a lot of questions and it looked like more than the ones I had left her with after our last conversation.

The room smelled of coffee, a carafe sitting on the long countertop that was a bar when this place was a saloon. And the Carterville Inn was not cheap, so the coffee was good. And eight ounces after five hours of sleep was no way to be in this world.

I tried to smile and the question on her face turned to

concern. She must have heard about my ambulance ride to Flagstaff last night. The whole town would have heard by now. I suppressed a groan.

"Do you mind?" I asked, nodding towards the carafe.

She shrugged but didn't say anything.

I walked over and pumped out a few ounces into a paper cup with the Carterville Inn logo printed on it. It's got the line of the mountains that rise behind us as part of the logo. Half the logos in town do.

I took a sip and sighed. It was good coffee. Drip coffee. Strong and bitter. Hot but didn't burn my tongue. Perfect.

When I looked back up, Annie had her arms crossed and her head cocked as she stared at me.

"I'm fine," I said.

"Looks it," she answered.

I stared at her blinking. I didn't know what kind of reaction I expected, but this wasn't it.

"I need to talk to Brooke," I said.

"So do I," she said.

God this was awkward. "When is her next shift?" I asked.

"Now," Annie said.

"Can I speak with her, then?" I asked.

She shook her head. "She's not here."

"You're making this hard," I said.

"Good."

Annie was mad at me. But then again, she had been mad at me since we broke up and especially since Lila's funeral and I told her—quite unnecessarily—why we would never be getting back together again. But this was another level. She was likely angry about how little information I gave her about what was going on with Smitty and Brooke's involvement last time we talked.

"I need to talk to Brooke," I said. "Did she call in sick? Do you know where she is?"

"No and no," she said.

"Please, Annie," I said. "This is important."

She shrugged. "Everything you do is important. You are Henry Carter, after all. You carry the name of our little town. You are this town, and we are the humble citizens that bow at your feet."

I drank more coffee to cover the sting of that. There was some truth to it. I was a Carter. My job was important, but I was not royalty, nor did I wish to be.

I cleared my throat. "I need everything you have on Brooke," I said. "A copy of her job application, her W9, her contact information. And I need you to document anything odd she might have said or done while working here."

Annie stood there staring at me, her lips pursed into a thin line, her blue eyes unrelenting.

I had come here for a simple interview that probably wasn't necessary of someone who was only peripherally involved. But Brooke missing a shift without notification and Annie's behavior had made me think I needed more.

I will admit that the list of things I had just given Annie was likely more than I needed. And I fully accepted that we have a past and I made many mistakes in our relationship. But I was here doing my job and I expected a little cooperation.

Annie just stood behind the counter, her arms crossed.

"What is her last name?" I asked, realizing that I had no idea.

"Jennings," she said.

I blinked. Jennings. That name was familiar, but I couldn't remember why. My heart sped up and I felt more awake than I had all morning. "I need the basic paperwork. Now, Annie," I said. "Please."

She nodded and opened the door behind the counter that led to her office. She slammed it behind her.

THIRTY-FOUR

TUESDAY JULY 3. THE CARTERVILLE POLICE DEPARTMENT

"Jennings," I said as I walked back into the CPD, the paperwork Annie had given me in my hand. It had that grey haze to it, just like Smitty's threat letters, having been printed out on the same printer.

"What now?" Annabelle asked, swiveling around in her chair. Ortega looked up from her computer, her smooth brow furrowed.

"Bring up your database, Annabelle," I said. "Is the name Jennings in there?"

She didn't tap on her computer but just shook her head. "No, Chief. There ain't no Jennings in Carterville."

I nodded. "But it's familiar, right?"

Annabelle shrugged and Ortega shook her head.

"Jennings is the last name of one of Annie's employees," I said. "Brooke Jennings. The one Ken Fischer was bribing to use Annie's messed up printer. She missed a shift today and isn't answering her phone."

"Probably had too much fun last night and is sleepin' like a babe," Annabelle said.

I shook my head. "Annie said the girl has never been late."

"A college student never late for a job 45 minutes away from where she lives?" Annabelle asked.

"I was never late for my college jobs," Ortega said.

Annabelle snorted. "But you're special. As a whole, nineteen- and twenty-year-olds are not the most reliable set of folks you'll ever see." She turned to me. "What's goin' on, Chief?"

I shrugged. "The name. It's ringing a bell. What if Brooke Jennings is not just a pawn in this whole scheme? Or what if she knows something and someone is cleaning up loose ends?"

Annabelle snorted again. "I think the lack of caffeine has gone to your head, Chief. That bottle blonde baby girl ain't no criminal mastermind."

I nodded. "You are probably right. You two get back to the warrant and affidavits."

"What are you going to do?" Ortega asked.

I went to the file cabinets. "Try to figure out what's so familiar about that name."

———

OUR OFFICE HAS A LOT OF PAPER FILES, WE ALSO HAVE SOME OF the newer cases in the computer. Digitizing everything is a huge job, one that Annabelle hasn't had time for—and let's face it, the will. It's boring as hell. The meteor hit six years ago and the first year is just a blur. There was so much going on and a lot of that stuff isn't in the computer. So I started with the filing cabinets at J.

There's nothing wrong with my memory which means it's as flawed as every other human's memory. Jennings was a name I should remember but I couldn't. Well, clearly there was some kind of memory there, I just couldn't make the connection.

I flipped through the Js, every single folder. I was glad to see things were actually alphabetized, but there was no Jennings. I searched through I and K just to be sure, but nothing.

I went into my office and searched our digital files and found nothing there. Maybe Annabelle was right. Maybe it was caffeine deprivation. The few extra ounces I had at the inn still left me far behind my usual quota.

I got on google maps and looked at the address from Brooke's W9. It was in Flagstaff, of course, on South San Francisco Street north of the university. But something wasn't right. I knew that part of the street and it was full of businesses, not residences. I zoomed in and saw the address she gave was for the Sunshine Rescue Mission. A homeless shelter.

I switched over to google and found there are a shocking number of matches for "Brooke Jennings." Facebook had a slew of them too with multiple variations on spelling for the first name. A bunch of them looked college age and quite a few were blonde, but I didn't recognize any of them.

Not that I ever paid much attention to Brooke. She was just one of Annie's college girls. They worked the summer or over the holidays and then they were gone. Not someone I needed to know. The kind of person I had zero curiosity about. If you wanted to insert someone in Carterville and have me not notice, a girl like Brooke working at the inn—where there is the ever-present distraction of Annie Smith—was exactly the right thing to do.

Okay, that in itself doesn't mean a thing. My town is full of tourists, especially in the summer and around Christmas. That means there are a ton of temporary employees, and unless they are involved in a crime, I don't need to know about them. But Brooke's intersection with this case meant that I did. And the fact that she was the kind of person I would have zero curiosity about made it all the more suspicious.

She was right in the middle of this thing, and without Martin Lester's work, I would have no idea.

I wrote Brooke's cell phone number on a Post-it and walked out into the main room of the office and handed it to Annabelle.

"Find out where this cell phone is," I said. "And I need to know the billing address."

Annabelle's forehead wrinkled. "Brooke's, I take it," she said.

I nodded. "The address she gave Annie was a fake. Something's not right here."

"It might take a warrant," she said, a sour look on her face.

"Then today's a day for warrants," I said.

I nodded to Ortega. "How close are you with those affidavits?"

She shrugged. "Another hour."

I nodded. "Be ready to go when you are done. I want to head out to the Winslow Ranch. At least find out if they are there."

Annabelle's eyes were narrowed as she studied me.

"You got something to say, Annabelle?" I asked.

She smiled, but it was a tense little thing. "In fact, I do," she said.

I nodded for her to continue.

She looked at Ortega and then back at me, asking if I wanted to have the conversation in private. I was impatient and nodded again for her to continue.

"I think baby-girl Brooke is a distraction," she said.

"Please elaborate," I said.

"As I said before, someone is just plain messin' with us. And I don't think twenty-year-old Brooke is capable. She's just another player just like Ken and Karen."

I took a deep breath and silently counted to ten. Not because I was angry, but because I trusted Annabelle and if she was hinting that I needed to slow down and think this through, then that's what I needed to do.

"If she is just a pawn," I said, "then whoever is behind this had to communicate with her and we need to know how."

Annabelle gave me a slight nod. Ortega was watching the conversation, her head snapping back and forth like she was watching tennis.

"And if she's just a pawn," I added, the picture finally coming into focus in my mind, "then she is in danger and we really need to find her."

THIRTY-FIVE
TUESDAY JULY 3. THE WINSLOW RANCH

Something wasn't right at the Winslow Ranch. I could tell as soon as the barn and the corral came into view. My breath caught and for a moment I thought my heart was going to seize up, that I was going to have another one of those coronary artery spasms.

Stress as well as caffeine is a major factor. And then I remembered my promise to my sister to see Doctor Lion today, and I hadn't even called.

I rolled down the window as the tires crunched against the gravel letting the air lick the sweat off my forehead that had appeared despite the air-conditioning in our old police SUV.

"Katie's gone," I said before the thought was fully formed. Karen adored that Appaloosa, and she was a curious animal, always trotting out to see who was coming. "And the other horse."

My stomach sank. How bad was this that Karen Winslow left her home with her horses and her husband to avoid this?

Where was she going to go that would protect them from the arrest warrants I would have to issue for both of them?

Karen Winslow would never leave Carterville.

I stopped the SUV on the driveway short of the house, the big red barn to our right, my eyes darting around.

"What is it, Boss?" Ortega asked.

"Something's not right," I said.

"Maybe they are out riding," Ortega said.

Perfectly logical except that they both knew what was coming and going out for a casual ride didn't seem right. I nodded and pulled out my cell phone and dialed Karen Winslow. The phone rang four times and went to voicemail, "Hello, you've reached Karen Winslow, mayor of Carterville, Arizona, the best little mountain town in the Southwest. Please leave a message and I'll get back to you just as soon as I can."

That "best little mountain town in the Southwest" was a slogan she had pitched to the town council last year that hadn't flown. Apparently she hadn't let go of it yet.

I dialed Ken Fischer's number and it went right to voicemail, a computerized voice just reciting the number and asking me to leave a message.

I sat there staring at the single-story log house nestled up against the piñon and juniper trees. The day was heating up and there was hardly a breeze, the trees barely moving.

The curtains to the house were drawn. There were no visible vehicles, although they could have been parked in the detached garage to the left of the house, also built of big pine logs. Nothing moved, the scent of the horse corral wafting in my window.

I watched and waited. After a few minutes, Ortega shifted

in her seat so she was facing more towards me. "What are we waiting for, Boss?" she asked.

I shrugged my shoulders. "It feels empty, doesn't it? No movement. No sound."

She nodded. "Yeah. But what are we waiting for?"

I looked at her and smiled. "I wish I knew. This whole case… something isn't right about it. I think Annabelle is correct. Someone is messing with us."

"Why?" she asked. "What do they have to gain?"

I shrugged again. "Control. Revenge. Why else would someone do something this elaborate and premeditated?"

"Control of what?" she asked. "Revenge for what?"

"That is the question, isn't it?" I said. "On the control side, you have Carterville and all its powers. Smitty's in particular. How much is that worth? On the revenge side you've got Smitty and all the people he's turned down or failed with that power of his."

She turned and stared forward, and we both watched for a few more minutes. I then put the SUV in gear and rolled up to the house. I got my phone and dialed Annabelle this time, putting her on speakerphone.

"Somethin' wrong with your radio?" she asked by way of greeting.

"No, just don't want the whole town knowing," I said. "Looks like Winslow and Fischer have fled and taken their horses. We're going to need to track their phones too."

"Got it," she said. Annabelle tended to be less colorful when you weren't in person.

"We're going to search the property," I said. "We'll check in in thirty."

"Be careful," she said.

———

MY BOOTS ON THE GRAVEL DRIVEWAY OF THE WINSLOW RANCH seemed loud in the strange silence. The sun wasn't high yet, but it was hot, with that intensity you get at higher elevations, especially on cloudless days like today.

The feeling that something wasn't right had deepened. This was a ranch, a small one, but a ranch nonetheless. There was always something going on. It was too still. Too quiet. Almost like we were on the other side of some kind of strange apocalypse and the place had been long abandoned.

Ortega was back and to the right and we were both looking, both listening.

The sound of my boots changed as I went from the gravel of the driveway to the wood of the covered porch, the crunch turning into a hollow thump.

Here, farther away from the barn, I could smell the dust and a whiff of the trees. I thought I caught a trace of something flowery, like Karen Winslow's perfume, but I could have been fooling myself.

Ortega hung back as I approached the door and knocked, careful not to stand right in front of it. The door was thick, solid wood, and the sound deep. I waited and knocked again.

I was mostly listening and watching, but in the back of my mind I was pondering if I had sufficient grounds to enter their home without those arrest warrants.

Was there evidence here that was likely to be destroyed? Was there someone in danger inside? Add on to that the complication that we were outside the city limits of Carterville and outside my jurisdiction. The last thing I would want to do was to have it declared an illegal search and evidence barred.

I knocked again. "Karen? Ken? Are you home?"

What if the person behind all of this had taken them and there was crucial evidence in there and their lives depended on it?

That's just a fantasy and not the way my world works. I did not have cause to enter their home. I knocked again and called, loudly this time. No response, only silence.

"Try the door," Ortega said.

I looked at her and she didn't meet my eyes. She was a "by the book" kind of cop, and while trying the door wouldn't be crossing a line, it would make it a lot harder not to cross the line.

I nodded and took the brass doorknob in my hand and twisted it. The door was unlocked. Still standing to the side of the door, I eased it open and called, "Ken Fischer. Karen Winslow. Anyone home? It's the Carterville Police Department, we have a few questions for you."

I know, overly formal, but I really wouldn't put it past Karen Winslow to be sitting inside watching all of this and trying to catch me doing something I shouldn't.

I peeked around the edge of the door and saw the big living room with its elegant furniture with rough wooden accents. The ceilings were high and vaulted and the décor was all horse oriented with a beautiful picture of Katie above the hearth.

That first glance didn't reveal anything disturbing so I stepped in front of the door and really looked. The center of the living room was an arrangement of three couches around a big, heavy coffee table that looked like it was made out of reclaimed wood, all dented and scuffed. The couches were made of pale wood looking like pine and the cushions had a southwestern pattern in pale red, white, and light turquoise reminiscent of a Navajo blanket.

On the couch most directly facing me was a white piece of paper. A steak knife had been thrust through the paper and into the couch. The edges of the paper had been ripped to make it look a little irregular and it had large letters on it, large enough for me to see, and the font made the letters look like they were beat up and moth eaten on the edges.

My breath caught. The same as all of Smitty's threatening letters.

Destroyer of Carteville
  can you save them
    in tyme

THIRTY-SIX

TUESDAY JULY 3. THE WINSLOW RANCH

Deputies from the Coconino County Sheriff's Office were on their way, but it would take time. Time Karen and Ken likely didn't have.

Or did they? There was most definitely a game afoot here and there seemed to be rules to this game. We were being strung along, fed just enough so that we followed the clues dutifully but never got anywhere.

Or was that even true? When I called Martin Lester back to town and he caught Ken Fisher in the act of bribing Brooke Jennings and mailing one of the threat letters to Smitty, maybe that forced them to speed up their plans. They couldn't predict that, could they?

My boots banged against the covered deck of the Winslow residence as I paced back and forth. Ortega was standing in the doorway looking at the note, her jaw agape.

Was that note meant for me? Was it indicating that I was

the destroyer of "Carteville" and not Smitty? And what was with the spelling of time, "tyme"?

And what about Brooke Jennings? She had given Annie a fake address which was suspicious, and her last name still felt hauntingly familiar, but she was apparently missing too.

Before all the pacing, I had also made a call to a detective friend of mine in the Flagstaff Police Department, and he was looking for Brooke for me.

The size of what was going on had just ballooned. First the threat letters that Ken Fischer sent guided by alleged mysterious messages popping up on his computer, the last threat setting up a confrontation between Smitty and me where one of us could have easily been hurt or killed.

Well, I was hurt, kind of, with that coronary artery spasm thing, but that couldn't have been part of the plan.

Now, the people we knew were involved in one way or another were all missing.

It was all too much for a small-town cop like me. I had done my time in Tucson, but there had been a reason I came back to Carterville. And the job had been a lot easier before the meteor hit and everyone got powers.

I pulled out my phone again and called Smitty.

"What?" he said, picking up on the second ring. It was annoying, but the last time Smitty and I talked to each other he thought I was there to kill him.

"Everything okay up there?" I asked.

"Why?" he asked. That last threat letter was a hell of a thing. He didn't trust me anymore.

"Just answer the question, Smitty," I said. "Has anything changed? Has anything happened?"

There was silence for a few breaths as I paced the length of the porch. "Clearly *something* has happened," he said. "Tell me."

"I don't have time for this," I said. "Yes, something has happened. No, I'm not going to tell you about it. At this point I am going to recommend that you leave town until we get this sorted out."

"Leave?" Smitty asked, his voice suddenly sounding younger, like a child's.

"Yes. Leave," I said. "For your personal safety. Steve can help you find a safe place. You don't even have to tell me where it is as long as it's a ways away from here."

Another pause. "Can we have this discussion in person?" he said, his words slow and tentative.

I wanted to shout something back at him and hang up, but I took a breath instead. Maybe he was worried that his phone was tapped, and given what Ken Fischer said happened to his computer, that could be true. He probably didn't trust me and maybe thought if he could see me he could tell whether I was lying or not.

"Fine," I said. "I have no idea when I'll be able to get up there. I still recommend you leave now. At least tell Steve about it and start planning."

"Okay," he said, his voice timid again.

I hung up and realized that Ortega wasn't on the porch anymore. We hadn't gone into the house yet. It seemed most prudent to wait until someone with jurisdiction got here.

"Boss," she called from inside the house. "You need to see this."

———

Ortega wasn't far into the house. She stood on the hardwood floor staring at the note.

"Get out of there," I said. "We need to wait for—"

"No," she said, her voice eerily calm. "You need to see this."

I looked around and the ranch was still strangely quiet. There was no sound of sirens coming closer, no telltale dust plume on the road that came out here. We had had the first brush of our monsoon season, but it was still quite dry.

I sighed and walked in and stood next to Ortega. She was staring at the note, the same note stuck to the couch with a knife. Up close I could see that it was a serrated knife with a black handle, the kind that lives in a butcher block in the kitchen.

"What?" I asked.

She pointed at the paper.

I looked but didn't see anything different. "Pretend your eyes are almost thirty years younger than mine and just tell me what you see."

She looked at me, her eyes wide and her cheeks briefly flushing red. I hadn't meant to shame the girl, but this was a difficult day already. I didn't need any puzzles.

"The paper," she said. "It's got that grey gunk on it from a leaking toner cartridge."

Shit.

I stepped forward until my older eyes could see it. It looked exactly the same as all the other threat letters that Smitty had received. Which meant it was probably printed at the Carterville Inn.

I turned around, grabbed Ortega's arm and guided her out of the house and started pacing again.

"Maybe Fischer printed it," Ortega said. "Not knowing

how it would be used."

"Maybe he's the one that put it there," I said, "and Karen and Ken are heading out of town laughing their asses off."

"Can we assume that?" she asked tentatively.

I shook my head. "We cannot. Annabelle has got an APB out on them by now. If they're in their truck towing a horse trailer, hopefully they'll be spotted soon."

"So they have either fled or have been kidnapped?" she asked.

I stopped pacing and stared at Ortega and blinked.

"Find them in 'tyme,'" I said. "T. Y. M. E. Why that spelling?"

Ortega pulled her phone out and jabbed at it and swiped a few times. "Not much with that spelling, but it is an archaic way to spell time."

"Screw it," I said, taking my phone out and calling Annabelle.

"What now?" she said. "There's not more, is there?"

I sighed. "Maybe. Get ahold of the sheriff, tell them we are entering the premises. We have reason to believe their lives may be in danger and time is of the essence."

"Well, shit," Annabelle said. "You all be careful."

I hung up and walked past Ortega and into the house. I might be stepping on toes here, but there were too many unknowns. Karen and Ken could be in danger. Or they were the danger. In either case I needed more information.

I pulled a pair of blue nitrile gloves out of my pocket and put them on. I could hear Ortega behind me doing the same.

"Just look for now," I said. "We are going to go one room at a time. Walk where I walk. Don't touch anything you don't need to."

I looked back and she nodded, her eyes wide and her jaw set, and I realized just how fond of the young woman I had become. She was this strange combination of competent and shy, brave and curious. I was really coming to like how young she was, the different perspective she brought and the lack of cynicism. This was all new to her.

I also felt a stab in my gut. If something happened to her like happened to Lila Chang, I don't know if I could bear it.

"I'll take the lead," I said quietly. "You cover my back."

She nodded, those big brown eyes still wide.

I pulled my taser and eased into the hallway. You might be wondering why I didn't pull my gun. Well, it probably was justified, but in my mind, if I fire my taser when I don't need to, the consequences are much lower than firing a gun. Much lower. We were in a quiet house, and while I felt the need for something defensive, it didn't seem like it was time for deadly force.

The hallway was clear, so I went across it into the kitchen which was gleaming granite countertops and stainless-steel appliances. The kitchen was huge, almost as big as my living room, and had French doors opening onto an expansive deck.

I paused and took a deep breath through my nose. I didn't smell coffee or the lingering scent of bacon or toast, making it doubtful that breakfast was prepared here this morning.

The kitchen table was clean and the counters sparkled. I moved through and peered out the windows, Ortega close behind.

There was a big barbeque out there sitting on a flagstone patio as well as a fire pit and elegant wicker patio furniture. Every chair and cushion in its proper place.

The perfection of it all was starting to spook me. The

house looked like it was for sale and staged for prospective buyers to come through and view. It didn't look lived in.

But then again, I had been here on numerous occasions, and it never looked that lived in. It was just the day, I think.

"It's too clean," I said.

Ortega snorted. "You can say that again." The girl was a slob. She always left used cups and food wrappers in our one CPD vehicle after she had been using it for a while, and her desk was always a chaotic mess.

"No," I said. "If they were fleeing, how did they have time to stop and clean like this? And if they were kidnapped, how did the perp have time to wipe everything down?"

Now I was really spooked. Did the perp, if there was one, have cause to wipe everything down?

We went through the rest of the house. A master suite, a spare bedroom, Ken Fischer's office, and what looked like a formal library that I knew was Karen Winslow's office.

It was the same throughout. Every bed made. Every throw rug in place. Every sink clean. In the smaller rooms I even got a whiff of some kind of cleaning product and the rugs looked to be freshly vacuumed.

"Was their housekeeper just here?" Ortega asked when we had finished and were back on the porch.

My shoulders relaxed a little. Why hadn't I thought of that? Maybe because I was in a hospital well past midnight this morning and hadn't had much sleep or nearly enough coffee. "Yeah," I said. "That makes sense." I rubbed at my face wishing I wasn't so damn tired.

"What now?" she asked.

I nodded to the garage and the barn. "We keep searching."

THIRTY-SEVEN
TUESDAY JULY 3. THE CARTERVILLE INN

THERE WERE TOO MANY MISSING PEOPLE. TOO MANY LEADS TO follow. Ortega and I had searched every building on the Winslow Ranch. No people. No horses. Everything in its place.

One of their trucks was gone along with the horse trailer.

Annabelle had tracked down their housekeeper and confirmed the place had been cleaned early this morning. That the horses were already gone and no one was there. That the cleaning crew had found nothing unusual.

Annabelle had also called the Carterville Brewery and found out that Karen had been expected in this morning and hadn't shown. It was inconceivable that she would abandon her fledgling business on its opening week. Add that to the note and I was starting to fear for their lives.

The Coconino Sheriff's Office had taken over the scene, but it was pretty clear there was nothing else to be found.

It really looked like they had fled except for that note with the knife through it on their couch. That happened after the house cleaners came this morning. Before Ortega and I drove out here, which was about a two-hour window.

Was that note a diversion, a misdirect, trying to send me out chasing them? Were they really in danger?

I mean, they were in some danger, from me. Ken Fischer had to answer for sending me into that situation with Smitty. Karen Winslow had to answer for being an accessory to it. But why were they fleeing? What was that going to buy them?

The warrants were issued. The APBs sent out. They would be found. What exactly were they running from? What did they know that they were not telling me?

I left Ortega at the office and walked back up to the Carterville Inn. It was past noon and my stomach was growling and my energy was waning, but this was the one lead I could still follow.

Annie was behind the long counter that used to be a saloon bar, a sour look on her face when I walked in. The room was otherwise empty and she was dressed in her black and white inn uniform. "I haven't heard from Brooke and I don't know anything else," she said. "Please leave me alone, Henry."

"I wish I could, Annie," I said. "Something dangerous is going on here and Brooke is part of it. Maybe just a bit player, maybe more. I don't know. But I do know that this situation is escalating, that lives will be on the line if they aren't already. Maybe hers. I know I'm the last person you want to be interacting with, but I need your help."

She crossed her arms and pursed her lips. "What exactly do you need?"

I smiled, or tried, but I was too damn tired and hungry

and beat for it to be much. "That's the tough part," I said. "I don't exactly know. Whoever is behind this has us on a wild goose chase. I need to know more about Brooke. I need to see any personal effects she might have here. I need to know if there is any other evidence of what's been going on in your office."

Annie stiffened during that last sentence. "Are you ready to tell me what's been going on?"

What she was really asking was, "Are you ready to trust me?" And I couldn't. Because of our past. Because of my job. Because this was a delicate situation. And because I didn't really know what was going on.

"Honestly, Annie. I don't exactly know," I said, looking around and making sure we were still alone. Out on the sidewalk tourists walked by looking around and the sun was shining which seemed incongruous with my last twenty-four hours. "What I can tell you is that Brooke was accepting bribes to let someone use your printer. Threatening letters were printed out on it. So far the letters were used to maneuver me into a situation where I might have killed someone or been killed. Besides Brooke, I know one other individual directly involved in this. They are both missing right now."

Annie just stared at me blinking. I hadn't meant to tell her that much, but after all the good times with Annie it was just kind of reflex. The vague way I used to tell her what was going on with my work. The way I could ease some of the burden.

"Shit," she said.

I nodded. I had no better word to sum up the situation.

Her brow furrowed and she really looked at me, those blue eyes finally looking familiar again. "Are you okay, Henry? You're kind of pale."

I nodded and leaned against the bar, the old wood smooth against my hands. "It's been a day," I said.

"And let me guess," she said, "you haven't eaten."

I shrugged.

She shook her head and rolled her eyes, but it felt familiar and that felt good. She pointed to an antique armchair on the other side of the lobby. "Go. Sit. I'll get you something to eat and then we can talk about Brooke."

———

WHEN IN THE ANNALS OF HEROIC FICTION WAS THE HERO felled first by a caffeine overdose and then low blood sugar? And yeah, while I may be writing my stories down, capturing a little bit of the strange things that have happened in Carterville, I don't view this as heroic fiction. But would Jack Reacher stop for a snack? Or Jack Ryan? Or Jason Bourne? Or James Bond?

Wait. What is with all those "J" names. "Ja" names. It seems there has been a bit of a boring trend in the selection of the names of white male heroes. At least the ones that I have paid attention to.

My name is Henry and I'm nothing like those guys. Marshmallow abs. Receding hairline. Decidedly middle aged. Divorced and living with my sister.

I shook my wrist, still not used to the fitness tracker, and remembered I hadn't gone to see Doc Lion yet. Now Doctor

Jenny Lion is a good name for an action/adventure hero. And with all her tattoos and bungee jumping, she was much more the sort for this. But I was the chief of police. I had run for the office many times. And while my first name might be the bland Henry, my last name is Carter.

All of these rather silly thoughts whirled around my head while I sat in the antique armchair in the Carterville Inn. I was looking out the big windows that fronted the place, at the tourists and the traffic, but I wasn't really looking. I could smell the faint musty odor coming from the furniture and a slight whiff of distant coffee, but I wasn't paying attention to that either.

I was exhausted. I needed to go have a drink or two and sleep for a week.

The enigma of Ken Fisher and the threat letters he sent to Smitty were a distant buzz in the back of my head. And why he and Karen ran—or seemed to have run.

The mystery of Brooke Jennings wasn't anything I was thinking about either. If the young woman was just making a few bucks on the side, why didn't she come in today and why wasn't she answering her phone? Why had she given Annie a fake address and a silly one at that? She could have given the address of a house and yet she gave the address of a shelter. It was like she wanted to be found out.

And the threats themselves with all the bizarre spellings were out of focus and buzzing in the background too.

Carteville

Comming

Retrobution

Firewerks

Sufer

Sekret

Tyme

It was that moment in neutral where the mind could actually do its work.

Maybe James Bond and Jason Bourne were never forced to sit down and just breathe because of low blood sugar, but maybe they should add it to their repertoire.

Annie came busting back in with a paper plate with a sandwich on it, some chips, and a bottle of water. She handed it to me and sat in a similar chair across from me while I started eating and drinking.

The thoughts weren't clear enough to form words yet and the baser needs of my body were in control, so all I could do was eat and drink.

"Thank you," I got out between bites.

Annie sat there, leaning forward, staring at me.

"Brooke Jennings," I said when the words started coming back. "*Jennings.*"

The sandwich was ham and cheese, which I was finally back enough to myself to realize. It was thick with meat and several pieces of cheese with lettuce and mustard. Annie knew me and knew me well.

Annie shrugged. "Yeah? That's her name."

"Don't you remember?" I asked.

She narrowed her eyes and shook her head.

I nodded. It was understandable. "There were some tourists here the day the meteor hit."

"Yeah…" she said.

"Like Carl George," I said. "Took Carl years and a trip back here to figure out his power."

She slowly shook her head. "You're not really making any

sense, Henry."

"Jennings," I said. "Don't you remember? His name was… Jason, no… Joe. Joseph Jennings. He was an anthropologist staying here with his daughter. Exploring Anasazi ruins around the Peaks. I didn't remember her name, but she was about twelve and had brown hair and glasses. She wanted to be an anthropologist like her father. She was quite social despite her lisp. Well, maybe not a lisp, per se, but some kind of minor speech impediment. She had trouble with the second R in Carterville, the one after the T. She would say 'Carteville.' It was adorable."

Annie was nodding her head now. "I kind of remember," she said. "But didn't Joseph Jennings die? Some kind freak accident early on. Smitty tried to save him but couldn't." Her mouth opened and she gasped. "Is this why Smitty is hiding out in his house? Has some security guard up there? He's the one that's been receiving threats."

I didn't deny it and I didn't confirm it. Secrets are hard to keep in this town. "Brooke Jennings," I said again. "She has come back for revenge. And she has a power… she must. And she plans to use it to destroy Smitty, but only when he knows it's coming."

What I didn't add, as the memories flowed back, was that Brooke had come back to destroy me too. I was right there with Smitty when Joseph Jennings died. That explained the clues we had been following and all the bizarre details that led us right to Brooke.

Annie stared at me, her hand going to her mouth. "Joseph Jennings was burned, right?" she asked. "Badly. And tomorrow is the Fourth of July, right? Maybe…" she didn't finish the thought and that was fine by me.

"Will you help me, Annie?" I asked.

She nodded, and for a moment it felt like old times. Annie and I were always good together, when we put our minds to it and when we weren't fighting, that is.

THIRTY-EIGHT
TUESDAY JULY 3. THE CARTERVILLE INN

ANNIE AND I DIDN'T FIND MUCH. WE SEARCHED THE OFFICE and the little kitchen in the inn which served as a breakroom. She let me go through Brooke's work records and her resume and employment application. Both of which weren't much because of how young she was.

What stood out were a couple of things on her resume. And while Annie had given me a copy of it earlier, I had only glanced at. But now that we had placed the name, it told a different story. She had listed Joe Jennings on her work history and as a reference. It said that she worked as an archaeological assistant with him from 2010-2018. There was a phone number listed next to the reference.

I pointed it out to Annie. "Did you see this?"

We were in her cramped office, smaller than even mine, the air still and hot. She grabbed it. "I asked her about this," she said. "She told me she had worked with her father, but he had died earlier this year and she just couldn't bear to take his name off of her resume. I can't believe I didn't put it together."

I shrugged. "That first year after the meteor hit was so chaotic. So, you never called the number?"

She shook her head.

She was digging through files, and I just watched her for a moment. She was the focused and driven Annie that I had known for so long and loved for so long. We were past that, I truly knew that we were, but so much of my life had been intertwined with hers that I couldn't help feeling something. Longing. Regret. Sadness.

She stood up and sighed, putting her hands on her hips. "Her interview was perfect and I was in a hurry. I didn't check any references."

Brooke had left a blue sweat jacket in the kitchen, but it was just a sweat jacket. Nothing in the pockets, nothing unusual about it at all. It had a vaguely floral scent, the remnants of her perfume.

Annie was standing in front of her filing cabinets, her arms crossed and her eyes staring at nothing.

"That's it?" I asked.

She nodded slowly, her eyes still distant.

I knew that look. The wheels were turning. I gave her a moment and scanned the resume again. There wasn't anything else that stood out, except maybe the complete lack of spelling errors.

On those threat letters, she had misspelled "Carterville" as "Carteville" as a clue. It represented her unique adolescent speech patterns.

But what about "comming" and "sufer," one with an extra letter, another one missing one. And "tyme" the archaic spelling of "time." "Retrobution" also hinted at something old with "retro" instead of "retri."

And "firewerks." Shit. Annie had just mentioned the Fourth.

I sat down and flipped through my little notebook and found where I had copied that one down:

Destroyer be warned
  I AM equalizer
    firewerks will ensue

I sank into the chair in Annie's office, and I tapped on my phone and found that "werk" is an archaic spelling of "work." I tapped some more and found that "comming" was listed as an obsolete spelling of "coming."

"Sekret" was listed in an urban dictionary as information that was supposed to be secret but actually had little or no value.

Were all of these misspellings hiding a meaning?

I typed in "sufer" and found it is urban slang meaning "beyond super." A clear reference to power.

"Shit," I said.

"What is it?" Annie asked.

I shook my head. "I think you should cancel the fireworks tomorrow," I said. Annie and the inn only handled a part of it, and it wasn't really hers to cancel, but my mind was overwhelmed at the implications of it all.

"Henry, tell me what's going on," she said.

I looked up and saw genuine fear in those beautiful blue eyes of hers. "I think you're right about tomorrow. And I don't think it's just Smitty that will be targeted."

I got up and shoved my notepad in my pocket and looked around. It was an impulse I couldn't explain. I felt like I was missing something, that I hadn't done something important. That we were being watched.

I no longer had any doubt that Brooke Jennings was behind this. I had no idea how she managed it, but I knew it involved her power and that it was a formidable one.

"Henry," Annie said. "Please. I need more than that."

I looked at her. "Just trust me. Do what you can."

She nodded. "I'll call Karen."

Shit. Karen had fled or was abducted. "She's not answering her phone," I said.

"What?" she asked. "What's wrong with Karen?"

I kept looking around the cramped, chaotic office. Desk. Filing cabinets. The printer all of the threats were printed on. Bookshelf. An old picture of Annie's ancestors in front of the Carter Mine in the early 1900s. I had been here so many times, but it looked foreign.

The hair on the back of my neck raised and a cold sweat broke out all over my body. I shook my head. "I'm sorry. I can't say any more. Stop the fireworks. Get out of town if you can."

She fired more questions at me, but I turned and left.

THIRTY-NINE

TUESDAY JULY 3. THE CARTERVILLE CIRCLE AND SMITH RESIDENCE

I walked the Carterville Circle, barely aware of the tourists. I should have headed back to the station, but after being in Annie's cramped office and all we had figured out, I needed to move. I tend to think better on my feet, and I needed to think. Boy, did I need to think. And I needed to remember as many details about Joseph Jennings as I could.

Brooke Jennings clearly remembered what happened and had been stewing on it for much of her young life. And she had obviously been thinking about this for a long time. And planning. And scheming. She had been manipulating us and had been ahead of us every step of the way. But how? Even with Martin Lester doing his invisible man routine and catching Ken Fischer in the act and getting us on her trail, she was still ahead of us.

How? Did she somehow know that I would pull him in when it became clear the threats were printed at the inn? That doesn't seem possible. But this is Carterville. Anything is possible with powers.

Something was tickling at the edge of my tired brain when my radio squawked to life. "Chief, come in. This is Mary. I…"

The aged voice was that of Mary Reilly and she was clearly holding back tears. As an unofficial member of the CPD she had a radio at her house.

I grabbed the mic clipped to my shoulder and squeezed it. "Go ahead, Mary. What's going on?" I dispensed with normal radio protocol. Annabelle had tried to teach it to her several years ago, but it hadn't stuck.

"It's… it's William," she said between gasping breaths and tears. "He… he's having a heart attack. Smitty… he's not answering his phone. Help, Henry. Help."

I turned around and ran towards the station. "Coming, Mary. I'm coming."

———

I RAN BACK TO THE OFFICE WHICH IS WEST OF THE CIRCLE, JUST down Cedar, jumped in our old SUV and started it up. I flicked on the siren and did a quick U-turn and headed back to the Circle. I don't have to run the lights on our police vehicle very often in Carterville, but this time I did.

I saw Ortega running out of the station in my rearview, but there was no time. As soon as I rounded the Circle and headed up Main, I took one hand off the steering wheel and squeezed my radio mic. "Dispatch, this is Carter. We've got a 10-56 at the Reilly residence and Smitty is not responsive. Heading up to get him now. Call emergency services. Over and out."

Fir Street was three streets above Cedar. I roared up, the hill getting really steep after the Circle, turned right, and stopped in front of Smitty's place.

I ran to the door and knocked. "Smitty! Open up!"

For a moment I forgot that less than twenty-four hours ago Smitty and I were trying to kill each other—well, technically he was trying to kill me and I just tasered him, not that it did much good. I also forgot that I had set him up with very competent private security, so it took me a moment to get my brain in gear when the door opened and it wasn't Smitty.

Steve Lancaster looked fairly grizzled, in his mid-fifties, with several days' growth of grey beard and close-cropped grey hair, his finely wrinkled face looking like he had spent a lot of time in the sun. He used some kind of body spray, the sharp scent of it filling my nose. He was tall and clearly athletic. He also had a gun in his hand and a grim look of determination on his face.

"Winston is not available," he said.

"This is an emergency," I said. "There's no time, Steve. Get Smitty."

"I am sorry," he said. "My orders are explicit."

I didn't know Steve all that well. Our paths had crossed multiple times, usually when someone of note came to Carterville. Northern Arizona wasn't the type of place that needed security as good as Steve very often, but he was an avid rock climber and when he got burned out on the West Coast scene, Northern Arizona caught his eye because of all the rock-climbing opportunities.

"Fine," I said. "He asked me to come talk to him about my recommendation that he leave town. Can you please go get him?"

Steve's brown eyes narrowed, and he nodded and closed the door.

I looked at my "watch" and it showed me that I had 6k steps today. Great. Just what I needed, a reminder about another way I was failing today. I tapped on it impatiently until it showed me the time.

This was all stupid—seconds were ticking by and William didn't have the time. I took out my phone and texted Annabelle, "Smitty not cooperating. Get Doc and call out the fire dept to stabilize. See if you can bring William up here."

And here's the problem with a superpower like Smitty's. Since it makes the impossible possible, no one faces reality in the same way they used to. Mary wasn't, desperately trying to get her husband the kind of attention just not possible in any other remote town like this. I didn't know it, but I was guessing that she hadn't called 911 but had called Smitty instead and then gotten on the radio to get me.

Sure, we don't have any ambulances nearby, but we have a volunteer fire department, and they have emergency gear including a defibrillator. But a power like Smitty's can make you react differently.

"On it," Annabelle texted back.

I don't know how long it took—it seemed like an hour—but the door opened and Steve signaled me to enter. I was glad to see his gun was holstered on his hip and not in his hand anymore.

Smitty was sprawled on his couch, a sneer on his face as he looked me over. "Looks like you survived well enough," he said.

"It's William," I said, ignoring him. "He's having a heart attack. He needs you."

Smitty sniffed and shrugged his thin shoulders, a weak display with them barely rising. "I'm not going anywhere. Apparently, I'm in great danger. At least that's what the chief of police of this fine town kinda, sorta told me earlier today."

"Between Steve and I," I said, "we can keep you safe. William needs you." I paused and lowered my voice. "Mary needs you."

I didn't need to spell the threat out any more than that. You didn't want to get on the wrong side of Mary Reilly. If she went bad, the whole town could suffer.

Mary was another one of those with a superpower. She may be a tiny, old-fashioned, white-haired woman nearly eighty years old, but when she put her mind to it and told someone to do something, they did it.

Smitty blinked and sat up and chewed on his lip. He was weighing the nebulous threat that he didn't know nearly enough about against the wrath and known power of Mary Reilly.

"What do you think?" he said, nodding his narrow chin at Steve.

Steve shrugged. "I don't know enough about the threat to assess in a meaningful way. I have to defer to Henry on this one."

"You know," Smitty said, leaning back on the couch and looking at me. "There's a reason I don't want to leave town. I'm a hell of a lot harder to kill here. But going out there… now… nope. Not gonna happen. Not with you keeping us in the dark here and not having a clue what—or who—we are facing."

I thought for a second. Even if I was willing, there was no

chance of bringing Smitty up to speed quickly enough, and if I did he probably wouldn't leave anyway.

"Fine," I said, my teeth grinding. "We're bringing him to you. Be ready."

FORTY

TUESDAY JULY 3. REILLY RESIDENCE AND SMITH RESIDENCE

MARY HADN'T CALLED 911. WILLIAM WAS UNCONSCIOUS BY THE time I got there. Doctor Jenny Lion was doing CPR on him while Annabelle was kneeling working the bag valve mask while Ortega watched.

Mary and William lived in a vintage Airstream. They've got two empty lots off Aspen Street where the land is fairly flat and have a total of six beautifully restored Airstreams, the five extra rented out as vacation rentals.

It was crowded in there with the very short and very grey Mary standing there crying, the thin William Reilly laid out on the narrow floor as the short, strong Jenny Lion administered CPR.

I hadn't been in here that often. Mary mostly entertained outside when the weather was decent. Inside it felt claustrophobic to me with the curving walls and narrow space. I mean, I didn't live in a large house, but it was huge compared to this.

The space was neat and clean with frilly touches like lace curtains and lots of pink, but all of that was lost on me today. It was just a hot, claustrophobic space.

When I crowded in past Ortega, Mary's eyes found mine and her lips formed "Smitty," but no sound came out. She was crying and it shredded my heart to see her like that. It hurt even more to see William laid out. He had just turned eighty and was one of the kindest men you could ever meet. His career had been in real estate, but they had started their Airstream park about twenty years ago, a labor of love for the both of them.

"We have to move him," I said, my voice sounding too loud and echoing in the tiny metal space.

"Are you crazy?" Doc Lion asked without missing a beat, her shoulder-length brown hair bouncing with each compression. Annabelle was at his head squeezing the plastic bulb to get air in him.

"No," I said. "Smitty won't come, we have to take him there. Now."

Mary's eyes were hard and accusing and I couldn't blame her. If Smitty and I hadn't been in the middle of this mess, Smitty would have answered the call, he would have come, William would be okay.

I saw something change on Mary's face. She took a deep breath and threw her thin shoulder's back. She's a tiny woman, all of four-foot-four, but she was formidable even before the meteor hit. She was dressed in dark capri pants with a simple white blouse and a pink sweater despite the heat, further deepening the impression of her as a kind old grandmother.

"You heard him," she said, her voice suddenly strong.

"We're taking William to Smitty. Let's get him loaded in the chief's car. Now."

Normally something like this would be fairly chaotic as the emergency mixed with people's doubts. But not this time. Annabelle got up and stepped back and held Mary while Doc Lion went to William and picked up his shoulders while Ortega brushed past me and picked up his feet. I hustled out and opened the back of the old Ford SUV and pulled out all the extra gear and threw it on the ground.

I found something then that chilled my heart and made me sweat even more, but I had no time. It was a manila envelope, like the one Ken Fischer had put Smitty's threat letters into. It was unmarked, new, and sitting under a duffle bag. I wanted to open it, I needed to open it, but William was the priority here, the only priority. I folded it up and shoved it into my back pocket and then ran around and put the back seat down.

Doc Lion and Ortega loaded William and squeezed in with him, the doctor continuing compressions while Ortega squeezed air into his lungs. Mary got into the front passenger's seat. I got in, flipped on the lights, and drove.

Annabelle was left behind to deal with all the gear I had dumped.

On our way out, the Carterville fire engine passed us, its sirens warbling, but they were too late.

Looking back, I marvel at our efficiency and wonder how much power Mary put into her voice.

You might think if her husband was dying, she would have used the full force of her power, but that might have left us doing exactly what she had told us instead of using our minds.

I have no doubt that her power was involved, though. I've rarely seen people work that efficiently in an emergency. And I felt this pressure in my head, one that broke through my fatigue. It was like someone was gently squeezing my brain. It was strange and a bit uncomfortable, but it wasn't painful.

I knew it was Mary's power, that she was gently compelling me, but it was what I would have done anyway so it was more like a boost to my will and my focus.

I turned right on Main Street and almost immediately ended up behind a clueless tourist in a pickup truck. I honked and they finally got a clue, but parking was full and there was nowhere for them to go so they sped up and I stayed on their tail.

"I think he's gone," Doctor Lion said from the back, her breath loud and rhythmic as she continued compressions, the slower woosh of the ventilator bag quiet in comparison and hard to hear with all the other noise.

I glanced at Mary and her wrinkled face squeezed in pain. "Just keep at it, dear," she said. "Please."

I don't know if there was power behind that, but Doctor Lion kept going. Ortega kept squeezing the bag. And I kept driving.

The truck hit the Carterville Circle and got off on Cedar and I got us around and back on Main and sped up. I went as fast as was safe up the hill and it didn't take long until I turned right on Fir and got us down to Smitty's house.

I jumped out, opened the back of the SUV and ran to the door and knocked. "We're here!" I shouted.

Steve Lancaster opened the door, his lips pressed into a thin line as his eyes took in me and the crew behind me.

Doctor Lion and Ortega had William, and Mary was behind, crying hard now as she followed them.

In Smitty's house, the coffee table had been shoved to the side and space had been made for William. Smitty was there, but he had changed. He was wearing his flowing New Age garb, soft fabric in light earth tones.

It didn't hit me then, but later when I thought about this the fact that he had taken the time to change made me furious.

The girls hustled him in and Doctor Lion resumed chest compressions while Ortega worked the ventilator bag. Smitty slowly leaned down and put his hand on William's throat. Not like he was checking for a pulse, he just gently rested his hand there. With Ortega at his head and Doctor Lion doing compressions, maybe it was the only place available, maybe it was some secret healing spot, maybe it didn't matter where he touched him.

Smitty's eyes fluttered and closed, and he let out a long sigh.

Mary hadn't said anything. She didn't need to. Her power even when it wasn't exercised loomed large over everything.

I was just inside the living room watching it all. Hoping William would be okay and this all wouldn't go sideways. The pressure I had felt, like my brain was being squeezed, was gone and I was left exhausted from it all.

"Stop," Smitty said, his voice low and husky.

Jenny Lion let out an exhausted sigh and stopped the compressions and leaned back. Smitty moved in and put both hands on William's heart. His eyes squeezed shut and I saw sweat bead on his forehead while he got even paler.

A minute passed but it felt like so much more. In the end, Smitty gasped and slumped to the side, his eyes fluttering open and finding Mary. "I'm so sorry," he said. "He was gone when you got here and beyond my power."

FORTY-ONE

TUESDAY JULY 3. SMITH RESIDENCE AND REILLY RESIDENCE

I didn't know if all the drama from Smitty was for show, to make it look like he tried when there wasn't anything to do, to build some kind of plausible defense against Mary's wrath.

Given Mary and her power, it was understandable. And given Smitty and his past and personality, it was probable.

Mary stood there, tears silently streaming down her cheeks as she stared at her dead husband. They had been married for close to sixty years, their fifty-fifth anniversary had been a big deal a couple of summers ago. What must it be like for her to face losing someone she had been with, and loved, for so very long?

I think we all expected something, all of us staring at Mary. William's lifeless body lay on Smitty's floor. Smitty just to the side, slumped and looking exhausted. Doctor Lion to the other side of William panting and sweating from her efforts. Ortega at William's head, her hand still on the big plastic bulb, her brown eyes wide as she looked from person to person.

I was just inside the living room and Steve Lancaster was to my right.

I felt a weight bearing down on me. If Mary was going to go bad, now was the moment. If she was smart about it, she would deal with Steve and me first.

I glanced at him at the same time he glanced at me. He gave me a small nod. Smitty must have filled him in on Mary's power and what we could be facing. That nod said a lot. It said, if you can't get her, I will.

My heart started thumping in my chest, the sound of blood whooshing in my ears. If Mary went bad, if she went bad now, could I shoot her? At her age even a taser could be life threatening, but her power was such that a taser wouldn't be wise. Could I shoot Mary Reilly, who looked like the quintessential kind old lady?

I don't know how long it lasted, all of us caught in that moment waiting for Mary to do something.

And then it hit me. Mary was a bomb and we were all expecting her to go off. All afraid to move lest we trigger her explosion.

And then Mary took a deep breath and spoke. "Thank you, everyone," she said, her hazel eyes roaming the room but not really connecting with anyone. "I know you tried your best. Doctor Lion, do you mind staying with the body? I will contact the funeral home."

Jenny Lion shook her head, her eyes wide. "Of course," she said.

Mary then looked up and her eyes met mine. "Henry, please take me home."

———

"WILLIAM ONCE TOLD ME HE HOPED IT WOULD BE QUICK," MARY Reilly said as I drove slowly through the streets of Carterville. No sirens this time, and I went slower than I normally would, still afraid I might jostle the bomb that was Mary Reilly and set her off.

"Did he?" I asked, not knowing what else to say.

She chuckled—it was quiet and dry like the sound of fall leaves in the wind. "The little shit also said he hoped he went first. That he couldn't bear being in this world without me."

"I'm so sorry, Mary," I said.

She laid her hand on my shoulder and it felt so light, like a bird had landed there. "Death is just part of the deal, Chief," she said. "I hope it's quick for me too."

Mary saying that had a lot of heft to it. She had Alzheimer's. William and she had been traveling a lot when she was diagnosed. When they came back to Carterville, it got better. Something about the town, or maybe her power, counteracted the disease. I could see how anyone facing that kind of death would want a quick one.

I didn't know if this was shock and Mary's anger would come later, or if this was how graceful it's possible to be in old age.

"This must be so hard," I said. It seemed all I could utter was platitudes.

"It is," she said with a hollow sigh. "And it will be for a very long time. But William and I... we talked about this a lot. We made plans. He handled the finances but started teaching it all to me a few years ago. Death is inevitable, Henry. We planned for it. And that doesn't make it easy, but it makes it so I don't have to rush around wondering what to do."

When she went silent, the sound of the wheels on asphalt seemed loud. She stared out the window the rest of the way and all I had to offer were hollow platitudes and my own blossoming guilt, so I didn't say anything.

But I thought it.

The threat letter that I delivered, that had me tasering Smitty while he tried to shoot me, it was built on the foundation of our long mutual distrust. What if I hadn't delivered it or just delayed giving it to Smitty until the morning?

Or if I hadn't called to tell him to leave town after seeing the note attached to Karen Winslow's couch with a knife.

Or maybe if I hadn't recommended Steve Lancaster, Smitty would have come with me and he would have gotten to William in time.

I don't really remember driving the rest of the way, but then we were parked in front of Mary and William's Airstream… well, just Mary's now.

Mary put her hand on my arm, her touch again so very light, and said, "You did everything you could, Henry. I know you did. Heavy is the head that wears the crown."

I swallowed hard and nodded and then dared to look at her. She was crying and looked so small, like a child. "Is there anything I can do to help you, Mary?" I asked.

She shook her head. "Not right now. I… I have calls to make. Family. The funeral home in Flagstaff. We prepared, but… you can never really be prepared for this."

I nodded dumbly. I wasn't nodding because I understood what she was going through. I couldn't even imagine how the two of them had the courage to sit down and have the difficult conversations about their mortality and actually plan for death. What I did know is that while you could plan for the things that had to be done, there was no planning for the emotional devastation.

She got out and so did I, the two of us standing in front of her Airstream while she eyed it suspiciously. When she went in there, I knew she would be imagining William on the floor having his heart attack. That it would be a very long time before she could see anything else.

And then she was in my arms sobbing hard and I held her.

I hate to say it, but I was relieved. She was having the kind of reaction I would expect. The pain was finding some release.

I don't know how long it lasted, but I held her until she pushed away, sniffing and wiping her nose. I pulled a handkerchief out of my pocket and gave it to her. She blew her nose noisily.

"Do you want me to stay with you, Mary?" I asked.

She shook her head. "No need. I have a niece in Cottonwood, I expect she'll come up and stay with me."

I stood there and nodded. Again. I just didn't have any words.

"But you could come around a little more now," she said, her tear-streaked face looking so sad my knees went weak.

"Yes. Of course," I said. "I will come by. And call whenever you like."

She took a deep breath, squared her thin shoulders, and walked into her empty home.

FORTY-TWO

TUESDAY JULY 3. CARTERVILLE POLICE DEPARTMENT

THE MOMENT MARY ENTERED THE AIRSTREAM thoughts of Brooke Jennings and all that we had been dealing with came tumbling back and I became very aware of the manilla envelope folded up and stuffed into my back pocket.

This wasn't the kind of day that had time for what just happened. Carterville being such a small town, this would have a big effect on us all. Everyone knew William Reilly and he was well liked, although Mary's power had left them more isolated since the meteor hit.

But we are a small town and we have to always make time for each other.

I felt frozen there. Mary's need was immense. Even though she hadn't asked me to stay, on most any other day I would anyway. No one should be alone in a moment like this.

But there was a threat to deal with. A threat to Smitty and to me. A threat to Karen and Ken. A threat to Carterville.

I shook my head, trying to gather my thoughts. I took a

deep breath and forced myself to turn away from Mary and her needs.

Yes, I felt guilty about what happened today and that was part of what made it hard to move. And while the difficulties Smitty and I were having were a part of what delayed Smitty helping William, it was Brooke and her campaign for revenge that had created these very strange circumstances.

It wasn't all on me.

I got in the SUV and fired it up and drove back to the station and parked outside. I pulled the manilla envelope out of my pocket and unfolded it. I looked it over carefully. It was unmarked and not sealed, the envelope just clasped. It was thin and light, like maybe it was empty, but I shook it and felt something sliding in there. A single piece of paper.

My heart started thumping and I looked around. It was a normal afternoon in Carterville right before the big summer holiday. Meaning it was busy with plenty of traffic and tourists walking Main Street behind me.

I couldn't see anyone watching me, but I couldn't shake the feeling. Brooke had been ahead of us every step of the way and my brain was starting to come around to how. As I unclasped the envelope, I was sure what it was.

I don't know if you have these kinds of moments, but I was so sure this was another threat letter and at the same time I was sure that I was being silly and it was just nothing. I was sure and not sure at the same time.

I inched the sheet out and my heart thumped up to a faster pace. The paper had that grungy grey haze all the threat letters had. It had been printed in Annie's office at the Carterville Inn. As it peaked out I could see the same moth-eaten font had been used and my hands were shaking when I pulled it out revealing the message:

Destroyer of Carteville
  ur too late for him
    too late for all

Sweat beaded on my forehead because the words weren't the most shocking thing about what I was holding. I had folded it hastily and poorly, but in each crease of the paper was a shakily drawn line in pencil as if someone knew exactly how this piece of paper would be folded. It wasn't exact, but it was close enough, the imperfection making it clear the pencil marks had nothing to do with the folding process. I couldn't rationalize it away as anything but what it was.

My breath caught and I knew what Brooke's power was—or at least what kind of power—and I had no idea how to stop her.

"SHIT. SHIT. SHIT," ANNABELLE INTONED AS SHE PACED THE scarred linoleum floor under the harsh fluorescence of the Carterville Police Department. I had shown her and Ortega the latest threat letter, explained it had been in the department SUV under a bunch of gear, told them how I hastily folded it up and showed them the pencil lines that almost perfectly predicted where the creases would be.

Ortega sat at her desk, her eyes wide and looking something like a child. I felt bad for her. She was still new to Carterville and hadn't had the depth of experience with powers that Annabelle and I had had. And she didn't have a power. She sat stiffly in her chair, her arms crossed as if she were trying to hug herself.

Annabelle kept pacing and saying "shit." Which was strange for her. She is a fluent and expressive curser and the fact that she could only come up with one word seemed to indicate that she was really losing it.

I stood there watching them, the threat letter still in my hand which had finally stopped shaking. But I felt like I was shaking inside now. This was too much. I didn't want this job. I didn't want this name. I wanted to leave. Right now, and never come back.

My heart galloped along in my chest, and I worried about having another one of those coronary artery spasms. Or maybe even a real heart attack. And part of me thought that wouldn't be bad. Maybe I could make a quick exit like William just had and get the hell out of this mess.

The air in the room was still and hot and the smell of fresh coffee didn't even make me want to drink some.

I wasn't up for this. I didn't know what to do. I had no idea how to stop someone that could predict almost exactly how I would fold an envelope and stuff it into my pocket. If Brooke could predict that, was there anything she couldn't predict?

She had clearly predicted that I would bring Martin Lester in after realizing the threat letters were printed at the Carterville Inn. She had known that would lead us to Ken Fischer and then back to her where she would disappear just in time. She had Ken Fischer mail the threat letter that almost had Smitty and I killing each other.

"How the hell do we fight a power like that?" I asked. The

words surprised me. I was thinking them and hadn't meant to say them.

"We don't," Annabelle said, her clicking heels stopping briefly as she stared at me. "We don't, Henry. We get the hell out and we get out now."

I nodded and did my best to smile. "I support that, Annabelle. If you feel the need to leave you have my blessing." I turned to Ortega. "And you too, Isabella. If you want to leave, I won't think any less of you."

"You're not leaving, Boss," Ortega said. It wasn't a question.

I swallowed hard and shook my head. "I can't," I said.

Now, I don't think this was some great act of bravery on my part. It was part ego—I was a Carter and Carterville was my town—part habit, and a big part of the job itself.

If we allow it, we grow into our jobs and the responsibility we take on. I know I have. I was the chief of police of Carterville, Arizona. I had to stay and fight even if it was hopeless. Especially if it was hopeless.

"If you're not leaving, I'm not leaving," Ortega said. "I'm with you, one hundred percent." She took a deep breath and rolled her shoulders and stood up. She's not tall but she's strong, and in that moment it showed. I felt a level of affection for the young woman that can only be described as love. She was starting to feel like the daughter I never had.

"Nice of you to offer, Chief," Annabelle said as she paced. "But I ain't goin' nowhere. Brooke could have used her powers to save William's life but instead she allowed him to die. No way I'm letting her have her way without a fight."

I smiled. "Good. Thank you both. But Brooke must already know this too. How the hell do we stop her?"

My question was met by the silent stare of Ortega and the click of Annabelle's heels on the linoleum while she started intoning "Shit!" again and again.

For a moment there, I considered leaving. I really did. We were all up for the fight, but if you don't even know how to begin fighting, does it make any sense to stay?

The answer was a clear "no." It makes no sense to stay, but I was going to stay anyway. We had a few things on our side.

First, whatever Brooke had planned was going to happen tomorrow on the Fourth of July so there was a little time. I told myself we could always leave in the morning if we didn't come up with anything.

Second, we knew Carterville much better than Brooke. Sure, she had a power, a power that let her see what was going to happen, but there are downsides to all powers. And my suspicion in that moment was that while she could see the future, she didn't necessarily understand the nuances of how the future came to be, or why a person did what they did.

Third, all the Carterville powers have limitations, and the big powers come at a cost. She couldn't be omnipotent, could she?

Fourth, Carterville powers only work in and around Carterville, and that meant...

"Brooke is close," I said aloud.

Annabelle stopped pacing and Ortega stared at me.

"She has to be," I continued. "For her power to work, she is close."

Ortega nodded, her brow furrowing. "But won't she know we are coming?"

I shrugged my shoulders. "We know she has some kind of

psychic power, but we don't know the extent of it. She can't possibly see everything that is going to happen."

"Carl," Annabelle said, her face lighting up. "Carl George. You saw him just yesterday, didn't ya?"

I nodded and pulled out the notebook from my back pocket and flipped back a few pages. "He told me it was a woman that was threatening Smitty. He also said, 'One with great power will die. One with a kindred power will leave.'"

"William didn't have a great power," Annabelle said. "He could make people laugh." Ortega was staring at her, so she continued. "He could tell you the worst joke in the world—which he was quite fond of doing—and you would laugh your ass off like it was the funniest thing you had ever heard." Annabelle paused and shook her head. "I'm gonna miss that old guy, but that couldn't be who Carl was talking about."

I looked at my notes. "He also said that the change he spoke of was going to take time so it might not have been this death that he saw."

"Shit," Annabelle said, but this time there wasn't much energy to it.

"He also told me, 'no knowing what will happen, only knowing what *might* happen,'" I said.

"Do you think that's true for Brooke?" Ortega asked.

I nodded, although I wasn't very confident of it.

"Can this Carl guy help?" Ortega asked. "I mean, he has a similar power. Maybe he can give us the edge we need."

I nodded again, feeling a trickle of hope start to combat the dread. "That's a great idea," I said.

"Except Carl's not been good this summer," Annabelle said. "Getting confused almost as soon as he gets here. Wandering around like when you found him yesterday."

I sighed, the hope retreating. "Any other major psychic or clairvoyant powers in that database of yours?" I asked Annabelle.

Her heels clicked as she walked across the floor and sat at her desk, her long-nailed fingers stabbing at the keyboard. "Steve Thompson has been banned from buying lotto tickets, but all he ever won was small prizes and no one will play poker with him anymore. Never heard of nothin' else." She tapped some more. "Lisa Cummings knows the weather with eerie accuracy, but I don't think she's actually psychic. And Trent Bashir has people from all over bringing their pets so people can talk to them, but I think that's the extent of what he can do."

I started pacing, letting the movement help my mind loosen up. Carl was a major psychic, a clairvoyant, but his powers seemed to have faded or gotten more complicated. I didn't want to drag him to Carterville if he wasn't going to be able to help, but we needed help. Desperately.

Before this summer, he would get confused, just like when I found him, but it would take days, sometimes a week. His power wasn't like a crystal ball or anything, he couldn't just tell you anything you wanted to know, but the things he saw happened. Not always exactly as he described, but close enough that we took him seriously… or we did.

"What happened to Carl?" I asked, more to myself as I continued to pace. The office wasn't big enough for it to be very satisfying, just the one room with my office and a bathroom on one side and the two cells on the other, the three desks, filing cabinets, and whiteboards dominating the space.

"Maybe he reached his limit," Annabelle said. "Maybe he used his power too much and burned it out."

I stopped and stared at Annabelle. She had saved my life during the Lila Chang case by overusing her power. She could levitate small objects, but she did way more than that to save my life. She took her minor power and made it a major one for just a few moments and had paid the price.

"I'm sorry, Annabelle," I said.

She waved her hand at me and shook her head. "I'd do it again, Chief. Besides…" She got a mischievous look on her face and grabbed a pen off her desk and placed it on her palm. Her eyes went unfocused and her face relaxed and the pen wiggled on her hand. It didn't really float, but it was way more than she had been able to do.

"That's great!" I said.

She smiled and nodded. "I knew it would come back. You been fretting over it for nothin'."

Ortega was staring at our interaction, a slack look on her face, her brown eyes wide and unfocused. A few long, black hairs had escaped her braid and rested on her shoulders. She was so still that for a moment I thought something was wrong with her.

"Brooke started working here this summer," she began slowly, her voice quiet. "And Carl George's power changed this summer. And they have similar powers… they both see the future."

I stood there staring at her, afraid to breathe. The idea was simple enough, but I didn't want to say it. There's so much about the Carterville powers that we don't understand.

"Do ya think…" Annabelle said, breaking the silence.

I nodded my head, still not wanting to talk. I stared at Ortega—it was her thought and I wanted her to finish it.

"Think about it," the young woman said. "If your power is

seeing the future then you can change the future. But if someone else with that same power is there seeing the future, maybe changing the future, then… wouldn't that be like standing between two mirrors? Wouldn't that mess with you?"

"That sure as hell explains Carl," Annabelle said. "He gets overwhelmed almost immediately."

"And that explains Brooke," I said, and they both stared at me. "I noticed it when I went in to question Annie on Sunday. Brooke was pale and it looked like she had a headache. That was when Carl was here."

Our theory was that Brooke was still here and the one other power that could help us wasn't functional when she was here, but he might make her less functional and that might—

"We need Carl," Annabelle said.

"It's all we got," I said.

"Will he help us?" Ortega asked.

FORTY-THREE

TUESDAY JULY 3. JUST OUTSIDE THE ZONE OF INFLUENCE

I could feel it. We were just outside the zone of influence of Carterville powers. The line was a sharp one. On one side of the line your powers worked normally and on the other they aren't there at all.

That limitation is what makes Carterville Carterville these days. Our powers are limited to a geographical region which is a circle that extends about five miles from the center of town.

It's hard to describe, but have you ever been in your house when the power goes off? When the fridge and the lights stop humming, when quiet takes on a whole new meaning. It's kind of like that. Like someone shut the power off.

Which, I guess, is literally what happens.

I was sitting in the department SUV with Carl George next to me in the passenger seat, the same position we both had sat in just a couple of days ago when I drove him outside the zone of influence.

It had taken some hours to track him down and convince him to come meet me. The sun was low on the horizon and the Fourth of July would be here soon and he was our only hope.

I had spent the last ten minutes filling him in and his jaw hung open and his brown eyes refused to meet mine. I can't say that I blamed him. He was a kind, gentle man and I had just told him he was our only hope in a fight we had no idea how to win.

We were parked on the shoulder, a wider section of it with his red Prius parked in front of us. The engine was off, and the windows were rolled down, the warm air faintly perfumed with the sharp scent of junipers.

"I rremember zis Joseph Jennings," he said slowly, staring out the window. "Very serious. Very studious. Wire-rrimmed glasses. Tall. Girl always in tow with glasses. Brown hair had just been cut short, just under her ears. She kept touching ze ends like she not sure about it. Zey at ze diner for breakfast every day like me."

I nodded. My memories, now that I had accessed them, agreed with his.

"Zey staying at ze inn too," he said. "I hear ze girl laughing sometimes. Happy girl. So bright. So curious."

I didn't rush him. It was a lot to take in and it made sense that he needed time. Not that we had any to spare. But spooking Carl would be very bad for all of us.

"Ze ground shook zat night," he said. "Night of meteor. Not a lot. Just enough to wake me." He licked his lips and looked at me. "I left ze next day, zey did not?"

I shook my head. "No. He stayed another month, until…"

"What happen?" he asked.

"No one really knows," I said.

"But you know something," he said gently.

"Yeah," I said. "It was bad. We found him badly burned up at the overlook. Barely alive. Brooke was with him." I sighed. That first six months after the meteor hit were so hard. Powers kept coming into play and we didn't understand what was happening, but we were starting to.

"We got him to Smitty," I continued, "but it was too late. He was beyond saving."

"And Brooke?" he asked.

"Inconsolable," I said. "Her mother had died a few years earlier and she watched her father die. I tried questioning her but got nowhere. A social worker from Flagstaff came and got her. And…" I stopped with a shrug.

It was one strange, unresolved thing that happened in that first year after the meteor hit. Which was why I had trouble placing the Jennings name. A lot of what happened back then is still a mystery.

"Zat adorable girl back for rrevenge?" he asked.

I nodded. "Yes. She seems to blame Smitty and me. And I suspect her revenge will extend well beyond the two of us. I fear for the town."

He turned and stared out the windshield at the two-lane blacktop and the juniper and piñon trees. Powers can be a burden and in ways you never expect.

Let me rephrase that. "Power" can be a burden and in ways you never expect. Not just meteor-granted metaphysical powers but the power of position or role. Power brings with it responsibility. And while we needed Carl, the boundaries of that responsibility are for each of us to decide.

"And she is why zis summer has been so… strange?" he asked, still staring forward.

"The coincidence is strong," I said. "But there is no way to be sure."

"Could she be here last winter?" he asked.

I shrugged. "I guess so."

"One of ze times I came last winter and… yes, and few times in ze fall, it like now."

"She could have been scouting," I said. "Planning. It makes sense."

"And tell me now, how you keep me safe?" he asked.

I swallowed. How could I keep anyone safe from a clairvoyant like Brooke Jennings who had demonstrated such remarkable abilities?

"You will be locked in one of my cells," I said. "Officer Ortega will be with you the whole time. We're not looking for you to do anything but hoping your power weakens her enough so…" I trailed off. Hope is a tough thing and, I have found, not always that helpful. The flip side of hope is despair, and hope can twist around to despair on you in an instant.

"What will you do, Henry?" he asked.

"We're going to find her," I said. "Find Ken Fischer and Karen Winslow. We are going to stop her."

"How?" he asked.

I smiled and shrugged my shoulders again.

"Maybe I do more," he said, still not looking at me. I stayed quiet and let him speak. "Now zat I know, maybe I see more clearly. Saw woman threatening Smitty and saw conflict you and he had even with her here."

"If you could, Carl… that would be so helpful," I said. "I know it is a lot to ask."

He shrugged and glanced at me, a fleeting smile on his face. "I am here to study zis phenomenon. What kind of scientist would I be if turn back on chance to understand better? What kind of man would I be if I turn my back now?"

PART 4
FUTURES: JULY 4

FORTY-FOUR

WEDNESDAY JULY 4. CARTERVILLE OVERLOOK

I was short on sleep but not short on caffeine as the sun rose on the Fourth of July. The air was crisp up at the Carterville Overlook, the sun kissing the desert with its golden light, the cinder cones in the volcanic field to the east of us throwing long shadows across the dry land.

Wendy and I fought about coffee this morning. I hadn't made time yesterday to see Doctor Lion—it's not like there was any time—and I needed to be sharp today. She didn't want me doing anything to compromise my health and I didn't think today was the day to try to get by on less coffee. Besides, I didn't think the risk to my health posed by a decent allotment of coffee was much compared to what we were facing.

She pointed out that I was addicted to coffee and my own judgment could not be trusted where it was concerned. It escalated from there, but at least I was awake. And after only a few hours of sleep, that was saying something.

Carl George had already made a difference. His courage and his willingness to help made me remember how half the town came together last Christmas to save my life during the Lila Chang case.

Before, I said one of our advantages against Brooke Jennings was this was our town. We knew the people and their powers. So after Carl had been safely locked up, Annabelle, Ortega, and I got busy making calls. Recruiting others into this fight.

"Good morning, all," I said to those gathered for this fight, taking a deep breath of the cool air and tipping my cowboy hat towards them. It was in the low fifties, but the forecast promised this was going to be a hot one. "Thank you for coming. I apologize for the early hour."

We didn't call out the whole town. We just targeted a few individuals with powers that could help.

"I know we talked to you all on the phone last night," I said. "Filled you in on what we are facing, but I wanted to take a moment and see if you have any questions. Make sure you want to do this."

Annabelle Unger was there, not because of her power—which I was so relieved was coming back—but because I needed her help to coordinate something this complicated.

Patty Walsh stood next to Annabelle, her curly red hair barely contained in a ponytail. We were hoping her powers of empathy would help us find Brooke, or at least figure out what she wanted.

Lisa Paulson stood next to Patty, her short blonde hair waving in the breeze, her soft green eyes serious. Her power was a long shot and not very well explored, but since the meteor hit, she was incapable of losing things and could often find things others lost. Which was good, because her husband Frank was always losing things. We were hoping she could help us find the lost Karen Winslow and Ken Fischer.

Harold Marin, short and seventy years old with a grey ponytail, stood off to the side, his brow furrowed. He was Carterville's very own hippy lawyer and his power—also not very well tested—was a kind of force field. Don't think super-hero movie, nothing that grand, but if he got scared, nothing could touch him. We were hoping to not need it, but it could be a very useful power.

Doctor Jenny Lion was there, not because of a power but because she found out and was a doctor and had insisted. She was also a tattoo-covered rock climber and bungee jumper and loved adventure. Not that I would call this an adventure, but it was sure to be interesting.

There were a few notable absences, ones that made me nervous. Officer Ortega was at the station guarding Carl George. We had considered getting a sheriff's deputy in, but with what Brooke could do we needed to be sure he was well cared for.

Smitty was locked in his house with Steve Lancaster. He certainly might be useful, but seeing that he was the main target and he was Smitty, it wasn't surprising he had locked himself away.

And Mary Reilly was missing. Her power could be invaluable if we found Brooke, but with William's death—which was just yesterday, if you can believe that—she wasn't up for it. Actually, I wouldn't have asked, but Annabelle insisted on going down to her Airstream when Mary wouldn't answer the phone. Annabelle didn't say much besides it hadn't gone well.

It was a small group and nervous, everyone standing with hands in pockets with their feet shifting. Some looking at me, some looking out at the early morning view of the desert. No one spoke.

"Patty?" I said. "I know this is not how your power usually works, but do you think you can tune into Brooke? Or Karen and Ken?"

She gave me a thin-lipped smile and shrugged her shoulders. She was dressed in jeans and a blue sweater that hugged her generous curves. It was nice to see her out of her diner outfit. "I'll do my best, Chief," she said. "But this is new territory for me."

"For you too, Lisa," I said.

She smiled nervously, her arms crossed like it was a lot colder than it was. "I'll just pretend I lost Ken. I don't think I have a chance in hell of my power helping me find Karen."

There was some nervous laughter, and I was grateful for it.

"Harold?" I asked.

The older man looked away from the view and at me. "I don't like this, man," he said. "I don't like this one bit."

"This is strictly a volunteer operation," I said. "No one will think less of you if you bow out."

He snorted. "Felicia will."

There were a few more chuckles. Felicia Marin was his wife, and while she was a lovely woman, she was also a lawyer and fierce when she made up her mind.

"And I don't need to check in with you, do I, Doc?" I asked.

Jenny just shook her head. She had one of those leather doctor's bags in her hand and a grim look of determination on her face.

"Okay," I said. "Lisa and Patty are going to take the lead. Clint Ryan has been kind enough to loan us his van. We will all be staying together. We're going to drive every street and see if they sense anything."

It was a long shot, and with the looks I was getting I wasn't the only one that knew it. But we all knew this town and we knew it well. With only 290 permanent residents we all knew every street and every person. Even if powers didn't come into play, I was hoping with this many eyes we would find something.

FORTY-FIVE
WEDNESDAY JULY 4. CARTERVILLE

Carterville is a small town with just one street running roughly north/south and six running roughly east/west. The town is draped over the north side of Carter Hill, the hill getting steeper as you go up.

And Carter Hill is just a small bump in the huge presence of the San Francisco Peaks, a volcanic mountain range where Humphreys Peak tops out at 12,633 feet, the highest point in Arizona.

We started at the overlook on top of Carter Hill which is dominated by towering ponderosa pine trees and would end up at the bottom of the hill where mostly juniper and a few piñon trees hold sway. The hill sits at this interesting elevation, between 6,400 feet and 7,100 feet, where the forest is changing from one type to another.

I rolled us out of the parking lot and down the single switchback that takes us to Carterville proper, keeping the speed low and giving Patty and Lisa a chance to do their thing. I drove us down Fir, the highest east/west road on the hill with houses only on the north side of the street. We quickly reached Smitty's house and the mess of the three other houses that were in the process of being bulldozed, the past being eradicated for the future Smitty wanted to build.

Fir is a narrow street, and while the road flares at the end, it's not what anyone would call a cul-de-sac. I executed a two-point turn and got us going in the other direction.

Annabelle was in the passenger's seat with Patty and Lisa in the bench behind us and Harold and Doc Lion in the back.

As I slowly rolled past Smitty's place, Patty said, "Stop." Her voice was low and her eyes were closed, her head tipped to one side.

Smitty's place was two-story and narrow like all of the houses up high. It had vinyl siding and narrow windows. A little spark of hope lit up in me, but I couldn't imagine that Brooke was this close to Smitty. That made no sense.

I twisted around and studied Patty. I mean, there was good reason to right then, but I never really needed an excuse to look at her. It had been seven months since Annie and I had broken up, but I still hadn't managed to do anything about Patty.

Which was complicated. First off, she knew I wanted to do something about it and didn't do anything herself. And second, if I thought it was hard living up to the expectations of Annie Smith, what about a woman that knows everything you want?

Patty hunched over a little and tilted her head more towards the house. Out of the corner of my eye, I saw a curtain moving inside.

I had talked to Steve Lancaster last night, giving him a

brief update, but hadn't talked to Smitty since the mess with William Reilly. I, frankly, didn't want to talk to him. Ever again, really. It was only my job and my sense of duty to my town that kept me at this.

"He wants safety, he's scared, but…" Patty said, her voice low. She shook her head. "There's something else. He has so many desires… so many." Her eyes opened and her green eyes connected to mine. "He wants you gone, Henry. I mean… he *really* wants you gone."

I nodded and smiled. "Well, the feeling is mutual."

"After you save him from this, of course," Patty added, a mischievous smile on her lovely face. Patty was a few years younger than me, and I thought that the deepening lines around her eyes and her mouth just made her more attractive. I wasn't young and young wasn't what I wanted.

I would have liked to have had a longer conversation about what Smitty wanted, but we had an audience.

"No Brooke?" I asked.

She shook her head and I got the van moving, driving back to Main Street and down a block to Engelmann. This was my street and we rolled down the west side of the street and then crossed Main and drove the east side.

This was something I had done more times than I could count. Slowly driving down the streets of my town, looking at the houses, waving at my neighbors, patrolling. Not because it yielded results too often, but because it was my job, because being seen was important in my line of business. But I was usually in the CPD SUV, not a slow-moving unmarked white van. Smitty's curtain wasn't the only one that I saw move.

Nothing on Engelmann, so we did the same routine on Douglass and then down to the Carterville Circle and Cedar

Street. The Circle held the main businesses in town and a few lights were on as people got their day started.

Patty was starting to look tired. She had told me that she often had to tune out her powers to keep from getting overwhelmed by what she could sense in other people, and I had asked her to turn her power all the way up as we drove by every house in Carterville. This was her town too, and it couldn't be comfortable tuning in to what every person wanted.

Annabelle caught my concerned look and said to Patty, "You okay, hun?"

She smiled but it was clearly forced. "Fine. Let's keep going."

Lisa Paulson, in comparison, looked relaxed, her head slowly turning back and forth as I drove the Circle and rolled down the west side of Cedar, past the CPD and to the end of the street. Cedar was on a mostly flat portion of the hill so there was a proper cul-de-sac at the end.

We did the other side of Cedar and then down Main past the Carterville Diner to Bristle Cone Street, and I was starting to get worried. Sure, it was a long shot in the first place. Sure, we had just started. But we were running out of town.

After Bristle Cone was Aspen, and after that there wasn't much. Aspen was the north-most road and after it, Main Street turned into Carterville Road and meandered out to Highway 89. But I kept going. On Main Street after Aspen there is a big parking lot for tourists and a lot of the newer businesses—it is the more industrial part of town. If you can even say that for a place this small.

There's a small grocery store, a bank, the post office, a gas station, and a couple of garages. All of it a bit out of place after all the historic buildings in Carterville proper.

As I drove us, I tried to put myself in Brooke's shoes. She needed to be in the zone of influence. She needed to be close if she was going to exact her revenge. But what form was that going to take? How would she extract her "retrobution"? Where would the "firewerks" ensue? How would we "sufer"?

I wouldn't say I was impatient, but I was anxious. I had recruited civilians, this van containing several of the women I cared most about in this town, and I worried that I was putting them in danger.

I drove slowly past the newer section of town and then out to the "Welcome to Carterville" sign.

Patty sighed and slumped back.

"Did you get anything, Lisa?" I asked.

She pursed her lips and shook her head. "I don't think Ken's in town."

"How do you know?" Annabelle asked.

The tall woman shrugged. "I tried finding some other people. I could tell Frank was at the diner, but that was no surprise. But before that I searched for Harold's Felicia. She wasn't in their house, but I sensed her on the stairs up to the top of the hill when we were on the switchbacks."

At Fir and Main there is a set of metal steps that take you right up to the overlook. While most of Carterville's streets have sidewalks, the switchback to the top does not and it's a lot quicker and safer to just go up the steps.

She turned around and looked at Harold who nodded. "She likes her early morning walks," he said. She turned back and looked at me, her green eyes mischievous. "And I'm pretty sure Isabella was at the brewery... probably grabbing coffee."

I glanced at Annabelle and she nodded and got her phone at and jabbed at it, texting Officer Ortega. She had been told not to leave the station for any reason.

"Did you look for Brooke?" I asked.

She shook her head, looking down. I can't say I blamed her.

"Confirmed," Annabelle said. "She was getting coffee. Your sister came by looking for you and she stayed with Carl."

Well, that brought up a small storm of emotions. The fight I just had with Wendy. My sister being directly involved in this. Ortega not following orders. Brooke having seen all of this and maybe put things into play to take advantage of it.

How can it be paranoia when you are talking about someone that can see the future? Well, hopefully she can't see it very well with Carl in town.

"Tell her to stay put," I said to Annabelle and then turned to Lisa. "So, your power works this way. That's great. Can we run through again and this time can you look for Brooke?"

She nodded.

"And why don't you save your energy this time, Patty," I said.

She looked up at me, a fierce look in those lovely green eyes of hers. "I'm fine."

I knew better than to say anything else. I turned us around and drove us slowly back into Carterville.

FORTY-SIX
WEDNESDAY JULY 4. CARTERVILLE

We did it two more times. Lisa searched for Brooke and then Karen Winslow. Patty opened up her feelings and let the desires of the whole town flow through her.

The second time made sense to me, but by the third time, I was worried. Was this what Brooke had seen? Was Patty getting exhausted and me worried about her part of the future that led to her devastating plan?

And what the hell was her plan? The note at Ken and Karen's place indicated their lives were on the line and said, "can you save them in tyme." And one of the notes to Smitty said, "I AM your end" and another "I will destroy YOU."

My working theory was that it was Smitty and myself Brooke wanted. Probably dead. Because we were the ones that tried and failed to save her father. Maybe she wanted to kill Ken and Karen too because Karen was mayor. And she probably wouldn't mind hurting whoever else got in the way.

I know revenge is not logical, but from what I remembered about what happened to Joseph Jennings, we weren't the cause. A power was. And we never figured it out. We failed to save his life, but we weren't the ones that injured him.

We were back at the "Welcome to Carterville" sign and Patty looked pale and Lisa looked frustrated. Doctor Lion looked attentive like she was ready to leap into action, and Harold looked bored. We had nothing.

"Well… it ain't like we're the Avengers or anythin'," Annabelle said.

"You watch those movies?" I asked, grateful for anything else to talk about besides our failure.

"It's about half of what my grandson wants to talk about," she said with a shrug.

While I didn't watch movies like that, I was familiar with the idea. A team of superheroes gathering together to defend the world—or the universe—from some existential threat. Superheroes needed supervillains for those kinds of stories to work. My understanding was they kept ratcheting up the threats until the heroes struggled… right up until the end, that is.

And we weren't the Avengers. Those in town with what you might consider superpowers, Mary and Smitty, weren't here, leaving us a band of folks with minor powers.

Well… my power isn't exactly minor, but it's not useful here and doesn't come into play in this story and I'm not talking about powers until they are relevant. I ranted about that in the last story I wrote, something along the lines of people are more than the powers and thinking about them as primarily their powers is just plain rude, so I'm not going to contribute to that.

"Well, what would the Avengers do right now?" I asked.

Annabelle shrugged. "If they hit a dead end, a crucial piece of information would suddenly come to light, or someone would remember something important."

I shook my head. "It doesn't often work that way in the real world," I said. "It takes hard work and time… it takes—"

I was ramping up to an unneeded lecture when my radio squawked to life. "Carter, this is Ortega. We've got a 911 call from the Smith residence. A 10-42. Services have been dispatched. I suggest you get up there. Over."

In our new coding system, a 10-42 was a fire. "Services dispatched" meant the fire department had been called out.

I squeezed the radio mic on my shoulder as I put the van into gear, "Roger that, Ortega. We are going there now."

My heart leapt into gear, and I turned us around and headed us back into town.

"You were sayin'?" Annabelle chuckled as we headed up to Smitty's house.

FORTY-SEVEN
WEDNESDAY JULY 4. SMITH RESIDENCE

CARTERVILLE MAY BE ON A MOUNTAIN IN THE MIDDLE OF A forest, but it is also in Arizona, which means desert. Kind of. Northern Arizona averages around 21 inches of rain a year, most of it in winter and during the summer monsoon season. For an area to be considered a desert it should get less than ten inches of rain, so we are not technically a desert, but it is dry around here. We are not talking the lush forests of the Pacific Northwest or a rainforest. This is land that goes long periods without much of any rain and fire is a constant danger.

So, Carterville is on a mountain in the middle of a dry forest and we take fires very, very seriously. We had some rain recently, early monsoons, so it wasn't bone dry, but it was dry enough.

In 1934 a fire took out a fair amount of the town and damaged a whole lot more. During the rebuilding of Carter-ville, the infrastructure that pipes in water from the three wells that supply us was significantly updated. But that was 1934 and this was something the town council had been talking about for the last few years. Were our water mains big enough? Was there sufficient water pressure to fight a major fire? Did our current well capacity work for the town now that it was frequented by so many tourists.

Geeky questions, to be sure, but the kind of thing that can keep you up at night in a small town perched on a big mountain surrounded by a huge forest.

The forest has been thinned somewhat. First when Carterville was settled, local timber was harvested first for the mine and then for building the town. And then in the last twenty years, the Forest Service has allowed some lumbering in our area with the expressed goal of thinning the forest down a bit.

The problem with the early cutting of trees is that forest management wasn't really a thing in the late 1800s. The old growth trees around here that were easily accessible were removed. Pretty much all of them. A hundred forty years later, that left us with a forest that was denser and full of smaller trees than was the natural state of the forest, making it a forest that was much more vulnerable to catastrophic fires.

Around here it wasn't an "if" there was going to be another huge forest fire, but a "when."

Sorry for the civics lesson there, but fire is a thing we take extremely seriously.

All of this flitted through my mind as my heart beat fast, as sweat beaded along my forehead, as I drove us as fast as I could up Main Street, around Carterville Circle, right at the switchback that leads to the top of Carter Hill and down Fir Street to the fire.

I heard the siren of the fire engine behind us and heard the crackling of a hungry fire as we turned down the street. It didn't take long. There are only about eight houses on Fir, and Smitty's was a little over halfway down.

His quaint two-story brick house was fully engulfed, dark smoke pumping out and huge orange flames leaping out of the roof and the upstairs windows.

As we approached, fireworks erupted from the house. I am talking literal fireworks. Rockets zoomed out of the hole in the roof the fire had made and exploded just above the house, the noise of the explosion louder than the growl of the fire itself.

This happened more than once and only took a few seconds, but it took my breath away. Not because it was all that spectacular, fireworks are best at night, but because of what one of the threats Smitty had received said:

Destroyer be warned
I AM equalizer
firewerks will ensue

Brooke saw this. She must have. But did she know everything that was going to happen? Was Carl's presence helping us at all, or was that something she saw too?

This wasn't the time for contemplating Brooke and her motives and abilities. Steve Lancaster jogged quickly to us, his brown eyes wide, his face and his short-cropped grey hair smudged with soot.

"He's in there," he shouted as he ran up. "Winston is in there."

It was weird to hear Smitty called by his first name. No

one around here called him that. But that didn't change the situation.

I backed away from the house a ways to leave room for the fire engine and put the van in park. I twisted around and looked at my humble team, this assemblage of my friends and neighbors who bore no resemblance to the Avengers. But this was our town. We all knew what was at stake.

"Harold," I said, nodding towards the burning building. "Do you think you can get us in there?"

"For Smitty?" he asked.

I nodded and for a moment I thought he was going to say no. That he wouldn't risk his life for Winston "Smitty" Smith, the town healer who used his powers to help others but always with an eye for how it benefited him.

I wasn't thinking of Brooke and if she knew what would happen. Or if this was foolhardy or wise. I was thinking about my town and how we had to look out for each other.

I could see the emotions running through his wrinkled face. Fear, first and foremost. Even back a house and a half, I felt the heat from the fire. Shame, maybe when he thought of walking away from this. And then, grim determination.

"Let's do it, man," he said.

I turned to Annabelle. "Get evacuations organized. See what the fire department needs. And make sure Ortega stays put."

FORTY-EIGHT
WEDNESDAY JULY 4. SMITH RESIDENCE

THERE'S NOTHING BETTER THAN A TAME AND WELL-CONTAINED fire. The heat and the beauty as the flames dance and slowly consume the wood. Popping. Sparking. It's why many of the houses in Carterville still have woodstoves when easier methods of heating are available. There is something so primal and comforting about a fire.

And there's not much worse than a fire out of control, that has escaped its boundaries and unleashed its unquenchable hunger for consumption. That is raging and growing and becoming more of the monster it really is.

Earlier I said that it was best not to think of movies when visualizing Harold Marin's power. But I was wrong. I had never seen it in a fire before.

"We have to stay together, Henry," he said. We were half a block away from the house and the heat was becoming unbearable. I was sweating, I'm sure of it, but the dry, hot air was evaporating it right away. "We have to stay connected."

He looked scared, as scared as I did, and given how his power worked, that was what we needed. He hooked his arm into mine.

"The bubble will extend to us both?" I asked, my voice a half an octave higher than I intended.

"Yes," he said.

"And it will protect us from the fire?" I asked.

He gave me a grim smile and said, "We're about to find out." And then under his breath, "For Felicia."

Which might sound a little strange. He was about to run into a burning building, doing something that could get him —and me—killed and seemed to be dedicating the action to his wife.

Felicia and Harold met during the summer of love in 1967. They had been together ever since. And while they were both excellent lawyers and spent a lot of time with books, they were always out there exploring. Whether it was rafting down the Colorado or exploring Machu Picchu, they were out living their lives.

The dedication to Felicia contrasted with his earlier fear and reticence about what we were doing. He was trying to make her proud. That's why he came along. That's why he was doing this with me.

It was a small realization as we jogged towards the burning building, our arms interlocked, but it tugged at my heart. I was long divorced. Annie and I were done for good. I had no one person to try to make proud of me. I had my job and my responsibility to this town. And that's not nothing, but as the crackling of the hungry fire became all I could hear and the heat grew from painful to excruciating, it occurred to me that my soulmate wasn't a person but this town that bore my name.

This was an interesting thought, but it wasn't a happy one.

The smoke became thick, and the heat became so extreme I was afraid my clothing would catch on fire, driving out all thoughts of pride and soulmates and anything else but getting in, getting Smitty, and getting out alive.

Harold groaned next to me, and with an audible "pop" the sound dampened, the heat backed off, and we were standing in the doorway to Smitty's house.

"Where?" Harold shouted.

It took a moment for my brain to engage. Flames were licking the edges of an invisible sphere that extended about three feet in front of us. We stepped into the living room. Smitty's couch was on fire, black smoke belching out. His wooden coffee table, the one the gun had been on that he had drawn on me less than two days ago, was on fire too. Flames were licking up the walls and dancing along the ceiling.

The usually tame fire had been unleashed and had turned into the monster it always was. This building wasn't going to stay standing much longer.

One small thing caught my eye. A picture of Smitty when he was a boy, standing with his father holding up a fish he had just caught. The flames gobbled it up while I watched, first distorting the color image as it shrunk under the heat, and then darkening and burning, the picture frame falling off the wall.

Everything was burning, but no Smitty.

I took a breath and noticed the air was stale in our little bubble, and I wondered how long our oxygen would last.

I pulled Harold deeper into the living room towards the

sliding glass doors that led to the deck and then to the right towards the kitchen, remembering the layout of his house as I went.

I had only been in the living room recently since Smitty had lived here, but when I was a kid, one of my friends lived here. The memories were old, but the layout wasn't complicated.

The front door opened up into the living room. To the right was the kitchen and to the left was a bedroom and bathroom. Immediately to the right of the front door were a set of stairs that went to the second floor.

We started moving faster. Into the kitchen, the bright flames lapping at Harold's shield. No Smitty. Through the living room and over to the bathroom whose door was cracked, I knocked it open with my shoe and saw that it was empty. Over to the bedroom as part of the living room roof fell down on us and slid off his shield.

The bedroom door was closed and it wasn't safe to touch it. And, oddly, Harold's shield bubble seemed to extend through the wall. Which made no sense to me. His shield was smart enough to keep dangerous things out but not interfere with normal things? Maybe every power is a superpower under the right circumstances, and this was certainly the right one for his power.

"I'm going to kick it open," I said.

Harold tightened his grip and I raised my leg and kicked at it, the door strong and unyielding. It was a solid wood door, and judging from the shape of it and the trim, it was brand new with a shiny brass doorknob and a deadbolt with the key side facing us. And, belatedly, I realized it opened out so there would be no kicking it in.

I turned around and looked back into the burning living room, the flames getting higher as another piece of the ceiling fell. There were the stairs and the second floor, but I didn't think we had time to get up there. We needed to check the bedroom, but how to open the door?

I stood there hesitating. It wasn't long, but it felt like a long time, the air in our bubble getting staler, and then I thought I heard a scream through the roaring crackle of the hungry fire and the dampening quality of Harold's shield.

I needed to use the doorknob, but I would burn the hell out of my hand if I did. I could take my shirt off and use it, but that would mean letting go of Harold and that was death. So, without really thinking about it, I took off my cowboy hat and used it.

It was so awkward, but desperation drove me and I shoved it on the door, the brass knob covered by the lovely brown felt of my hat, and squeezed and turned. It slipped and I swore I heard that scream again.

I squeezed harder and turned… nothing.

I did it a third time, pulling Harold with me as I yanked hard on the doorknob. The door flew open, barely missing us, and we rushed into the room. With the back and forth, Harold would have fallen, but I pulled him up and we stood there taking in the scene.

It took a moment for my mind to put it all together.

It was a nice bedroom, but not one I would have thought Smitty would have. A big bed with a large wooden backboard and four ornately turned posts on each corner. There was a bedstand with an antique stained-glass lamp, but the rest of the bedroom was bookshelves made of dark wood. Floor to ceiling, overflowing with books.

It made me wonder if this was the real Smitty, a book-worm who had a soft spot for antiques, or was this the way the room was when he bought the house?

All of this was a diversion my mind played with to distract me from what was really going on in the room. It too was on fire, but not as hardily as the living room. There were two windows in the room but they were both barred—recent additions.

Smitty stood in the corner of the room, the one least engulfed in fire, which at this point meant the flames were starting to lick up the wall. And lick up his body. A piece of the ceiling had fallen on him and lit him and his clothing on fire. Well, not clothing, per se, but pajamas. He had on loose white pants, a lower quality than his New Age getup, and a white T-shirt. He must have been asleep when the fire started. He was screaming and ripping off his clothes, coughing when he wasn't screaming, his eyes wide in terror.

The heat and the flames were trying to use him as fuel, his skin puckering and blistering but then his power fought back, white skin being restored so quickly that at first it was hard to see what was going on. And then another part of his skin would burn and then heal. This was happening over and over.

With his clothing off he was dancing on the floor trying to keep away from burning bits that had fallen onto the hard-wood, trying to avoid burning chunks of ceiling that were falling on him.

It was a nightmare. He was quite literally experiencing the agony of being burnt to death over and over.

I don't know if it was Harold or me that pulled us forward, but we didn't watch long. We ran over to Smitty and I grabbed his bare arm.

His skin was hot. Too hot, and I almost let go. Harold groaned next to me and, with a pop, the bubble grew bigger and encompassed Smitty.

"About damn time," he said through gritted teeth that were holding back more screams.

His skin was rapidly repairing itself, forming smooth, white patches. I could feel it healing under my hand and it was the strangest sensation, like bugs were crawling on my palm. And even glancing at him, it was clear that there were many such patches all over his body.

We turned to go when the house shook underneath our feet and much of the second floor fell onto the first floor. Large portions of the ceiling above us fell, but Harold's shield protected us.

It wasn't that bad here, but through the door I could see that in the living room where the fire had been more fierce, the damage was greater, and the house had nearly collapsed on itself.

We were cut off, stuck in Smitty's bedroom with all the window's barred, a pile of burning rubble between us and escape.

At this point, even though we were just standing there, Harold was slumped against me. All powers have a price, even if it's just the energy they sap, and it seemed he was just about out of both. And with Smitty in the bubble, the air was getting stale and fast. We didn't have long.

FORTY-NINE
WEDNESDAY JULY 4. SMITH RESIDENCE

Had Brooke Jennings seen all of this?

That Smitty wouldn't leave town when I told him to. That I would help him bring in private security and that he would fortify his home. That a fire would break out in his old home and trigger fireworks shooting out the roof just when we arrived. That he was in the bedroom napping when the fire started and by the time he saw the flames he instinctively stayed there. That he wouldn't realize that with his powers he could plow his way through the fire and recover just fine. That he would be in his bedroom with brand-new bars on the windows that he didn't have a key to unlock so he couldn't get out.

Did she see that I would use Harold Marin and his power? That the three of us would get trapped in here with the house coming down, the oxygen in Harold's bubble running out, and no way to escape?

All of this flashed through my mind as the three of us

stood arm in arm staring at the conflagration that used to be Smitty's living room. My mind and the hormones running through my system were way past such moments of reflection. My body was screaming that I needed to do something to survive. My mind was telling me there was no way out.

"Shit, man," Harold said. "I think we're screwed."

"You think?" Smitty asked, the pain in his voice clear.

"Stop talking," I said. "We don't have much oxygen left."

"You stop talking," Smitty said.

I looked at him, his eyes were dull green in the flickering light and defiant, half of his head shiny white skin contrasting sharply with his scraggly blond and gray hair.

"Brooke must have seen all of this," I said, mostly to myself.

"What?" Smitty asked. "Who? What the hell are you talking about, Henry?"

I ignored him. I didn't have time to fill him in on the details of the case. And I hadn't done it earlier because it hadn't been relevant. But Brooke clearly saw this future. She wants Smitty and me dead, to suffer a fate like her father did. How can there even be a way out of this?

I wasn't a firefighter, but I knew enough to know with a fire this far gone it wouldn't be about saving this house but keeping the fire from spreading. It wouldn't be about sending firefighters into a building this engulfed in flames, it would be about evacuating everyone around this house.

And that is the way it should be, but it left us trapped without hope of rescue.

My head was pounding and I could feel my heart clanging in my chest, feel the pulse of blood at my temples. My body was full of adrenaline, ready for flight, but I needed to think.

How could I fight a future already seen, one where we had been expertly maneuvered into this very circumstance?

But then I remembered what Carl said, "No knowing what will happen, only knowing what *might* happen." His power was similar enough to hers that they interfered with each other. So, hopefully, Brooke just saw what *might* happen here, not what *will* happen.

Harold groaned and slumped against me, the bubble shrinking. I was having trouble holding on to him with only one arm.

"Grab me," I said to Smitty as I pulled my arm out of his.

I didn't wait to see what he did, but scooped Harold up and held him in my arms as Smitty grabbed my bicep.

Harold was shorter than me, but he wasn't slim. I was feeling the weight.

I took a moment and stared at the flaming rubble out Smitty's bedroom door. It was hard to say how high it was, the flames obscuring what was underneath. A chunk of the bedroom ceiling fell on us and slid off the shrinking bubble. It was getting hotter, and I was having a hard time getting a full breath of air, my heart beating even harder.

"We're going to make a run for it," I said.

There was nothing else to do but to let the chemicals coursing through my veins have their way. It probably wouldn't work. We would probably die the horrible death that Brooke saw, that was so similar to the way her father died, the way she clearly wanted us to die. But I had to try something.

Smitty was saying something, probably objecting, but I didn't listen. I took the deepest breath I could and ran right into the heart of the fire.

FIFTY

My power has nothing to do with strength or stamina. I don't turn into a green monster when I'm angry. I'm just a middle-aged man with some heart problems that eats and drinks a little too much and exercises a lot less than I should.

I am no action hero, just a small-town cop in a town that got very strange six years ago when the meteor hit. But I was fighting for my life and my body did everything it could to give me the energy I needed.

Holding Harold in my arms and with Smitty clinging to my arm, I plunged us into the flames. The bedroom door was about halfway back into the living room, the route in my mind was a quick diagonal across the living room to the front door.

But it wasn't that simple.

We were in the conflagration, Harold's shield was smaller, but holding, and all I could see was the roaring, licking flames, the orange and yellow all around us like we were inside of the sun, the heat becoming painful despite his shield, the brightness hurting my eyes.

I hit a barrier and couldn't go any farther. I could see nothing but flames. Maybe it was the remnants of Smitty's couch, maybe it was rubble from the second story.

Without really trying, my direction shifted, to my right a little, like Harold's shield was slick and slid off the flames and debris.

I glanced down, worried about the floor, which was on fire too. Harold's shield wasn't a perfect sphere there, it flattened against the floor and I could see a few remnant flames dying beneath it on the blackened hardwood floor. There was an intelligence to his power and a good thing.

Smitty's house sat on a hill which meant there was a crawlspace, which meant once the floor was burned through, it would collapse and there would be no chance of escape.

Harold groaned again and went completely still in my arms.

I would like to say I held my breath, waiting to see if the bubble would collapse, but I was panting hard trying to get any oxygen left in the bubble. Sweat covered my body and my head was getting light.

I surged forward through the flames, and because it was almost too bright to see, I was essentially blind. I thought I was heading for the front door but there was no way to be sure.

"Harold," I said, jostling him a little. "Come on. Stay with us."

He groaned, it was a sound that came deep from within, sounding almost like he was an old wooden beam under too much pressure.

The shield didn't get bigger, but it seemed to change. I more felt it than saw it. It wasn't quite a circle anymore but seemed to come to a sharp point in front of me. We hit another barrier but didn't slide off this time.

I pushed hard, a groan escaping me. "Push," I cried, hoping Smitty could hear me. I felt him change position until he was behind me, pushing me.

At first nothing happened. I pushed. Smitty pushed. We all groaned.

"More, Harold," I gasped. "More!"

He groaned again, now sounding like an old beam about to break, and something changed. Given that we were in the middle of swirling, hungry flames and sweat was flowing into my eyes, and I was starting to see spots, it wasn't anything I saw. But it felt like the shield became sharper, maybe became more than a shield. We started to move, slowly, like we were plowing through the rubble.

The heat went from painful to excruciating, it felt like my clothes were about to catch on fire. My feet were moving, it felt like we were moving, but my view didn't change. All I could see was the swirling conflagration of Smitty's burning house, the crackle of the fire loud and painful.

I was panting hard. Getting dizzier. I could barely hold on to Harold much less stand, but I kept pushing. And Smitty kept pushing me.

Harold went quiet and still again, the shield shrinking more. I had no strength left. I couldn't breathe. It felt like I was on fire. But I pushed. We pushed. One last shove with our failing energy and...

We stumbled forward and it suddenly seemed dark. I heard a pop, the heat got so much worse and then I felt water smack into me. I tripped and fell, letting go of Harold and going down hard. Smitty fell on me. The three of us a tangle of limbs on the hard ground. I sucked in air as fast as I could, taking in huge gulps of it, feeling my heart slow just a touch, feeling stinging water sprayed on me.

The world was indistinct shapes, a swirling darkness as my eyes tried to adjust.

And then there were strong hands pulling me forward.

"Harold…" I mumbled.

"We got 'em, Chief," someone said.

My pupils had been so constricted from the fire that the normal light of day seemed dark, but soon they adjusted. Two fire engines were at what remained of Smitty's house, a couple of ambulances just beyond, people rushing about. I had a fireman on each side, and I thought I could see them carrying Harold. Smitty, nude and covered in white patches of newly healed skin, was stumbling forward on his own, Steve Lancaster running over to him.

"Good," I mumbled. We had escaped the fire. We had survived. "Good," I said again, and promptly passed out.

FIFTY-ONE
WEDNESDAY JULY 4. FIR STREET

"There's work to do," I said, my voice muffled from the oxygen mask on my face. I was lying down on a gurney in the back of an ambulance. I was dizzy, nauseous, and being merely exhausted was a fond memory at this point. I also had second-degree burns on my left arm and face, and the deep pain of them brought me back to consciousness.

"Sorry, Chief," Annabelle said. "But you are goin' to the hospital."

I shook my head. "This isn't over. Get Smitty."

Her eyes widened and she slowly nodded her head. We may have survived the "firewerks" Brooke Jennings had seen and maneuvered us into, but she was still out there, and Karen Winslow and Ken Fischer were still missing. It was early in the morning and there was a long way to go in this Fourth of July.

I tried to sit up, but I couldn't. My heart was still galloping along and despite the oxygen it didn't feel like I could get a full breath.

"Now!" I said to Annabelle with as much force as I could muster. She scurried out of the rig. There was a paramedic in there with me, getting ready to treat my arm. She was a young woman with blonde hair and a round face just like Brooke.

Now I may be a middle-aged white guy and I will admit the age of the young are getting harder for me to discern, but I don't normally confuse people. But I had just been through something and been deprived of oxygen, and my mind, for a moment, told me it was Brooke.

I tried to get up again, my heart beating faster, too fast. I needed to escape. I needed to get away. What was that needle in her hand? Where was everybody? Was she going to kill me now? Was this really her end game to take me out while looking in my eyes when I was too weak to defend myself?

It was only a moment, maybe the length of two breaths and then she spoke. "Please try to be calm." She had an accent that I didn't recognize. It was vaguely British, but it was most certainly not Brooke. She wasn't a Carterville local, but she wasn't Brooke either.

I lay back down, trying to calm my freaked-out mind. Focusing on my breath. Feeling the deep burning pain in my arm and head grow worse with every heartbeat.

It helped, but not a lot. My body was still full of all the fight or flight chemicals from the fire and flight is what I wanted. What I needed.

"I got this," Smitty said from the back of the ambulance, and I have to tell you I had never been happier to hear his nasally, condescending voice.

———

I'VE FELT SMITTY'S POWER BEFORE. LAST CHRISTMAS DAY during the mess surrounding Lila Chang's murder after my long hard fall. He saved my life when nothing else could. So I knew what to expect, but still, it was…

Words cannot contain the feeling, but I will try.

It was waking up from the worst dream you've ever had and realizing everything is okay. It was like making up with someone you adore after a terrible fight. It was warm and sweet and full of hope like playing with a pile of fuzzy puppies or the embrace of a mother to a scared child.

And I didn't want it.

Well… I needed it, but I didn't want it. Smitty and his superpower had a super price.

"We're even," I growled as the warmth of his healing energies flowed out of his hands into me. We were in the ambulance, alone. I had asked for privacy and I guess there are some perks to being the chief of police. The oxygen mask was still on and my voice was muffled.

"You mean back there?" he asked, his eyes back to looking hazel and mischievous. He was a mess, wrapped in a thin wool blanket and patches of new white skin all over his face and scalp. He looked like he had walked out of some deranged horror movie.

"We. Are. Even," I said.

He nodded and licked his lips and pulled his hands away. "Okay," he said, holding his hands up. "We are even. I'll give you that, Henry. What you did back there was more crazy than brave, but you saved my life. We are even."

The cessation of his healing energies was jolting and made

me want to cry. My body had been sucking it up and we had just gotten started. I needed it, certainly, but after he withdrew his power, I wanted it. I wanted it like a sober alcoholic wants a drink after a particularly bad day. No, I needed it and I hated myself for that.

It became completely clear to me how Karen Winslow and Lisa Bass and all his other regulars had gotten addicted. The first time he did this, I was dying and unconscious for most of his healing. This time… there was nothing more in the world that I wanted than to feel his power again.

And he knew it.

I tried to sit up, but I couldn't, the world spinning around me. I hadn't had enough from him to make an appreciable difference.

"You better lie down, Chief," he said, moving to get up. "You really do need to go to the hospital."

I pulled the mask off. I couldn't stand how I sounded with it on. "Good luck with everything while I'm gone, Smitty," I said, my voice so weak I hated it. "Brooke isn't done and it'll be fun to hear what happens without me standing in her way."

His face puckered up, like he had just bit into a lemon, and he sank back down. "Who the hell is Brooke?" he hissed. "Are we talking about the blonde wannabe Annie Smith that has been working at the inn?"

I nodded. "She can see the future."

His jaw hung open and his eyes widened, glancing out the back of the ambulance where the flickering light and heat from his burning house was visible. "So she saw that electrical fire starting?" he asked.

I hadn't known that's what it was, but it made sense. An old house like that. "And she maneuvered things so you would be asleep in there with newly barred windows," I said. "She knew you had some trauma around fire. That you wouldn't react very well."

I didn't know he had trauma, or at least I didn't remember any stories like that, but it explained his behavior. It was a guess, but judging from his reaction a good one.

He hugged himself, his hands shaking. Gone was the cockiness, revealing a much more human Smitty.

"Can you… can you stop her?" he asked.

"I can try," I said.

His face hardened and he shook his head. "Not good enough."

I shrugged, or at least tried to. It's not quite the same when you are lying down. Now that the mask was off, the smell of smoke was thick, the dark heavy kind of smoke that comes from things burning that shouldn't.

I wanted to get up. To get out there. To help defend my town from this immediate threat. Make sure people were evacuating, do anything I could to slow down that fire. But I was a mess. I needed Smitty.

"She has Karen and Ken," I said.

I didn't say this thinking it would open his heart and make him help me without condition. The mayor was someone he needed on his side, and I was hoping that her being in danger would wake him up to what we were facing.

"What?" he asked.

"Brooke," I said. "It looks like she took them. She left one of those notes, challenging me to find them in time."

"Brooke?" he said, shaking his head. "How… She's just…"

I got the confusion. It's hard to imagine her as some evil mastermind. Frankly, it's hard for me to imagine that of anyone in this town but Smitty. "She can see the future and she wants revenge."

"Why?" he asked.

I shrugged again, or tried to. "It doesn't make sense yet, but do you remember the guy that was burned badly, found up on Carter Hill not long after the meteor hit? Was found with his daughter—she was twelve or thirteen."

His forehead furrowed, an interesting show with the missing hair and patches of new skin. And then he relaxed and nodded. "He was an archeologist or something, right? I tried to heal him, but I didn't have a clue."

"The girl was Brooke," I said. "She blames us, not that it really makes sense because no one knows what happened to him."

"Jesus…" he said, shaking his head and putting his hands back on me. "That girl has one hell of a power. You are right, Henry. We're even."

I closed my eyes and sank into the healing warmth of Smitty's power and let it all go for just a few moments.

FIFTY-TWO
WEDNESDAY JULY 4. FIR STREET

After Smitty took care of me, I extracted a promise from him to heal Harold and to make sure he and Felicia lived long and healthy lives. Harold was the real hero here. It was my job to try to help, not his.

When it was over, I felt… It's hard to explain. I felt cleaner than if I had scrubbed my body for an hour in the shower. I felt more awake than I have in my entire adult life and was more energetic than I had been since my twenties. I felt an unreasonable sense of hopefulness.

It was extraordinary. It was intoxicating. It was entirely clear to me how easy it was for Smitty to addict people to his power.

And I hated it. My body loved it but my mind, my psyche rebelled against it.

I had never felt like this from my beloved coffee—there was no buzzy edge to what Smitty had done. My good friend gin never made me feel this way. And while I was as fond of sex as the next guy, I had never felt like this after the most passionate encounter.

The feeling made the rest of my life look dark and dingy and dull and somehow inferior to just a few minutes with Smitty's power. I wanted more and knew I would never ask Smitty to heal me again. Never.

"Now go stop her," Smitty said when he was done.

"We even?" I asked.

He rolled his eyes and shook his head. "Yes. Just stop her, okay?"

I sat up and wasn't dizzy, the golden glow of his healing gift still surrounding me. I suppressed a goofy grin and said, "Go take care of Harold, and call me if you remember anything about the Jennings that might be relevant."

He stared at me for a moment and then nodded. He looked tired, like all that energy he had just given me had left him drained and wrung out. He nodded and scurried out of the ambulance.

I took a deep breath, glad to take a normal one, despite the heavy smoke in the air, and followed Smitty out.

I felt ashamed. I didn't want to be seen. Like I had just slept with my best friend's girl or done something a hell of a lot worse.

Fir Street was chaos. Two fire engines, one hooked up to a red hydrant not far from Smitty's house and another spraying foam on a neighboring house.

The smoke was thick enough to blunt the light of the sun a bit and it looked like disaster had been averted. I could see that Smitty's house was just a pile of burning rubble and the debris of the houses Smitty had knocked down was burning, but the house next to Smitty's only had minor damage.

"You okay, Henry?" Annabelle asked as she ran up to me. I had no idea how she could move that fast in her heels.

I nodded. "Smitty took care of me."

She cocked her head. "And let me guess. Now ya feel as guilty as a hound that got into the chick coop?"

I had no good answer, and it didn't seem to be the time, so I ignored her question. "Looks like the fire is under control."

She nodded. "We got us some Forest Service help down on Engelmann. They're on the hill dealing with spot fires. Gonna lose a couple of trees but it looks good so far."

"And the rest of our team?" I asked.

"Doc Lion is with Harold, just saw Smitty get in the ambulance with them," she said with a wry smile. "Hopefully Harold won't come out lookin' as guilty as you. Lisa and Patty..." she looked around, her head snapping back and forth. "They were by that engine. Told them to stay put."

My heart sank and my stomach twisted into a knot. Maybe Brooke not only saw Smitty and me dying in that fire, maybe Brooke saw different possibilities, one of them being that chaos that would ensue and the opportunity to take some people truly close to me. Patty was my dream and Lisa was my best friend's wife and one of my oldest friends. I had drawn them into this. If Brooke had taken them, then this had turned into something else entirely.

"I'm sure that they are just..." Annabelle began, but I wasn't listening.

I was still high from Smitty's healing and feeling confident and powerful. I strode towards the chaos, my eyes searching every face. Brooke could be here. Part of me believed that she was. That this was the kind of dance someone who could see the future, who truly believed in their power, would do. She could know exactly when to duck out of sight or turn her back and watch everything unfold up close.

Given how personal this all seemed, that made perfect sense.

But how did she manage to take Karen and Ken? Could her powers give her insight so she could just threaten to release their most damaging secret and make them come with her? But she had already done that, using her knowledge of Karen's addiction to Smitty's power to get Ken to create and mail all those threat letters.

Did she use force then, pulling a gun on them and knowing what it would take to get them to respect it and come quietly?

And what of Patty and Lisa? How in the hell could she just snatch them away from here with so many people around?

I wound my way past the first engine, jumping over the thick fire hose as it carried water to the fire. I dodged a couple of firemen dressed in their gear, local boys that I recognized. As I got closer to the fire, the heat and the smoke intensified. The new skin on my face particularly sensitive to the heat. I started coughing, pulled a handkerchief out of my pocket, and covered my mouth.

Patty and Lisa weren't anywhere near the first engine, so I went to the second, the one pumping foam. It was a big splurge for the town to get that second engine, but the council had been worried that our water supply wouldn't be enough for a major fire.

They weren't at the second one.

I walked across the street to get a better view of everything and to get farther away from the smoke. And then I remembered that Ken Fischer had described the videos and photos of Karen Winslow leaving Smitty's house. It had to be shot from this side of the street.

There are no houses on this side of Fir, the hill too steep. It's mostly pine trees growing out of the hill with a few scrub oaks mixed in.

It didn't take long to find it. A white piece of paper stuck to a pine tree with a knife. I knew what it was at a glance, that moth-eaten font, that grey haze over the sheet. And the knife was the same as out at the Winslow Ranch, a simple steak knife.

Destroyer of Carteville
   you can't save all
      who will you chose?

My heart started pounding in my chest, clanging around like a pinball stuck between a couple of bumpers. The note was pinned low on the tree, but because of the slope it was at eye level.

This was meant for me. It had to be. And why the hell did she use "chose" instead of "choose"? Was this just sloppiness or some kind of sign? Was she indicating that in her mind I had already chosen so it wasn't really a choice?

I wanted to rush up and grab the note, but I just stood there staring at it. This was evidence. I needed to take care. I needed to slow down.

As I looked, I saw in the branch of the tree above the note a black plastic sphere that looked like an eye. Shit. She was watching. She had been watching. I should have looked for this as soon as Ken told me his story. But I had been busy, there had been too many damn things to track down.

Heat and smoke from the fire and the crackle of it in the background provided sensations and a soundtrack to the dread that was filling me up, creating the feeling that I had just descended into hell.

"Henry!" Annabelle called as she ran up to me, her heels clicking on the pavement. "Did ya find… what the hell?" Her breath sucked in and she swore. "Brooke has Patty and Lisa too."

FIFTY-THREE
WEDNESDAY JULY 4. FIR STREET

While Carterville has a high number of police officers per capita, two for the 290 of us, it's not nearly enough for when things get crazy. And if you count Annabelle, and you should even though she is not technically a police officer, the ratio is higher and it's still not nearly enough for a situation like this.

"Go get the CSI gear," I told Annabelle as the fire crackled behind us and we both stared at the threat letter pinned to the tree. "I'll stay here while you do that and then you can collect the evidence. And get on the phone and get some sheriff's deputies out here. We need some help, and now. And check on Carl, see if he can help us at all."

She nodded and ran off, pulling out her phone from her back pocket as she ran.

I stood there and stared at the sign and then felt the hair on the back of my neck stand up and felt like someone was behind me. It was then that I recalled that I lost my cowboy hat in the fire, and I felt exposed.

I turned slowly and watched the organized chaos. Two crews of firemen fighting the blaze. One engine dousing the remnants of Smitty's house with water, the other one foaming down the neighboring house. Things were fairly well under control, but things were still pretty dry and an errant spark could start another fire.

There were some locals farther down on Fir watching what was going on, but they were actually keeping their distance.

There were two ambulances, the one I had gotten out of and the second one which the tall Steve Lancaster stood by. Smitty had to be in there working on Harold.

No Lisa. No Patty. They wouldn't just leave.

I pulled my phone out and called Patty. It went to voice-mail. The same for Lisa. Their phones were off.

The knot in my stomach turned into a pretzel. My worst fears were starting to look well founded.

I turned the last few days over in my mind as I stared at the chaotic scene. Part of me was convinced that there was no defeating Brooke. That her power was too much. Even with Carl here and likely interfering with her powers, she probably saw all of this before now. Maybe before anyone knew she was in town, those times last fall and winter when Carl first had trouble keeping his head on here. It was a choreographed dance in her mind leading to her desired revenge.

But what the hell was that? This fire, if things had gone slightly differently, could have taken out most of the town, could have killed Smitty and me, and in the same way her father died. If she didn't want that, then what did she want?

And a part of me, a much quieter part of me, said that was exactly what she had hoped for, but we had managed to sneak through and now we were in her fallback scenario. Which meant there was more coming, but it was possible to defeat her.

Carterville powers have a price. What is the price of Brooke's power? If I understood it, that could point to a way to defeat her.

And I had to wonder at the early days, the month after the meteor hit when Brooke was twelve or thirteen before her father died up on Carter Hill. What was her power like then? Did she know what was going on or was she as confused as most of the rest of us? Maybe her power only manifests when she sleeps, and she thought it was just dreams and then those dreams came true. Maybe it took time for her powers to mature and the teenage Brooke didn't have a clue as to her power.

I didn't have enough information. Not even close. I felt powerless myself as I stood there guarding the crime scene watching everyone else do things that mattered.

Smitty hopping out of the ambulance caught my eye. It wasn't the graceful hop of a young man, but sloppy and he would have fallen badly if Steve hadn't caught him. He was stooped and looked exhausted. He had used his powers extensively this morning, first to save his own life and then on me and Harold.

He looked around, nodded towards me, and spoke to Steve. They were too far away for me to hear them over the rest of the noise.

With his arm around Smitty, Steve helped him over to me. His eyes widened as he saw the threat letter behind me and maybe the camera, his mouth opening and then closing. He shook his head as if trying to clear a thought.

"I'm leaving town," he said.

"Good," I said. "I don't want to know where you are going."

He snorted, his eyes flicking to the camera. He had seen it. "I wasn't going to tell you, Henry." He nodded back to the ambulance. "Harold will be fine."

He wanted me to thank him, that was obvious. But I wasn't in the mood to thank Smitty for doing the right thing and I wasn't into whatever show he was trying to put on for the camera.

"You should have told me about Brooke," he said after the silence got awkward. "I would have left sooner understanding what her power is."

I smiled, but it was a twisted little thing. "No, you wouldn't have," I said. "Something would have changed your mind, kept you in that house this morning. She saw it."

"Then she also saw me leaving town afterwards," he said.

I shrugged. Smitty was speaking of the future with a confidence, something I wasn't currently capable of.

He blinked and looked around. Maybe he was having the hair on his neck stand up. He shook Steve off and took a deep breath, standing up straight. He looked past me, up at the camera. "He's all yours, Brooke. Do what you will with Henry but know that if I live, I'll owe you one. You know what I can do."

My hands formed fists without me thinking about it. I wanted to punch Smitty, and I was wishing I had left him in that burning building. But only for a moment. I do my job to the best of my ability. I do my best for this town. And I do it for those I love and for those I hate.

Steve's brown eyes widened briefly. He didn't really know Smitty before he took this job, and now he was getting a clearer picture of the man. I think he felt bad for me. I certainly felt bad for pulling him into the job. When I called him in, I had no idea powers were involved, much less one this formidable.

I relaxed my hands. It took an effort of will, but I did know Smitty. It wasn't personal. This was just his basic nature showing. He was always using his power to get as much as he could from the world.

Smitty turned and walked away. He wasn't steady but he was staying on his feet.

"We'll be ditching our phones," Steve said to me. "Shoot me an email if you need to get ahold of me." He turned to go but then turned back, his eyes wide as he took in the scene. "Good luck, Henry. I think you're going to need it."

I nodded and Steve turned and caught up to Smitty. For a moment the two of them were haloed against the burning remnants of his house making it look like flames were licking around the edges of their bodies.

I'm not very superstitious, but it sent a chill through me despite the heat of the fire.

FIFTY-FOUR

WEDNESDAY JULY 4. FIR STREET

When Annabelle got back, she was white as a sheet. She hadn't been gone long, maybe twenty minutes, but it had seemed like a long time.

The fire was still burning and the street was still busy, but nothing had gotten out of control. I had just stood there with my back to the note and the camera feeling like I was being watched. Because, of course, I was.

And not just the camera. I didn't understand the full extent of Brooke's power, but it was like she had watched me stumble through these last few days before they even happened. Knowing what I would do. Knowing what I would get right. Knowing each and every mistake I would make.

The time alone with nothing to do wasn't good for me, so when Annabelle pulled up in the CPD SUV, got out, and stared at me with her face pale, I felt my heart lurch in my chest and feared another coronary artery spasm or something worse was about to take hold.

"Is Ortega okay?" I asked. I didn't think, just spoke. With Patty and Lisa apparently taken, Ortega being taken too would gut me.

She nodded, her brown eyes wide. "She's pacin' like a caged animal, that one. Stir crazy, too. But she's just fine."

"Then what?" I asked.

Her wrinkled brow furrowed like she was searching for the words. "I saw Smitty and his bodyguard hightailin' it outta town," she said, her words coming slowly. "I think you should consider leavin' too, Henry."

I took a deep breath and squared my shoulders. "Just tell me, Annabelle."

She looked down and scuffed her sneakers on the pavement. She had changed her shoes. Gone were the usual heels, instead she was wearing red sneakers. A dim part of me was glad to see that level of practicality. She was going to have to scramble up the hill a bit to get to the camera and the note.

"Annabelle!" I said, my voice louder than I intended.

She jumped, just a little, like I had struck her, and I felt bad.

"Please," I said, my tone normal. "Please, just tell me."

She looked up, her eyes haunted. She glared at the camera and leaned close and whispered in my ear. "Carl... he... he says he saw ya die."

I stood there hearing my breath, feeling like I wasn't in my own body, like it wasn't mine. "In the fire?" I asked. I didn't whisper because I didn't think it mattered. Brooke knew or knew enough about what Annabelle was about to tell me.

She shook her head and grabbed my arm, her long fingernails jabbing into my skin as she pulled me away. It was a silly thing, but I noticed how dirty my uniform was, covered in soot, the edge of the short sleeve burned on my right arm next to the white patch of healed skin. The blue slacks wrinkled, and the edges of the cuffs singed. I was gripped by the desire to go change. To go get another hat. I shouldn't be seen like this.

Annabelle pulled me about ten feet away from the camera and whispered again in my ear, her breath warm. "He said somethin' about agents and tunnelin' and an explosion that will rock the town."

For a moment it was like I couldn't even feel my own body. Like I was looking out of the eyes of a character in a movie. I mean, I got the dire nature of what she just told me, but I couldn't feel it. I couldn't feel anything.

I remembered Carl's words. It seemed like months ago, but it was only three days.

"Agents here," he had said. "Zey study us, you know. Zey want to extend our powers outside of ze mountain." He looked at me and his eyes were all the way crazy. "Sacred Kachina of mountain have granted us powers. Zat makes us more zen human and our powers will never leave zis mountain."

And then I was back in my body, my heart thumping fast, my breath coming quickly. Carl's visions can sometimes be confusing, but I didn't understand what was going on when he told me. Now it almost made sense. I at least knew what the next thing to do was.

Annabelle and I argued. It wasn't loud and it wasn't long, but it was serious. Low hushed tones because we knew we were being watched. She wanted me to leave town. I told her I couldn't. I tried to tell her why, that people I loved were in danger, that Carterville was all I had left, that it was my job.

"At least wait for the deputies," she said, no longer whispering. "At least do that, Henry."

And that was the smart thing to do. Wait for help. But I was conflicted that there would be a price to be paid for delaying and that price would be the life of someone I loved. This was Brooke's game and I had to play it.

"I'm heading to the mine," I said. "Over around to the old shaft on the east side of Carter Hill. Send the deputies there."

She blinked and stared at me, her mouth twisting into a bitter frown. "You're a goddamn fool, Henry," she said.

I shrugged. There was no denying it. "She has Lisa and Patty."

Annabelle's eyes flicked down to the pavement and she nodded. I had to try. Even against an unbeatable power, I had to try.

FIFTY-FIVE
WEDNESDAY JULY 4. EAST OF CARTERVILLE

THE VAN WOULDN'T START. CLINT RYAN'S WHITE VAN, THE ONE I was driving our crew around in as we searched for Brooke. It wouldn't start.

I felt anger spark at the delay, but it fizzled out. Maybe because I knew it was a useless emotion at this point, maybe because despite Smitty's healing, I had been through a hell of a lot in the last couple of days and I didn't have the energy. Or maybe because the sensation of fate pressing down on me was so heavy that it smothered any real feelings I had.

Brooke saw this too. I popped the hood and got out. Walked over calmly, lifted the hood and peered in. The thick black wire that led from the battery to the starter had been cut. They hadn't even bothered to try to hide it.

Earlier, I had thought that Brooke had been here, that she had seen the future in such detail that she could walk through the scene and not be noticed, ducking here at the right point, turning her head at exactly the right time. Now I had evidence of it.

I nodded once and let the hood slam shut and started walking. I didn't want to take the CPD SUV away from Annabelle and, more importantly, I didn't want to fight with her again. It was a relief to get the fire behind me, to get away from its heat and its noise.

I walked to Main Street, down to Engelmann, and over to my house. This street was busy too, several Forest Service vehicles parked and hot shots up on the hill back behind the houses on the south side of the street.

I hardly paid any attention. My house was on the north side of the street. I hopped in my old Toyota pickup truck and started it up. Which it did without hesitation, and that gave me pause.

The disabled van had slowed me down by maybe five minutes. Why had Brooke needed to slow me down for five minutes? What difference could five minutes possibly make?

The curiosity didn't last. The weight of fate soon pressed down on me again, extinguishing the curiosity. I drove back to Main Street and headed down Carter Hill.

———

I DROVE SLOWLY, DELIBERATELY, WATCHING EVERYTHING around me. It was fairly early, just after 9:00 a.m. and the town was still waking up. Some of the tourists that were staying here were out already, walking the streets or grabbing breakfast at the Carterville Diner. There was a crowd waiting outside for a table in the bright sunlight, the fifties-style neon sign looking a little out of place on the plain brick building.

I felt a stab of guilt as I passed. Frank Paulson was in there and didn't know his wife had been taken, that Patty Walsh had been taken.

I drove the rest of the way down the hill and past Aspen Street where the more industrial buildings stood, nestled in the piñon juniper forest. I turned right between a gas station and a garage onto an unmarked road.

I hadn't driven us down this road earlier, when our non-Avengers team had been assembled, because I didn't really think about it. There wasn't much back here. Our small water treatment plant and the yard where the city stored equipment and cinders to spread on the roads when it snowed and a few more things like that.

But the road went farther. Even though there wasn't a street sign, everyone around here thought of it as the Old Mine Road. It swung around the east side of Carter Hill to the mine. It was built in the early 1900s when the mine was most productive.

The main part of the mine is past the overlook down on the south side of Carter Hill. Technically you can drive to the mine from the overlook, but it's been fenced off for years and I don't have a key. The Carters haven't owned the mine for about a hundred years now. Various corporations have owned it since then. It was open to tours briefly in the 1960s when the town was trying to reinvent itself as a western tourist attraction but has been closed since.

It's changed hands about three times since the meteor hit. This was more in Karen Winslow's purview and not something I paid much attention to. As long as nothing was going on there, all I had to do was walk the fence occasionally and make sure it was still intact and drive out Old Mine Road on the weekends and roust the kids having parties in the forest and put out the fires they somehow couldn't bring themselves to douse properly.

It was an oversight on my part to not consider Brooke being back here. Because it made too much sense. This whole road and much of the area was inside the zone of influence. Her power would work and she'd be isolated.

And Carl's ramblings should have tipped me off. He had said, "Zey have tunnel to ze east," but his powers were haywire because Brooke was in town. There was a mine shaft on the east side of town, one that was dug late in the life of the mine and never turned into much. If you could get to it, it would be a perfect place to hide out.

The road turned to dirt right after the wastewater treatment plant as I drove across a cattle guard. Soon the buildings were behind me, and the San Francisco Peaks rose in front of me, the bowl of the inner basin visible. Aspen, fir, and spruce trees dominated the inner basin, and then above that, the bare grey rock of the mountains rose higher than the tree line. Humphreys, Reese, and then Aubineau Peak to my right, Agassiz, Fremont, and Doyle peaks to my left. The six peaks lined up on either side of the inner basin like sentinels watching over the deep bowl with Carterville down below it all.

The view struck me almost like it was new. Maybe it was my weird mental state, maybe it was the recent brush with death, maybe it was because Carter Hill often interfered with this view, and it had been a while since I really took it in.

It is said that the Peaks used to be a single mountain

around 16,000 feet tall. A single towering volcano until it blew its lid carving out the inner basin and creating the six peaks we have today. From this angle, it's not hard to believe.

And I had to wonder if Carterville with all its powers and with Brooke and her power manipulating things was about to blow its lid.

There wasn't much time for reflection because I was soon at the turn for the eastern mineshaft. It wasn't much, a badly degraded two-track that turned towards Carter Hill and was easy to miss if you didn't know where it was.

I stopped on the road and got out. The day was getting warm already and the sky was a deep azure blue, a soft breeze blowing. I still smelled fire, the stench of it in my scorched clothing, stuck in my nose. The populated part of Carter Hill was out of sight here, but I could see the grey plume of smoke rising in the air. I stood and stared at it. From this distance it was a thin column rising lazily into the morning sky.

The Old Mine Road had swung away from Carter Hill a ways, so the mine shaft was a few hundred yards off the road which ran through an open meadow—around here we call it a park. At first, I just listened and watched the smoke. Breathing the fresh air. Trying for a moment of calm.

The smoke plume wasn't getting any bigger, and that was reassuring. I didn't hear anything out of the ordinary, just some ravens cawing.

The road to the mine shaft had been used recently. There were tire tracks clear in the dry dirt. Not a lot of traffic, but vehicles had been up and down this road since the rain a week or so back.

If it had been anyone else I was after, I probably would

have set off on foot or waited for backup and entered with force. But with Brooke, it just didn't make any sense.

I got back in my truck and drove down the two-track.

FIFTY-SIX

WEDNESDAY JULY 4. EAST ENTRANCE TO
THE CARTERVILLE MINE

This portion of Carter Hill is steep, the final ten feet of it a cliff of dark grey volcanic rock. The mine tunnel started as a cave in that cliff which is now fronted by a rough rectangular structure made of local pine trees jutting out of the cliff.

At a glance it might look like an oversized log cabin except for the flat roof, the rusted steel railroad tracks sticking out, and the faded and flaking plywood nailed on to the opening.

The area was fenced off with an eight-foot chain link topped with razor wire. There was a gate, of course, and a lock on the gate.

To my left was an old Chevy pickup truck from the nineties, empty with the hood still warm. There were plenty of footprints in the dirt, and I knew they were here.

Brooke Jennings. Karen Winslow. Ken Fischer. Patty Walsh. Lisa Paulson.

At first, I just stood there. I felt the weight of fate, or destiny, or whatever you want to call it when I drove out here. And I still felt it now, but I also felt this dread.

Brooke saw this. Whatever I was going to do was what Brooke had seen me do and it worked to her advantage. What the hell should I do? What could I do to change anything?

Walking in seemed utterly foolhardy. I'd likely accomplish little beyond making sure my friends didn't die alone. Waiting also seemed risky with the threats that Brooke had issued.

There was a raven in a pine tree on the other side of the fence and it was cawing at me. Over and over. Like I was trespassing in its territory. Like it was berating me for my cowardice. Like it was laughing at my hesitation.

The tree was an old one, a two-hundred-foot giant with the brown bark that is called a "yellow belly." The raven was perched about twenty feet up on a dead branch, its beady eyes staring at me. I really just wanted to pull my gun and shoot it.

Don't get me wrong. I like ravens. They are smart and curious and look beautiful in flight. But they'll dig through your trash given half a chance and they can be loud and annoying too.

I sighed and kicked at the dirt. With that racket the raven was making they had to know someone was here.

I stepped closer to the fence and looked at the padlock on the gate. While it looked intact from farther away, it had been cut.

The raven continued to caw as I stared at the lock, the insistent sound drilling into my head. "Caw. Caw. Caw."

Except to me it sounded like, "Fool. Fool. Fool."

And I am a fool. In so many ways. A fool to stay chief of

police after the meteor hit. A fool to be constantly standing in the way of Smitty and Karen and their visions for Carterville. A fool for all the time I spent with Annie Smith. A fool for this little town I loved so much. And really a fool for going up against someone that can see the future.

"Shut up," I muttered to the raven.

Without thinking, I pulled the lock off the gate, threw it to the ground, opened the gate, and walked through.

I stood there and nothing happened. I don't know what I was expecting, maybe something like a random rock tumbling down the hill and bonking me on the head, delivering a quick and useless death.

I took another step forward and the raven just cawed at me. Another step and I smelled him before I heard him, that sharp scent of too much body spray.

I reached for my gun, but he said, "Sorry, Henry, but you are not that quick."

I turned my head and saw the tall Steve Lancaster right next to that yellow belly pine with a gun, a matte black 9MM Luger, pointed at me. He had been behind it the whole time, the raven probably more upset about him than me.

"Brooke will see you now," he said with a grim smile.

I had been such a fool. Brooke saw that I would bring Steve in and got to him before I even thought of calling him. Steve installed those safety bars on Smitty's house right before the fire and made sure he didn't have the key. Steve cut the battery line in the van delaying me coming here. Steve didn't leave town with Smitty but brought him here to Brooke. He was a prisoner too.

Steve had me disarmed and even knew about the pistol

strapped to my ankle and the penknife in my back pocket. He then gestured me forward with his gun and the oppressive weight of fate was bearing down on me so heavily I could hardly breathe.

PART 5
AMOR FATI: JULY 4

FIFTY-SEVEN
WEDNESDAY JULY 4. THE CARTER MINE

Steve Lancaster was both careful and talkative as he marched me down the old mine shaft, his overpowering body spray not quite enough to drown out the dusty smell of the mine.

Voices echoed weirdly and the shaft was well lit by light bulbs strung along the ceiling, the distant rattle of a generator giving away the source of the electricity.

"It's not like she's ever been wrong about anything," he said as I marched in front of him. "Ever. Not in the two years since we met."

That stopped me short, my feet locking in place, but I didn't look back. "Two years?" I asked.

"Keep moving, Henry," he said. When I started walking again, he added, "Yes. Two years. I thought she was just a stupid kid, but she knew things. Important things."

"That's before you came to Flagstaff," I said.

"It is," he said. "She's why I came. For this. For you. For

Smitty." He chuckled. "I gotta tell you, it took some convincing, she wasn't even out of high school then, but she knew things. She told me the exact date I would get some terrible news and she was right. She… well, you'll see."

I stopped again, my heart rattling in my chest and sweat prickling across my skin despite the cooler temperature of the mine shaft. If Brooke had been maneuvering towards this for years, what the hell was I going to do?

That sense of the weight of fate went from oppressive to impossible, like the weight of the mine shaft, of Carter Hill itself, was pressing down on me. My knees almost gave out, but I gritted my teeth and just stood there, my hands forming fists and my fingernails digging into my palms.

Most people I know overestimate how much they can influence what goes on around them. Especially people in power. And, yes, I am guilty of this too. My position lets me do quite a bit, but it's also one where I am constantly confronting my limitations. Like when Karen Winslow and the business interests of the town oppose me. Like Smitty exerting his considerable control over the town. Like our small staff and the big issues we face these days. But this feeling was something completely different. I felt like I had no power whatsoever. No ability to affect the future at all.

It was devastating.

Behind me Steve chuckled. "I know," he said quietly. "Believe me, I know. We are all her pawns. It takes some getting used to. The Stoics have a saying, 'amor fati.' It's Latin, but basically means 'a love of fate.' I suggest you embrace it, Henry, and quick."

I didn't know a ton about Stoicism, but I did know the most famous Stoic, Marcus Aurelius, had been a Roman emperor as well as a philosopher. I knew the Stoics believed in accepting what they couldn't control but were also ethical and thought a lot about virtue.

Caving into the desires of a woman that can see the future and using Stoicism as a justification seemed to run at odds with the deeper precepts.

"Is that what you are doing?" I asked. "Justifying your crimes just because she can see how it will turn out?"

"Shut up, Henry," he said. "And get moving."

"Because I think murder is just about to be added to the list," I said. "Can you be a Stoic about that? When you have our blood on your hands?"

His invocation of philosophy had woken me up, given me just enough room to think. And, yes, part of me was still despondent, curled up into the emotional equivalent of the fetal position, but Steve's rationalization enraged a part of me, and I needed the anger.

I'm human, so it's not like I haven't rationalized away some terrible stuff, but this was just too far.

When he didn't say anything I turned around. His face was flush with anger, his hand tight on his 9MM.

When he still didn't say anything, I forged on. "Because I don't think cowardice is a virtue of the Stoics. And doing whatever Brooke tells you without question may be *amor fati*, but it's also cowardly. I would think the Stoics would be more into something like courage. Or maybe even valor."

His mouth opened to speak, but the flood gates were open and I cut him off. "And you realize, she set you up for this moment right here. If she's all powerful, then she saw my reaction. She saw my utter disdain for your bankrupt philosophy. My contempt for your hollowed out life. And she knew that you still wouldn't pull that trigger when I told you what I thought. That you would be the good little soldier she needs you to be. It's why she picked you. It's why you are the one here and not someone with a backbone. It's why I can tell you what I really think. It's why..."

The energy had mostly escaped, and I shrugged my shoulders, turned, and trudged down the mine shaft. He wasn't worth it. I needed to nurture that anger so I could at least die with some dignity and not be like Steve Lancaster.

"I used to get angry about it too," Steve said quietly from behind me. "I used to fight it. I used to think I could make a difference. But that date she gave me, the one where something terrible would happen. It's the day I was diagnosed with stage III colon cancer. It's also the day she told me there was only one way I would survive, and that was to get Smitty to heal me. And there was only one thing I could do to get Smitty to heal me in time. What choice did I have but to come here and do this?

"Your anger is understandable, Henry, but it's no use. She knows too much."

FIFTY-EIGHT
WEDNESDAY JULY 4. THE CARTER MINE

I don't know what I was expecting. Maybe Brooke Jennings on some kind of ornate throne with her followers bowing before her and her victims strung from the ceiling of a high cave. Maybe it was because this whole mess started out with me finding out how people in this town almost worshiped Smitty and his addictive healing power and now I was about to confront a woman with a power that could really engender worship and made Smitty's power seem almost superfluous.

I was expecting something dramatic, something big and bold and flashy. The details I imagined varied as we marched silently forth. I had nothing else to say to Steve and my anger seemed to have snuffed out his need to talk.

I nursed the anger, like there were just a few coals left in the woodstove and I was out of kindling. Just enough so I could summon the heat if I needed it and not so much that it would expend all its fuel.

It was a long walk, longer than I expected, and the air had grown damp and stale. The footing was challenging on the old narrow-gauge railroad tracks, stepping from railroad tie to railroad tie.

The tunnel at times seemed natural with the dark volcanic rock flaring out some and twisting this way and that. At other times the tunnel was straight and true, the mechanical gouges visible in the walls telling the story of its history.

I don't think we were quite below Carterville, but we were several hundred yards into the hill.

When the tunnel opened up into a cave it wasn't dramatic at all. There were six people tied up in chairs and Brooke Jennings pacing in front of them.

Six people.

It took my brain a moment to parse it. I was expecting the five people she abducted. Karen Winslow, Ken Fischer, Patty Walsh, Lisa Paulson, and Winston "Smitty" Smith. But there was a sixth.

Isabella Ortega.

My anger was gone and terror gripped me. I suddenly understood why the battery line had been cut in the van. Steve needed the extra five minutes to go get Ortega.

Our eyes met, but only for a moment. I saw a flash of shame and then her face scrunched up as she struggled against her bonds.

The young woman had been in the office guarding Carl George while all the drama went on with the fire. It must have driven her crazy. I'm sure all it took was Steve Lancaster telling her I had sent for her to get her to leave.

The scene took time to assemble in my brain. There was

just too much to look at. Too many people and too many expressions.

The cave was roughly oval, the ceiling about eleven feet high with two other tunnels coming into it. The railroad tracks continued down one of the tunnels, the larger one that was roughly straight back.

The chairs the six of them were tied to were wood and worn, looking to be at least fifty years old. To one side of the cave was a cot, a cooler, a jerry can, a big ammo box, and an old bookshelf with a camp stove on top and foodstuffs on the shelves.

The six of them were all tied the same way, their ankles were tied together, their hands behind the chair tied at the wrists with a piece of rope running under the chair and attached to their ankles. More rope was wrapped around their chests and the chair, all of it making sure they could barely move and making it quite hard to untie them. The rope work was neat, tidy, and nearly identical for all six.

The expressions on their faces varied. From Ortega's struggle, to Smitty's resigned sneer, to Karen's pursed lips that looked to be holding back terror, to Patty's brief flash of hope collapsing back into fear when she saw me.

Everyone was a mess. Smitty was wearing baggy grey sweats too big for him with his burned off hair and patches of pink new skin. Karen and Ken look disheveled and tired, Karen's black skirt torn and dusty, a bruise on Ken's right cheek. Lisa and Patty looked unharmed but scared, and Ortega just looked mad, her black hair partially out of her normally perfect ponytail giving her a wild look.

There were light bulbs strung on the ceiling giving a harsh

glare to the space. And there was something else there—two blocks of C-4 with the tips of metal blasting caps visible and wires running from the explosives to a little black box.

At the front of the scene was Brooke Jennings. I hadn't seen her out of her Carterville Inn uniform, and she looked different in jeans and a dark blue sweater. She was still young, still blonde, still petite and round faced with grey eyes, but she was no longer the meek employee of Annie Smith. There was a set to her jaw as she paced, her hair loose and flowing down her back, her eyes sharp as they flitted from me to the trussed-up people and back to me.

It was only seconds as I stood there, as I took in the scene, as I smelled the sharp scent of fear, as my stomach clenched into knots, and as my heart started up into a gallop.

But it felt like ages, and after her last note, the one pinned to the tree across from Smitty's burning house, I knew the general shape of what was coming.

Destroyer of Carteville
  you can't save all
    who will you chose?

I ignored the people, ignored the fact that Patty, Lisa, and Ortega were some of the most important people in my life, and stared at the C-4. The setup was neat, just like the rope work, and well done. The two chunks of C-4 were six feet apart and there was something else, a small black plastic device attached to the end of the metal blasting cap, something that would likely detect movement and fire off the cap if it was tampered with.

The two blocks of C-4 were encased in clear plastic and the wiring between everything ran through clear conduit. A fair amount of time and energy had been put into this arrangement. Besides the C-4 being on the eleven-foot ceiling and nearly impossible to reach, the rig had been clearly set up so you could see exactly what it was and that it couldn't be tampered with.

"You are right, Chief. There is no disarming it," Brooke said, still pacing, and I swear she sounded bored, as if she had seen this so many times that actually experiencing it was deadly dull.

I nodded and shifted my attention to her.

"I am sorry about what happened to your father," I began. "I am sorry that we didn't do better, but all of this won't—"

"This is not about him!" she snapped, her voice suddenly brimming with manic energy. "How can you be so stupid to think this is about him?"

Really looking at Brooke, I could see she was in pain. She rubbed at her right temple as she paced, and her young face had this clenched look that made her look older.

Those five minutes Steve bought by disabling the van had been enough for them to add Ortega to the list of victims but not enough to get Carl George out of town.

And this gave me a sliver of hope. It meant that Steve didn't just shoot him, that there were limits to what they were willing to do... or maybe how they wanted it to all look in the end. Or maybe it was some bizarre, tortured logic that came from Brooke and her power.

"What is it about then?" I asked, doing my best to keep my voice calm when I was anything but.

"Carteville…" she began, her old speech impediment coming through and showing a high level of stress which also gave me a little hope. She stopped pacing and took a deep breath, her grey eyes drilling into mine. "*Carterville*. This is all about Carterville."

Smitty gave a snort and said, "She thinks we are going to destroy it, Henry. You and I. As if either of us would do something so—"

While Smitty talked, Brooke marched over to him. He was on the far left end of the row of trussed up people and slapped him. Hard. The sharp sound echoing in the cave. "Shut up," she said. "That goes for all of you. One word and I'll have Steve taser you."

Smitty's left cheek was beet red and his eyes showed raw hate as he stared at the young woman, his jaw clenched shut.

It was a small thing in the scheme of what she had done, but the little hope I had slipped away and I started nursing the anger again. "How the hell can this be about Carterville?" I asked.

She stared at me, looking me up and down, and shook her head. I was a mess, soot covered, my clothing singed, my hat gone and my hair some kind of a mess I didn't even want to imagine. But it felt like that look had nothing to do with my appearance and was about something much deeper.

"You," she said and then turned to Smitty. "And him. You are the destroyers of Carterville. Your rivalry. Your petty disagreements. You and your enablers." Her hand encompassed the rest of the tied-up people. "You are destroying this town."

The silence was thick and the large cavern felt small. We

are the destroyers? How the hell can Smitty and I hating each other destroy this town?

"But that can't happen anymore," she said, a smile replacing her pained look and lighting up her face. "No matter what happens today, Carterville is saved."

FIFTY-NINE

WEDNESDAY JULY 4. THE CARTER MINE

I think what the meteor gifted Brooke with can be labeled more as a curse than a power. She had spent the last few years seeing the destruction of Carterville because of Smitty and me—whatever the hell that means—and trying to see a way through. Trying to see enough futures so that she could manipulate things here and there and cause it to turn out better.

Despite her threat and her treatment of Smitty, everyone started talking at once.

"You call this saving Carterville?" Smitty asked.

"I'm sorry, Boss," Ortega muttered as she continued to struggle against her bonds. "I should have known. I should have…"

Karen Winslow said, "I am not an enabler. What the hell do you mean by that?"

"Are you crazy?" I asked.

Everyone else said something, but those are what I could

hear. And then everyone was talking, and Brooke was telling us all to shut up, her tone getting more and more strident.

And then a gun went off, the sound of it in this small space absolutely painful, and everyone shut up. Steve Lancaster was at the cave entrance, and everyone seemed to have forgotten about him. His face was flushed and he looked angry.

"What do you mean 'no matter what happens today,'" he said to Brooke. "I thought you knew exactly what was happening today."

She rolled her eyes and shook her head. "I am not a god, Steve," she said. "I am a woman that sees the future. But I can't see everything. And I can't..." She ended up rubbing her temple. "There's too much interference. And I've never been able to see these moments that clearly."

Steve's jaw was working, like he was struggling to find the words. I am guessing that was the first time she represented her power clearly to him. All the tricks she used to pull him into her orbit were when she could see the future clearly.

"You lied to me," Steve said, his tone almost plaintive. "You used me."

"Oh, please," she said to him, her arms crossed. "This changes nothing. You no longer have cancer because of me. You will be rich soon because of me. I'm so very sorry it's a surprise that I am not totally omnipotent, but it changes nothing. We need to finish this."

His jaw muscles bunched up and his brown eyes narrowed. "Very well then."

His gun, which had wandered and was pointed at the floor, zeroed back in on me. His doubt, while hopeful, was never useful. He was too far away for me to try anything. And if I did and he fired and missed me, there was a good chance he would hit one of the hostages.

Brooke turned back to me. "No, I am not crazy," she said, answering my question from before when everyone was talking. "I am quite sane. And since I am tired of this, all of this, let me just answer your questions."

I nodded.

"First," she said, a bitter grimace forming on her face. "My father was a fool. A loving fool, but a fool at that. I don't blame you for his death. I blame myself."

I caught Patty's eye and she nodded to me. Maybe she was telling me that Brooke really wanted to save Carterville or that she could sense Brooke's emotional state enough to believe what she was saying.

Maybe it was the crisis we were facing, but in that moment, I wanted nothing more than time with Patty. I had no idea if a real relationship was possible, but I desperately wanted the opportunity to try.

"I was having dreams then," Brooke said, starting to pace again. "It was the first manifestation of my power. I saw him on the overlook reaching his hand up and summoning lightning. I didn't understand my dreams yet, but I think he did. I was a stupid kid and scared. I told him about it. The next storm that came, he was up there trying to summon the lightning." She stopped, her eyes haunted as she looked right at me. "And he did."

"I am sorry, Brooke," I said. I know, showing empathy for our seeming deranged captor seemed out of place, but I couldn't help myself. I remember Brooke as the precocious girl that loved her father so much and wanted to be just like him.

"Shut up, Henry," she said. "I don't want your pity. I want to save this town."

"Then why all of this?" I asked, nodding at the elaborate C-4 arrangement on the ceiling and the carefully tied hostages. "There are much easier ways to get rid of Smitty and me."

"Murder you and make you a martyr?" she asked. "No. No. That wouldn't do at all. But if you died in a house fire or in an unfortunate mine collapse… well, that would do."

"No one is going to rule this a mine collapse," I said. "And how the hell are you going to explain our presence or what is found when things are excavated?"

She stopped her pacing and stared at me and then shrugged. "I'll be here. I'll see a way through. There will be no excavation."

There was something else, otherwise we would all have been shot by now and our bodies buried under tons of rock. Annabelle knew I was here, and I had to guess that she wasn't a hostage because of her telekinetic power. Even though it was just coming back, she had proved she could do more than just tricks in extreme circumstances.

And Annabelle had called the sheriff and they were headed here. But maybe Brooke didn't know that. Maybe Carl's presence was interfering just enough. But why didn't they just shoot us? That would seem to make the future she wanted much more likely.

And then it snapped into focus. "So, you couldn't talk Steve into killing us in cold blood," I said. "And you don't have the stomach for it yourself."

She flinched like I had slapped her. She clearly didn't expect me to say that. Her cheeks flushed and her face twisted into something cruel that seemed less human and more animal.

"You never did find out who made the 911 call last Christmas morning and reported the dead elf up on Carter Hill, did you?" she asked.

My heart fluttered in my chest and a cold sweat sprung up on my forehead.

"Did you ever wonder where Annie got the idea to give you that cowboy hat on Christmas Eve?" she asked, a sneer on her face. "I'm guessing she never told you about the young woman with dark hair who made a casual comment about men in cowboy hats a few weeks earlier at just the right moment."

My mouth went dry and my heart seemed to stop for a beat or two. I didn't say anything. I didn't want to give her the satisfaction, but she was behind what happened to Lila Chang. Without her Lila wouldn't be dead.

"Yes," she said, her voice growing louder. "I was behind that. And I knew that you two would be too late to save William Reilly and made sure that happened." She was almost yelling now. "It was necessary so that we would get here. Some people have to die for the greater good. So don't you dare tell me what I do and don't have the stomach for."

The crushing weight of fate was lying on me again. I looked down at the hard rock of the cave and tried to concentrate. I was breathing as deeply as I could, but it didn't feel like I could get enough oxygen.

Brooke hadn't murdered Lila, but she had catalyzed the circumstances that led to her death. The same for William. Maybe she couldn't get Steve to murder us in cold blood and maybe she couldn't pull the trigger herself, but that doesn't mean she wouldn't make sure we all died.

She had set events in motion years ago to create this moment right here and right now. All in the name of saving Carterville from Smitty and me. It was too much. Too damn much.

When I looked back at Brooke, she was smiling softly and nodding. "Now you see it. Now you understand."

I just nodded. I had no words.

"So let me explain what comes next," she said, her voice gentle. "There is a five-minute timer on the explosives. I will trigger it when Steve and I leave. You will have enough time to untie one person and escape."

I opened my mouth to speak. There was nothing intelligent ready to come out, just a "What…?" but she cut me off. "It will take you a bit over two minutes to untie one person if you have your wits about you. You might think you can untie two, and you can, but then you won't have enough time to escape the explosion."

When she stopped talking, the cave was silent. No one spoke. No one moved. It seemed like no one was breathing.

"Six people, Henry," Brooke said. "Who will you save? Or will you take on too much—as we all know you are prone to doing—and die trying? Will your ego let you do anything less?"

She took a deep breath and smiled brightly. "I for one have no idea and that feels really good. I don't know about you all, but I can't wait to find out.

"Shall we do this?"

SIXTY

WEDNESDAY JULY 4. THE CARTER MINE

ONCE BROOKE AND STEVE WERE GONE, ONCE THE TIMER ON the ceiling came alive and started beeping every second as the five minutes leaked away, I felt free. Now that fate or destiny or whatever you want to call it was here, I didn't feel that oppressive weight anymore and I acted.

I rushed to Isabella Ortega on the far right side of the line of hostages. There was no thought, it was just my gut.

As I moved, Ken Fischer shouted to the retreating Brooke, "Wait! We had a deal. You promised me Karen and I would walk away from this. Wait!"

I heard the words but didn't really think about them and got to work on the knots at Ortega's wrists. If I freed her hands, she could do the rest. The bundle of knotted rope between her hands was thick, this first layer was the rope that bound her wrists to her ankles.

"Henry!" Smitty yelled. "What are you doing? You know

what I can do. You know I can save some lives here if I get clear."

He went on but I tuned him out and worked the knots. The rope was nylon and Ortega's struggling had tightened them up.

"You made a deal with her!" Karen said to her husband. "You told me you were blackmailed. You made a goddamn deal with her!?"

The air was thick with nervous sweat, and it smelled like someone had been here long enough that they had let the bladder go.

"Help someone else," Ortega quietly said to me. "Please, Boss. Help someone else."

Her tone was pleading and there was pain behind it. Maybe guilt for letting Steve capture her, maybe something deeper. It didn't matter.

"No," I said, my tone flat and calm.

The fight between Ken and Karen was escalating but I ignored it. Smitty was yelling and I ignored that too.

"When you get out," Lisa said to Ortega, "tell Frank I love him. Tell him I said he's the best man I know, and it has been the honor of my life to be his partner."

She went on giving Ortega small messages for their three kids and two grandchildren, but I couldn't listen. I had to focus. I had to work the knots.

There was a clatter and I glanced up and saw that Smitty had tried to move himself towards the entrance still tied to the chair and hand fallen over. "You've got four minutes and thirty seconds, Henry," he yelled. "You can do this. See those knots. Find the path!"

Was Smitty hoping I would untie him next, or had he shed

his selfish skin now that his fate was clear and he was actually trying to help?

I don't know what kind of knots Steve used but they were extensive and difficult, designed to both stay tight and take a long time to untie. I got the first set of knots undone, unwound the rope between Ortega's wrists and ankles, and started on the knots at her wrists. Her struggles had made them very tight.

Ortega kicked her feet out with a groan of relief, her hands had been tied tightly to her ankles, pulling on her shoulders, and she rolled them, making it harder to do my work.

I needed a knife. I needed time.

Sweat started trickling down the side of my face as I dug into them.

"Four minutes, fifteen!" Smitty yelled.

When Patty started relaying messages to Ortega, started relaying a message for Frank, I couldn't take it. I tuned everything out except the knots and Smitty's countdown of the time.

My breath was loud in my chest, my heart hammering in my ears, sweat running down my forehead as I dug my fingers into the rope. It was a strange moment that seemed to draw out. For once in my life, I knew exactly what I should be doing and had no doubts. If no one else survived, Isabella Ortega needed to survive. It was this crystal clarity, and while I felt the urgency of the situation and the adrenaline flowing through my veins, I also felt a contentment I rarely had.

After this, after this one last thing, the struggle will be over.

It wasn't like I had had a lot of time to contemplate my

own death lately. Sure, a decade ago when both my parents died within eighteen months of each other, I had spent quite a bit of time pondering my mortality. But since then, I had had more pressing matters. If I did think about it, I hoped that death wouldn't be long and drawn out like my parents, but not so quick that I didn't have time to say goodbye. I hoped that I would be good and old and ready to let go of the struggle of life.

I didn't expect the feeling to come at the age of fifty with death imminent in the flash of an explosion.

But I leaned into it, letting the chemicals that had been dumped into my system drive me forth and keep me quick, not caring about the torn fingernails and raw fingers as I kept at Ortega's knots. And I let the peace of acceptance deepen as the words of everyone washed over me.

"Four minutes!" Smitty said.

As I finished with Ortega's wrists, I did the math in my head. A little over a minute for the wrists. Hopefully less for the ankles. And two minutes to get far enough down the tunnel before the explosion. Ortega would have the time, and maybe one other, if my degrading fingers didn't slow me down and Ortega helped.

"Three minutes and fifty seconds," Smitty said.

I released Ortega's wrists and she groaned again with relief, and I moved to Lisa who was next to her. I didn't think about it, I just knew.

"Are you sure?" Lisa asked me as I started at the rope that connected her wrists to her ankles.

"Yes," I said, my voice still calm. "For Frank and your kids and your grandkids." I didn't say the name of her children or her grandchildren. I knew them all, their names, what they loved, where they lived. They were all family, and I didn't think my calm could handle it.

"Come on, Henry!" Smitty said. "Seriously? You're not even going to try to untie me, are you?"

I just worked the knots.

"Shit!" Ortega said. She had shoved down the ropes wrapped around her chest far enough so that she could bend over and was working on the knots at her ankles. "My hands are numb, Boss. Not workin' so good."

I almost stopped and went back to her but did the math again. Even if it took her twice as long as me, she would still likely have time to escape.

Likely.

There was nothing guaranteed here. Nothing certain. I kept working on Lisa's knots.

"Three minutes, twenty seconds!" Smitty said.

Steve was nothing if not meticulous, each knot tied the same way. Despite the damage to my fingers, I knew the tricks now and it was going faster.

Ken and Karen's fight was reaching a shouting crescendo with her saying things like "How could you be so stupid?" and him saying things like "But I did it for us. For you." But I didn't care about their fight, and I didn't feel guilty about the choices I had made.

To distract myself, my mind wandered a bit and I imagined sitting at the long counter of the Carterville Diner, Patty serving me coffee with a bright smile on her face, Frank working the grill, and the air perfumed with the smell of bacon, syrup, and coffee with the town peaceful outside so I could just have a moment, just take a breath, just be.

"I want that too," Patty said, her tone gentle.

I wasn't surprised, Patty's empathetic power was something that was quite intriguing to me.

I glanced up. She had twisted around and was looking at me, her green eyes intense. "You've made the perfect choices here, Henry. Anyone that thinks or says differently just proves that you have."

It was just a moment, but it was almost as nice as that calm cup of coffee would be. I had felt sure, but now I felt validated and that was exactly what I needed. Patty, of course, knew I needed that and gave it to me. I took a deep breath and redoubled my efforts.

SIXTY-ONE
WEDNESDAY JULY 4. THE CARTER MINE

M

OMENTS DON'T LAST. THEY CAN'T. OTHERWISE THEY wouldn't be moments. I know, I know, way too vague and philosophical. But that time in the cave where I knew my purpose, where I could gracefully accept my mortality, where the comfort Patty gave me was the perfect thing, was just that, a moment.

It didn't last.

As I worked the knots on Lisa's wrists, as Ortega cursed as she worked the knots at her ankles, as Smitty grew angry with me for not untying him, as Karen and Ken redoubled their commitment to fight until the moment we all died, I felt doubt creep in.

Who was I to decide who lived or died? Who the hell was Brooke Jennings to put me in this situation and why had she done it? She had been so sure that I could only untie one person and get out alive and now that was looking like it was true. She also seemed quite sure that my ego would keep me here working until the explosion and I could believe that too.

But the thing that really twisted me up was wondering how much Brooke had said was affecting my choices right now.

The noise of the fighting and the shouting and the cursing echoed in the small damp space, and I was having more trouble keeping the anger and the accusations out.

Another fingernail tore, badly, and a couple of fingers were bleeding, staining the rope red and making it harder to grip.

"Three minutes," Smitty called. "Can't you even untie a couple of ropes, Henry? At this rate we are all going to die."

And maybe that was why Brooke said what she did. So I would believe I could get two people free, so I would not concentrate my time on one person. She knew that all their hands would be numb so they would have trouble helping.

"You got this, Henry," Patty said, her voice kind and gentle, trying to nudge me back to where I had been.

I nodded. I almost asked her to keep talking, but this was Patty Walsh, I didn't need to.

"You were why I stayed, Henry," she said. "You and Frank. You were the first person I met in town writing parking tickets and being so kind. Walking me up to the diner. And Frank is the gentlest man I've ever known. And that's what I needed. That's exactly what I needed.

"I remember the day, it was late summer, the sky so crystalline blue, the air warm and still, the scent of the junipers floating in the air like subtle perfume."

"Two minutes and fifty seconds," Smitty called. "And do you two need a room? Because it's kinda now or never, kids."

He chuckled, a manic high-pitched twitter, but no one else did.

Patty kept talking to me, her tone low, and while it wasn't the same moment, the same level of peace, it was what I needed. I finished Lisa's wrists and she too groaned in relief and started rubbing her wrists. I stood up using her chair, my knees creaking in the way they had started doing that was just a constant reminder of my age.

I moved around to the front and saw that Ortega hadn't gotten very far.

"Let me," I said.

The young woman looked at me, her brown eyes moist, her face scrunched up in pain. "No," she said. "No… I…"

"Yes," I said. "I need you to survive Isabella. Please."

She sniffed and nodded, and I kneeled down and got to work on her ankles.

"Two minutes, thirty," Smitty said. "Halfway done. I would say that it's been nice knowing you all, but you know, it hasn't."

Patty, who had paused while I was speaking to Ortega, started talking again, resuming her gentle retelling of the day she came to Carterville, the day we met. This was before the meteor and powers, when things around here were a whole lot simpler. When I was just a small-town cop in rural Arizona, and I actually had time for things like parking tickets and welcoming new tourists.

It was her curly red hair, freckled cheeks, and sharp green eyes that caught my attention. Her ready smile and her intriguing curves. I was with Annie Smith at the time and that day I didn't think I'd ever see Patty again, but she stayed. She became a friend. And now that I was free of Annie, I still hadn't had the courage to ask her out.

Patty stiffened and I thought I heard a sound echoing down the tunnel.

"Someone's coming," she hissed, and Ken and Karen actually shut up.

As I wound the sound back, I became convinced it wasn't anything. It was the sound of a chair scraping on rock as one of them shifted position that just echoed funny. It was nothing important.

And that feeling felt familiar. I had experienced it before. But it couldn't be that. It couldn't be him. He told me he was never coming back.

"It's Martin," Patty whispered, hope filling her voice. "Martin! We're here," she yelled. "Hurry!"

SIXTY-TWO
WEDNESDAY JULY 4. THE CARTER MINE

Martin Lester. The quiet man. My former colleague and friend.

That feeling I had when I heard the noise echoing down the tunnel and immediately dismissed it as something easily explainable was Martin's power. He wasn't invisible and he wasn't silent, but when he put his mind to it, he was very hard to see or hear.

I had experienced his power often enough and that feeling was part of my mind recognizing it, not that it did any good. I still rationalized away the sound.

But Martin couldn't hide his desire from Patty's empathetic power. She felt him coming.

Hope blossomed in me, and it was everything I could do to not turn around as I kept working on Ortega's ankles.

"Two minutes, ten seconds until this is all over," Smitty said.

And then the hope came crashing down. Even with

another set of hands it wasn't going to be enough time. Martin was just adding himself to the list of victims. I almost shouted at him to turn around and save himself, but I couldn't. I just couldn't.

I'd like to tell you that I was too focused on freeing Ortega's ankles to do anything about it, but that would be a lie.

The words rose in my throat, I almost turned around, but then I just let it go. I've thought a lot about that moment, and I have to say that I am not proud of it. Martin deserved to know what he was getting into with as much time as possible to make up his mind.

But that was just it. There was no time. I worked the knots.

"You gotta be…" Martin Lester said behind me when he entered the cave.

"Cut me loose!" Smitty yelled.

"Hell with that," Lester said.

Everyone started talking again, their voices echoing in the cave, and I couldn't make much of it out.

"Two minutes!" Smitty yelled, punching through the cacophony. He then chuckled manically. "Time to run if you're going to run."

Lester was close, touched me on my shoulder, and handed me a knife. It was just a penknife with a three-inch blade, but I recognized it—the bright yellow case was unmistakable. It was Lester's and I knew it was razor sharp.

"You should go," I said as I took it, finally finding my voice.

He kneeled next to me in front of Lisa Paulson and said, "What? And miss the fun?" Out of the corner of my eye I saw that he had another knife, a fixed blade hunting knife with about a ten-inch blade.

"Brooke?" I asked, my head down as I sawed through the ropes.

"Cuffed to an unconscious guy with short grey hair," he said, and I could hear the amusement in his voice. "Down the tunnel a bit."

He finished with Lisa's ankles, damn he was good with that knife, and moved to Ken Fischer who was sitting next to her.

"Run," I said to Lisa as I finished cutting through the rope and freeing Ortega's ankles. "You too," I said to her. "Get Lisa out of here. Secure Brooke and Steve. That is an order."

I didn't bother to look, but heard them scurrying behind me as I went over to Karen Winslow and started working on her ankle ropes.

"One minute, forty-five," Smitty said. "And of course I'm last. Why would anyone cut free the guy who can heal people? Why?"

"If he don't shut the hell up," Lester said, "I think we should leave him. What do you think, Chief?"

I didn't answer. I focused on cutting through the ropes at Karen's ankles. I was following Lester's lead here—he was working on Ken's ankle ropes. At the time, I was way too focused to think much about it, but looking back, I should have only focused on ankles and not wrists. You can run with your hands tied behind your back. It might not be pretty on the rough floor of a mine tunnel with train tracks running down it, but it was better than nothing.

"If we survive this," Karen said, her voice low, "we are going to have to have a nice long conversation about what happened here."

I snorted. "If we survive," I said, "I think you are going to have much more important matters on your hands."

It was silent then, the beeping of the timer above us sounding loud.

"How?" I asked Lester, not having the time or focus for the full question, but this was someone who had known me my entire life, so I figured he'd get the question. I wanted to know how he had gotten here just when we needed him.

"Annabelle," he said. "She called as soon as the fire happened."

Of course. I had promised him that I wouldn't call again, so I hadn't, but Annabelle hadn't made any promises.

Lester finished with Ken's ankles and moved to the ropes binding his chest to the chair.

"One minute, thirty," Smitty called, but he didn't say anything else. Maybe Lester had actually shut him up.

Lester finished with the ropes at Ken's chest and Ken stood up. I was focused so I didn't see his face, but I know he was looking at Karen and Karen was looking at him. But only for a moment and then he was stumbling away down the tunnel, leaving his wife behind without a word.

Lester moved to the ropes at her chest and cut through them just as I finished with her ankles.

"Get her out of here," I said to Lester.

He nodded and grabbed her arm and levered her up. Karen yelped in surprise, or maybe pain. They had been here a while.

"Don't lose it," Lester said as he handed me his big knife. He knew me so well. I did my best to smile and nod as he hauled Karen down the tunnel.

"Just you and me now, Henry," Smitty said. "The destroyers of Carterville."

This was the kind of situation for a dramatic moment. Me standing over him with a sharp hunting knife, him tied up to a chair and helpless, half his hair gone, patches of newly healed skin all over his body, all with the relentless beeping of the timer in the background. It would have been good to watch him squirm, good to hear him at least trying to be nice.

But there was no time.

With him on his side, the ropes around his chest were right there, tight against the side of the chair. I hacked at them hard with the wood backing it and it took maybe fifteen seconds to slice through.

I was then at his ankles.

"Do it," Smitty hissed. "Now. And don't worry about cutting me."

It was a bundle of rope with his ankles tied together and then more rope and another knot wound between his ankles trussing his ankles to his wrists.

But I took him at his word. I hacked at the ball of ropes, using the long sharp knife as a saw.

"She's not right," Smitty said as I worked. I wished he would just shut up, but I didn't say anything. I couldn't spare any energy or attention. "Pacing. Chewing her fingernails. Mumbling to herself which always sounded like arguments."

He was talking about Brooke, and while it was interesting, it sure as hell wasn't the time. I kept cutting.

"I wouldn't want her power," he said. "That's a curse. What would seeing enough futures to create this do to you? And imagine if this was the best future you could find? And why the hell didn't she see Martin coming?"

He was nervous. This wasn't Smitty pleading for his life or expressing gratitude, but it was the stress of the situation coming out.

"One minute, Henry," he said. "Nice of you to try. Stupid, but nice. I—"

He cried out in pain as the knife hit flesh. I can't say that I enjoyed it. I had cut myself enough and badly enough that it just made my stomach tighten in empathy. I pulled back, adjusted the trajectory of the knife and kept sawing away.

And then I was through. Smitty jumped up, which at first surprised me, and then I remembered his power. Of course he wasn't stiff and cramping up. Even with all he'd been through today, his body was still healing itself.

I was squatting down and for a moment I thought he was going to leave me there, but then he extended his still bound together hands.

There was no time for words. I let him help me up, took him by the arm, and we ran.

SIXTY-THREE
WEDNESDAY JULY 4. THE CARTER MINE

WHY DIDN'T BROOKE JENNINGS SEE MARTIN LESTER COMING?

And she didn't. She couldn't have. If she had, she wouldn't have let Lester knock Steve Lancaster out and cuff her to his unconscious body halfway down the tunnel. It would have been too easy to avoid. Leave a little sooner and get out of there before he arrived. Or tell Steve of the danger and he could have rigged something to capture him even with his power.

The clairvoyant couldn't see the quiet man.

Maybe there's something deep in that statement, but as Smitty and I ran down the tunnel, the noise of our rush echoing around us, the beeping of the countdown timer getting fainter, my brain put that much together.

It was better than thinking about dying in an explosion or when tons of rocks fell on me. It was better than regretting that I just might die because I took the time to try to save Smitty.

As we ran down the tunnel, the uneven surface a challenge, I was awake and alert and energized. Running strongly, carefully placing my feet so they avoided the old railroad tracks and bigger rocks. Not just because of the adrenaline of the day but because I was touching Smitty. I felt the faint golden glow of his power seeping into me, and I ran like I hadn't run in twenty years.

My heart beat fast but smoothly in my chest, clean sweat helped cool me down, and my lungs sucked in deep breaths of cool air.

I loved it and I hated it because I understood the source. I didn't know if Smitty was doing it on purpose or if it was just the side effect of skin-to-skin contact, but it made me hate him just a little bit more and relate even more to those that had become addicted to his power.

The tunnel curved and in the distance I could see a spec of light that was escape and safety. That was survival. There were people up ahead of us, close to the entrance, and for a moment I hoped. I hoped that we had escaped this trap and Brooke had been wrong despite her power.

And then the distant beeping stopped. For a moment I thought we had just run out of earshot but then I wound back the last beep in my head and that couldn't be the case, it wasn't that dim.

The thought sparked in my mind just as light blossomed in the cave, light too bright to look at, and then we were flying, the wind knocked out of me as the sound of the explosion crashed into us. And then we were on the cool floor of the tunnel, rocks, railroad ties, and rails under us, dust engulfing us and the mountain rumbling under us.

My body was a constellation of pain again. Not as bad as

what happened with the Lila Chang case last Christmas, not like in the fire only an hour or two ago, but I could taste blood and it was hard to breathe and everything hurt.

I hate to say this, but while I did throw my free left arm over my head, I also held tight to Smitty. Even if what I had been feeling from him was just residual, I was hoping it was enough to survive.

It felt like the tunnel was a wild horse beneath us trying to buck us off. Rocks fell on us, adding to the constellation of pain. I couldn't breathe, the air was so choked with dust.

I wondered for a moment if Smitty could survive without oxygen. I worried that the figures I saw ahead had been caught in this too. And I worried that a rock might hit Smitty in the head hard enough and we both would die.

But this was all just a flash in my mind as rocks and dirt rained down on us.

SIXTY-FOUR
WEDNESDAY JULY 4. THE CARTER MINE

I STILL DREAM OF THAT RUN. MY LEGS PUMPING, MY LUNGS filling easily, my heart beating strong. In the dreams, I feel like I can run forever. It's hard, yes, it's taxing, but none of that matters. I love to run and it feels so good.

Sometimes the dream twists and that light at the end of the tunnel keeps moving away from me. Sometimes it's not Smitty's arm that I'm clinging to but Brooke Jennings or occasionally Annie Smith.

Sometimes I am running away from something terrible, and every so often I actually make it out of the tunnel. And sometimes Smitty's power fades and I am just a pitiful middle-aged, out-of-shape man trying to run.

Even when it's a bad version of the dream, I just so love the feeling of being able to run easily, as if I will never run out of energy.

As I lay there under the rocks, coughing and gasping for

breath, my grip on Smitty's arm tight, I wished we were still running, wished that we had made it.

I've faced death enough lately to know how and where I'd like to meet my end. I'd like to be in the Carterville Diner with Frank and Patty and my son Tom. Shooting the shit and drinking a little gin and soda with a twist of lime and a dash of bitters.

I get it that it would be hard on my friends and my son to have me drop dead with them right there, but it would be a hell of a lot better than dying buried under rubble with Winston "Smitty" Smith.

The weight of the rocks was heavy, but it wasn't crushing. Or was that Smitty's power? Would we lie here with his power healing us, hacking our lungs out until his power finally failed? That gave me even more empathy for what Smitty went through in the fire, burning and healing over and over again.

But the rocks weren't that heavy, and while I hurt, everywhere, I had experienced much, much worse.

I tried moving my left arm which was protecting my head. It moved easily, the rocks that had fallen on me small. I got my arm under me and levered myself up, slitting my eyes open. In the distance, the light at the end of the tunnel was still there. The cave had gone dark, so its presence was clear. I heard the echoing of the others coughing down the tunnel.

"Come on," I said through the hacking and tugged at Smitty. I wasn't going to let go of him. Not yet.

He didn't move and my heart skipped a beat or three, which it had been doing entirely too much lately. He wasn't coughing and I couldn't tell if he was breathing or not.

Thoughts raced around my head, like horses on the track trying to win a race.

If Smitty was dead, did that mean Brooke had won and Carterville was saved? Not that I knew how the hell Smitty and I were supposed to destroy it.

On the other hand, another death on my watch was not something that I could easily stomach. And Carterville would reel if their superpowered healer was dead and a source of tourist traffic would end.

I shook my head at that last thought. That was how Karen Winslow and the town council thought. Not me.

This was a small moment with these thoughts flashing through my mind. It didn't matter what Brooke had seen and it didn't matter how much simpler my life would be without Smitty, there was only one thing to do.

I let go of him and pulled my T-shirt up from underneath my short-sleeved button-down and covered my nose. I needed to be able to breathe. I pulled a flashlight from my utility belt and clicked it on, the beam of light sharply defined in the dusty air. I set it aside and started pulling rocks off of Smitty.

None of them were that big, fist-sized at the largest. But if it hit you in the right spot, you were done for.

"Help!" I croaked between wracking coughs. "We need help down here! And someone call 911."

I could hear other coughing and the echoing sound of movements. "Roger that," I heard a woman's voice say, echoing down the tunnel. It was Ortega and I breathed a sigh of relief.

The light from the flashlight was low, casting weird shadows as I worked, but it was enough. I got all the bigger rocks off Smitty and grabbed the flashlight and assessed the damage.

His chest wasn't moving, he wasn't breathing, he needed CPR, but if he was bleeding out that could take precedence.

With the dust on him and in the air, I couldn't see much. There was some blood oozing at the back of his head and some blossoming bruises on his body, but that was it.

I didn't know how far his power could go. Did it work when he was unconscious? Did he simply run out surviving the fire, healing Harold and me, and now this? Did something happen in the explosion that ended our powers?

The last thought lodged in my brain, and it spun around as I continued to work on Smitty. Would I be happy or sad if Carterville was suddenly without powers? If we were just a struggling old mining town in Northern Arizona off the beaten path with not enough tourism?

Maybe that was it. Maybe Smitty's power had been the only thing keeping him alive and now that Brooke had blown up the source of our powers, he was dead. The explosion had been large, shaking the whole tunnel. I was no explosives expert, but it seemed to be more than what I saw rigged in the cave.

I turned him over as gently as I could, coughing the whole time. The shirt wasn't helping much, the air still thick with choking dust, and it was hard to keep over my nose.

I knelt next to him and quickly checked his pulse. Nothing. I took the position with my elbows straight and my hands on top of one another and began compressions.

It was hard. With the coughing and my eyes watering and I was starting to get dizzy. But I let it all go and just did CPR. After thirty quick compressions, I leaned down, tilted his head back and did my best to get some air in him. I mostly coughed but it was something.

And then back to compressions.

While it was still cool in the tunnel, I was soon sweating. Compressions. Breaths. Compressions. Breaths.

The air had cleared just a little and I was coughing less but still getting dizzier. My body hurt everywhere, and it felt like this was useless. Stupid. Unwise, even.

I needed to get out of here and get some air or I would just die with him. Maybe there was something else wrong with my heart beyond the spasm. Maybe it pointed at a bigger problem, and putting my body under this kind of stress would just lead to a heart attack. And was Smitty really worth it? What the hell was I doing? And were our powers really gone? Wait, could I feel the background buzz of them? Not with all of this going on.

Did I want our powers to be gone? Did I want Carterville to go back to being a sleepy little mountain town?

Two days ago, when I had the coronary artery spasm, I wasn't having a panic attack, but I was close to one there coughing and sweating and trying to revive Smitty.

I wanted to run and leave him. Go get some help and really breathe and then come back. My body was telling me to run. My mind was freaking out.

But I stayed. I worked it. I did what the job demanded of me. What my humanity demanded of me.

It seemed like forever, but I'm sure it was only a minute or two.

"Nine one one is on the way, Boss," Ortega called down the tunnel. "And everyone is out safe. Martin and I are headed your way."

SIXTY-FIVE
WEDNESDAY JULY 4. THE CARTER MINE

THE SUN WAS SHOCKINGLY BRIGHT AS WE RAN SMITTY OUT OF the tunnel. It hadn't been an easy decision, but we had to be able to breathe. I had his feet while Ortega and Lester each had a shoulder.

We set him down right out of the cave, and while I tried to hack a lung out, Ortega and Lester started CPR. She was doing compressions while he was at his head.

Besides the brightness of the light, my eyes were watering and I couldn't see very well. But I counted quickly.

Patty. Lisa. Karen. Ken. Everyone was here.

I also saw two people sitting against the fence. Brooke and Steve.

The raven up in the big yellow belly pine was making a racket, cawing indignantly at this incursion onto his territory, demanding that we leave immediately.

There were too many thoughts running around my head.

Smitty dead? Powers gone? How had so many of us gotten out of there alive if Brooke could really see the future?

If Smitty was dead, what would my life in Carterville actually be like? I had been watching him, arresting him, trying to blunt his damage to my town since he was a teenager. What would Carterville be like without him? Who would I be without him?

We all fight our demons, plenty internal, some external. What happens to us when they are suddenly gone?

When I could get a breath, I wiped the tears out of my eyes and walked over to the fence. I could see that Brooke was cuffed to Steve and Steve was cuffed to the fence. She was glaring at me. He still appeared to be unconscious with a blossoming bruise on his forehead.

"Is this what you saw?" I croaked as I got close but stopped short of being in reach.

Her lips formed a smirk and she nodded her head. "Not my preferred outcome, but, yes, within the realm of possibility."

"And you still 'saved' Carterville?" I asked

She smiled but it was a hard little thing. "Yes. As I told you, all outcomes led to my goal." She paused, staring at me, and then winced and rubbed her temple. "Or at least all outcomes will lead to my goal."

"So Smitty had to die?" I asked.

She shook her head. "No." Her eyes left me and went to Smitty.

I turned and looked. Patty and Lisa were standing watching, looking dirty and bedraggled. Ortega had stopped compressions while Lester filled Smitty's lungs with air.

When Lester leaned back and Ortega raised up to begin

compressions again, Smitty pulled in a big shuddering breath and started coughing.

We all froze, staring at him. He weakly raised his hand. "I like you just fine, Martin," he said, his voice low and weak, "but not like that. Let's just be friends, okay?"

There was nervous laughter and I turned to Brooke and said, "I don't understand."

She nodded and smiled, fully. "But you will, Henry. One day, you will."

EPILOGUE
WEDNESDAY JULY 4. THE CARTERVILLE OVERLOOK

As inky blackness finally started creeping into the sky on the longest day of my life, I breathed a sigh of relief. Me, most of the town, and a gaggle of tourists were up at Carterville Overlook awaiting the fireworks show.

The western horizon was lit up with quickly dimming yellow and orange against the northernmost flank of the San Francisco Peaks as night finally took hold. The air was warm and calm and perfumed with the smell of grilling meat.

I had had a shower, changed clothing, and gotten one of my old cowboy hats on my head and felt something starting to approach human. I hurt all over from the explosion, but I was in a strange place and even grateful for that. The pain meant that I was alive and alive was good.

Brooke Jennings and Steve Lancaster were gone, locked up in the county facility in Flagstaff. Carl George was home in Flagstaff, probably sleeping by now.

Smitty was striding around, laughing and telling stories,

dressed in his flowing off-white New Age clothing, happily telling everyone of how his power saved his life over and over when he was trapped in his house as it burned to the ground. I don't think Harold or I ever got mentioned.

Patty and Lisa were at the Carterville Diner booth with Frank at the grill, as usual, and the two women were selling burgers, hot dogs, and watermelon. Frank and I needed to have a long conversation, the kind we had out in his greenhouse with multiple beers. Lisa was okay, but she had been in danger and I hadn't told him. I hadn't been able to catch his eye all evening.

But I had caught Patty's eye earlier, and she flashed me a kind smile that made my knees go a little weak. It was clear there was a lot more to be said there too and a lot more to be processed there.

Karen Winslow was dressed in a long skirt and a flashy cowboy shirt flowing through the crowd with a smile on her face. Her absent horses had been found at a nearby vacant ranch, just part of the show Brooke put on making it look like they had fled. Ken Fischer was noticeably absent. I kind of expect this to be the new norm.

Martin had left town as soon as he'd given me his statement and I had given Ortega the night off, so it fell to me to be up here.

"You're quiet tonight, Henry," Annie Smith said. She smiled shyly and was dressed in her black and white Carterville Inn outfit. This was her show, and it was the flyer for this event that got me on the trail of Brooke only three days ago. It seemed like a lifetime.

"It's been a day," I said with what smile I could manage. Everyone knew about the fire. No one but those involved knew about Brooke, her powers, the hostages at the mine, and the threat to the town.

"A fire and an earthquake," she said with a shake of her head. "What more disasters can possibly land on us today?"

The explosion in the mine had been felt by everyone here, causing minor damage to a few buildings. Everyone figured it was an earthquake and we had decided to let that be. At least for now.

"We" being Karen and myself. She was shell-shocked after we all escaped but it didn't take her long to come back to being mayor. This was a small town and word would get out, but it seemed best to breathe for a moment or two before the wagging of tongues started.

I let Annie's question sit there for a bit. She knew about Brooke and about Karen and Ken being missing. She was fishing, but we both knew this wasn't the time or the place. Not that I knew if there ever would be a time or place for this.

"I can't imagine anything else happening," I said.

There were portable lights set up, a long extension cord ran from the church, but the light was dim and Annie looked lovely. I caught the faint floral scent of her perfume and briefly wished things were different between us… but only briefly.

She rested her hand on my chest and my body responded to our long intimacy. "Maybe after this is over, you and I can have a long talk," she said quietly.

I would be lying if I said I wasn't tempted. Our breakup last Christmas had been spectacular and brutal, but when we were in her office working together yesterday, trying to figure out what Brooke was up to, it felt like old times to me.

I guess it felt like old times to her too. The very nature of our relationship has been on again, off again since we were teenagers. And that meant there were plenty of difficult times, but there were also plenty of good times. Realistically, though, seeing Annie as a murder suspect last Christmas had changed something for me and that wasn't going to change back.

"Sorry, Annie…" I began, the words feeling like they were sticking in my throat. "I don't think that's a good idea. Besides, after this, I plan to sleep for a week or so."

Her face hardened and she nodded once, turned, and walked away. There was something there that felt final.

That's the trouble with small-town relationships. After they are over you can't get away from your ex. I was the chief of police, Annie ran the local inn, our paths would always be crossing.

It's why we had gotten back together so many times and it's why being apart for good would always be awkward and painful.

I moved away from the booths and the crowd to the far end of the overlook. There were plenty of people here, sitting on the low wall built of local volcanic rocks, eating, looking at the quickly darkening desert, talking. But I found a place that was quiet. I needed time. I needed to think. And God knows, I needed a few drinks and lots of time to sleep.

It's one of the benefits of the uniform. It's often easy to be alone in a crowd, which was what I wanted, but it wasn't to be tonight.

"You'll see Doctor Lion tomorrow," my sister Wendy said as she strolled up. She was dressed in jeans and an oversized Carterville PD sweatshirt, her shoulder-length brown hair pulled back into a nub of a ponytail. Her tone was casual, but it wasn't a question. "I chatted with her earlier." She nodded back towards the crowd. I had seen Doctor Lion, but we hadn't talked. "She's got you booked at 2:00 p.m.."

I just nodded. Wendy was my older sister and when she was worried about me it was like when I was five and she was seven, when the two years between us actually made a difference. "Sure," I said, just in case she didn't see the nod.

"I know Smitty healed you after the fire," she continued as if I hadn't spoken, "but that was a hell of a thing you did. Seems like you've got a few reasons to get checked out."

This was my sister, arguing her point after I had already conceded. It was sweet and it was annoying. She was opening her mouth to say more when I said, "I agree with you, Wendy."

Her jaw worked and she stared at me. I hadn't told her about the mine, and with a few drinks in me, I probably would. I was moving slow, bruises all over my body from the explosion, but none that were noticeable with my cowboy hat and a long-sleeved shirt on.

She cocked her head and kept staring at me. "You seem different," she said.

I shrugged my shoulders and suppressed a groan—a big rock had hit me between them on my back. "An old friend recently told me about a Latin saying," I said. "*Amor fati*. Love your fate. Seems like a good lesson for me today."

I smiled and it was a real, albeit tired, smile. Maybe Brooke had set things in motion to make sure Smitty and I didn't destroy Carterville. Maybe I couldn't see it. And maybe I should do my best to enjoy the ride, to change the things I can and accept the things I can't. Seems to me the serenity prayer has a lot in common with "amor fati."

Except I don't want to be like Steve Lancaster and give up

on the fights that are important. I don't want to let fate turn me into someone I can't look at in the mirror.

And let's be real. I'm human, so some days looking in the mirror is hard, but you know what I mean.

Wendy stared at me for a bit. She's my sister. She knew me. She knew there was more, but she also knew that I'm not about to talk about it here. She smiled and nodded. "I like that saying."

We chatted more, just bits of small-town gossip, and soon she wandered off and was quickly replaced by Smitty.

He was clean, but still looked a fright with missing hair and white patches of new skin. He had buzzed his hair down to about half an inch, but it was still clear that a bunch of hair was missing, and I think that was the point. His wounds and his survival would only serve to grow his legend.

"I've been thinking," he began, looking around, but no one was currently close to us, the uniform keeping the tourists away. "Adding things up in my head."

I nodded and turned, looking out at the desert. There wasn't much to see now, but I could still feel the calm of the desert rolling forth and see the lights of our little town winking on below us.

"I put you back together after your fall last Christmas," he said. "And then you were stupid enough to drag Harold into my burning house and pull me out."

I nodded. "Yup."

Smitty wasn't looking out at the dimming view. I could feel his eyes on me.

"You kept your word and found out who was behind those threats and stopped her," he said. His tone was strange, restrained and sharp at the same time.

"Had some help," I said.

Out of the corner of my eye, I saw him nod. "But she set up that test in the mine for you," he said, his tone lowering. "The 'which lives does Henry Carter value the most' test."

He took a deep breath, and I was so tempted to look at him, but I kept staring out at the desert right where I knew the cut of the Grand Canyon was, even though it was far too dark to see it now.

"First, Isabella Ortega," he said. "Frankly, kind of surprised there. I figured you'd go for your eternal crush and save Patty Walsh. Mind telling me why she was first?"

I shrugged, this time a groan escaping. Smitty knew what I had been through—there was no need to hide it. "Just went with my gut," I said.

"But you've thought about it by now," he said.

I nodded but didn't say anything.

"Mind telling me?" he asked.

I sighed. "Brooke convinced me I could only save one person. And without Martin, I think that would have been true. Ortega was the youngest with the most life to live."

I wasn't going to tell him of my growing attachment to the young woman, how I was starting to think of her as the daughter I never had.

"Okay," he said. "Makes sense. And then Lisa Paulson?"

"Family," I said. There was more. Her husband was my best friend and she was one of my best friends. I was the best man at their wedding and the godparent of their eldest child. But he knew all that.

He nodded. "And then good ole Martin came in and you had him help Karen and Ken."

I finally turned to him, and I could see hate in his eyes.

Which was fine by me—he probably saw it in mine. "If you've got something to ask, Smitty, just ask it."

"I was last," he said.

It wasn't a question, so I just nodded.

"I could have helped. I could have healed people," he said.

I snorted. "Your powers ran out," I said. "In fact, I suspect they haven't come back yet, not in full at least. Despite your bravado amongst your loyal followers, you're probably as bruised up as I am right now."

My time this afternoon with Annabelle had included her levitating a pen for me so that I knew that the explosion hadn't taken our powers away. And once things had calmed down a little bit, I could feel that background buzz that is a sure sign of being in the Carterville zone of influence.

Smitty's face blanched for a moment, and I knew I was correct. But soon a familiar sneer took over. "Anyway, Henry," he said. "I saved your life. You saved my life. And we'll just ignore the fact that you recommended Steve and how all that turned out."

He paused, giving me a chance to say something, but I just stared at him. "I just wanted to thank you and tell you that we are even," he said. "Your debt is paid."

There were so many things I wanted to say. I wanted to point out that I had risked my life to save him today. That I had done it twice. And while he had saved my life last Christmas and healed me today, his life was never in danger when he was healing me. It wasn't the same and we were nowhere close to being even.

I swallowed all of that and said, "Glad to hear it, Smitty."

As he walked away, I could see a subtle hitch in his step. He was hurting. And I was glad.

"It's almost dark, everyone," Annie said from behind me, her voice amplified. "Who is ready for some Fourth of July fireworks!"

There was cheering and clapping. Little did they know the real fireworks were over and Carterville still stood with Smitty and me in it despite what Brooke had said.

My mind started chewing on the future, on Smitty and me and how we might destroy the town, on Brooke and her power and the future she gave so much of herself trying to create.

She was going to jail. I don't care how many futures she could see, all of them led to jail at this point. Kidnapping. Attempted murder. The list was long and there was no way of getting out of it.

And that was puzzling. Why had Brooke created a future that led to her going to jail? What was so important to her that she went through all of this?

I didn't dwell on it for too long. I couldn't do my job and live my life always wondering about Brooke and her machinations here. I couldn't see the future, so I would just have to meet it when it came, just like everyone else.

I turned around and watched the crowd as they watched the fireworks, bright flashes of light illuminating their happy faces. The loud bangs of the fireworks drowning out the noise of the crowd. The smell of freshly burned gunpowder wafting up the hill.

The fireworks were being launched from down in the desert and the view was spectacular from up here. I also knew there were a bunch of folks lined up on Highway 89 watching from a distance with the looming darkness of the San Francisco Peaks behind the fireworks.

This was a celebration. It took a while, but it eventually settled in. I had no idea what kind of future Brooke had seen, but from what she had said, it had to be one where her actions somehow "saved" Carterville from the "destroyers," from Smitty and me.

Carterville was my town, and my job was to take care of it. That's what I needed to focus on. Not the past or the future, but the present and these people. With all the powers and all the egos and all the challenges, that was a hard job, but one I felt like I was born to, one I would keep doing until the day I died.

That thought resonated in my mind and chased away thoughts of Brooke. I took a deep breath and smiled as fireworks exploded and blues and whites and golds flashed in the sky above us, the light briefly illuminating the faces of those looking up in awe.

The future makes fools of us all, especially when we are as sure of ourselves as I was of my place in Carterville. Brooke had set events in motion, and while I couldn't see it yet, more changes were coming. Big changes. But that's another story.

WANT MORE CARTERVILLE?

THERE'S MORE CARTERVILLE FOR YOU. *THE BLOOD OF Carterville* takes place over a years after the events in this book and all the brewing conflicts come to a head. There is more information on *The Blood of Carterville* below.

The best way to find out when things happen in Carterville is to sign up for my email newsletter at RobertJMcCarter.com/newsletter. When you subscribe you'll get a free 750+ page ebook, *Bits, Bites, and Rarities: The Worlds of Robert J. McCarter*, that introduces you to my many series, and has four stories you can't read anywhere else!

Or, if you'd like a different kind of mystery, check out my *Walter Anchor, Ghost Detective* series. That's right. A ghost who solves murders. The ebook of the first case, *Detecting Haley*, is free when you sign up for my newsletter.

———

The Blood of Carterville

CARTERVILLE, AZ. POPULATION: 286. PEOPLE WITH powers: 198

Just a sleepy former mining town turned tourist haven in the mountains of Northern Arizona until the "incident." The meteorite that gave everyone in the town powers, but only while near Carterville.

Some people think that the blood of Carterville bestows powers, but when a tourist stabs police Chief Henry Carter's best friend, everything changes.

Henry will do the unthinkable to save his friend. But when the crime gets complicated, can Henry find the culprit and save his town, much less survive?

From Robert J. McCarter, long-time Arizona resident and the author of *Shuffled Off: A Ghost's Memoir*, comes a mystery and a town you will never forget.

Get a copy today!

ACKNOWLEDGMENTS

Carterville is a fictional town set in Northern Arizona, my long-time home. It's pretty natural for writers to pull from what they know when they write and that is, in part, what I am doing here. I write a lot of stories in Arizona, particularly in Northern Arizona, but not just because it's nearby and convenient, but because it's a stunning landscape where you can quickly go from tall pine trees down to barren desert, where awe-inspiring views are always nearby, and where opportunities to be out in nature abound.

All of that is to say, I owe a debt of gratitude to the beauty of Northern Arizona for this book and for years of having the privilege of living here.

My next debt of gratitude goes to Stephen King. Carterville is my version of his Castle Rock, a fictional town where strange forces live and a variety of stories can be written. To tell the truth, Carterville is also inspired by the TV show Haven, about a strange town on the Maine coast which is loosely based on King's *The Colorado Kid*.

Big thanks to my beta readers, Roni Hornstein, Peter Klein, and Eliot Schipper, and to my proofreader, Diana Cox. Thanks for catching so many of my goofs and making this book better.

As always, huge gratitude to my wife Aleia. She's my first

listener (the first time these stories leave my brain is when I read them to her), my partner, and my constant cheerleader. None of these books would exist without her.

Special thanks to Elizabeth Fitzekam. She created the series bible for Carterville which helped immensely in writing this book.

Thank you so much for reading! Hope you'll come visit Carterville again soon.

ABOUT THE AUTHOR

Robert J. McCarter is the author of more than ten novels and over a hundred short stories. He is a regular contributor to *Pulphouse Fiction Magazine* and his short fiction has also appeared in *The Saturday Evening Post, Andromeda Spaceways Inflight Magazine, Everyday Fiction,* and numerous anthologies.

Robert writes in a variety of genres from contemporary fantasy to science fiction and just about everything in between. His diverse background–including a career in software engineering, growing up on a ranch riding horses, and acting–colors the stories he tells.

He lives in the mountains of Arizona with his amazing wife and his ridiculously adorable dogs.

Find out more at:
RobertJMcCarter.com

BOOKS BY ROBERT J. MCCARTER

Carterville Mysteries

- **Out of a Christmas Sky**
- **Destroyer of Carterville**
- **The Blood of Carterville**

Walter Anchor, Ghost Detective Stories

- **Case 1: Detecting Haley** (also part of *Life After: Stories of Life, Death, and the Places in Between*)
- **Case 2: The Ghost Bride's Gift**
- **Case 3: A Long Hard Fall**
- **Case 4: Death of a Dentist**
- **Case 5: A Hollywood Kind of a Murder**
- **Case 6: The Red Arrow Murders**
- **Unfinished Business: The Cases of Walter Anchor Ghost Detective**

For a complete list of Walter Anchor stories, go to RobertJMcCarter.com/WalterAnchor

Novels in the "Ghost's Memoir" world:

- Shuffled Off: A Ghost's Memoir, Book 1
- Drawing the Dead

- To Be a Fool: A Ghost's Memoir, Book 2
- Of Things Not Seen: A Ghost's Memoir, Book 3
- A Boy, a Girl, and a Ghost

For a complete list the "Ghost's Memoir" novels, go to ShuffledOff.com

The Woody and June versus the Apocalypse Series

Find out more at WoodyAndJune.com

The Neutrinoman and Lightningirl Series

Find out more at Neutrinoman.com

Other Novels:

- Seeing Forever
- Where the Past Belongs: An Angelica and Ash Time Travel Adventure

For a more information, go to RobertJMcCarter.com